DEVIL IN FALSE COLORS

JACK WINNICK

Dedication

Every day, throughout the world, there are individuals and groups of armed men and women whose sole aim is to spread terror among civilian populations. Their reasons are inexplicable to normal people, no matter their religion or personal philosophy. But they are bent on disrupting or ending our lives. In many cases they are, unfortunately, successful. In many others, they are thwarted by the tens of thousands of brave individuals who risk their lives to protect our way of life.

These people, whether they are part of our CIA, FBI, Joint Terrorism Task Force, or the military and security agencies of other free countries, go about their dangerous job without expectation of fame or monetary reward. This is especially true for Israel's security forces, whether it be Mossad, Shin Bet, AMAN, or other anonymous organization. Their job is even more critical, if that could be possible. The future of their very nation is at stake.

It is to these unnamed individuals to whom we owe so much, that this book is dedicated.

Acknowledgements

DEVIL IN FALSE COLORS is a work of fiction. It is a story based on events that never occurred. However, it has strong ties to historical events that are not fiction, events that are happening more and more often in the real world. As such, it was necessary for the author to rely heavily on news items from the recent past and present, as well as true historical events.

Much of the information is available in the open literature; some is not. The author wishes to acknowledge, anonymously, the aid granted him by officials of the U.S. and Israeli governments in the creation of this fictional tale.

But the most important aid is that granted lovingly by one person: my sweetheart, Gisel, who kept me afloat during this long and difficult process with her constant help and encouragement. Perhaps most important was her work as editor, tirelessly checking and re-checking the manuscript for errors, but also adding immensely to the actual tale. She is responsible for much of the story itself, and in keeping the author within the bounds of reality, while allowing for the creativity of the fiction.

Jack Winnick, Los Angeles
August 2016

Chapter 1

Judith Levy wasn't worried when Michael didn't show up on time after preschool. "Mazeltov" was considered one of the best Jewish preschools in the area, and was not far from their house. But the young school bus drivers were not all that prompt and often changed their routes; for example, when new students enrolled. Their neighborhood in a modest part of the upscale suburb was well patrolled by the highly regarded Beverly Hills police. The houses were all priced well over $2 million, protected by expensive alarm systems, and crime was virtually nonexistent. So when the doorbell rang, and she promptly answered it, the pair of men standing at the door caused her quite a start.

Patrolman Ed Henderson was the first to arrive on the scene. His beat covered a section of Beverly Hills that included a medium-sized shopping mall and several blocks of single-family homes. Henderson was thirty-two years old, married, with three young children. He was a quiet man, and if you didn't see him in uniform, you would take him for an accountant or lawyer. He had actually been in office work for ten years after finishing junior college, but found it boring, and so enrolled in the Los Angeles Police Department (LAPD) Academy. After six months of tough training, he became a regular police officer.

Henderson's normal day in Beverly Hills consisted of reporting minor automobile accidents, uprooting vagrants, and answering calls from store owners about kids who were shoplifting. It was not as exciting as the six months in South LA, but not as bloody either.

He had just exited a snack shop when a young woman, quite hysterical, ran up to him, screaming and crying. "Come quickly," she said, gasping for breath. "Over there!" she shrieked, pointing across the street and grabbing at his arm. Henderson saw she was indicating a small house in the middle of the block that had been converted into some sort of school. Over the door he noticed a large, six-pointed Star of David. Watching out for traffic, he ran alongside the woman to the house, tossing his doughnut into the gutter.

They entered the living room and he was first struck with the small size of all the furniture. A group of five adults and about a dozen young children were formed into a group in one corner of the room. The adults were trying desperately to control and console the youngsters; but all were clearly in various straits of distress. He noted that the adults were in tears, the children seemingly in shock. The woman who had grabbed him outside the snack shop pointed to a room near the back of the house, but didn't say a word.

Henderson strode cautiously toward the room, drawing his .45 caliber Glock from its holster. He pushed open the door, peered around the corner, hearing nothing and seeing no movement. His pistol at the ready, he barely entered the room in a crouch, and quickly took in the scene. His fast-food lunch rose up into his throat as he saw the sight. Blood was splattered everywhere. Tiny, headless bodies were strewn around the room. The tortured heads were piled up in one corner. It was worse than any gang fight he had ever seen.

As soon as he was certain no one was in the room, no one alive that is, Henderson called into headquarters on Rexford Road and asked for Lieutenant Jerry Spencer, whom he knew was in charge that afternoon, adding "Code Red."

"Lieutenant, this is Ed, uh, Patrolman Henderson..." his voice shaking. He stopped to catch his breath.

"What is it, Henderson, you got a situation?"

"Bad one, sir. Multiple homicides. Need backup, patrol car and ambulance." The hoarseness in his voice was evident to Spencer.

"This an active situation, Henderson?" he barked into the microphone.

"Uh, no, sir, I got some, uh, several DBs here, no assailants" he croaked.

"I got you pegged at the, uh, 'Mazotol' preschool on Elm Drive, that right?" Spencer said sharply, as he looked at the green dot flashing on the large widescreen map in front of him.

"Roger, sir, that's a positive. Except I think it's called Mazeltov, whatever that means." Ed had seen the name above the door as he had rushed in. But he had temporarily lost the correct vernacular; his hands were shaking, and he felt he was going to be ill, seriously ill.

"Stand tall there, officer, help's on the way. Over and out."

Dead bodies were not common in Beverly Hills. Perhaps after an automobile accident, but that was generally at night when the drunks staggered out of the clubs. There was also the occasional celebrity murder. This was obviously something different, something the folks who lived in Beverly Hills weren't going to like. Lieutenant Jerry Spencer decided quickly that he himself had better be part of the cover team.

Spencer was a large, heavily-muscled man in his early 40s. He had over twenty years experience on the force, much of it on tough assignments. He wore his thinning hair in a buzz cut, giving him the appearance of a Marine Sergeant. His uniform was tailored, fitting tight to his upper body.

"I'm headed out to location," he said to the desk Sergeant. "I'm taking Hodges and Barrett in a car. Send an ambulance with a team," he ordered, nodding his head at the green dot flashing on the screen.

Spencer hustled out back toward the waiting cars, waving at officers Hodges and Barrett, who were sitting in the squad room to his right. They slapped on their caps and ran out the door right behind him. They didn't often see the Lieutenant exhibit this much haste; something big was up.

They pulled up to the preschool and parked in the drive, lights flashing but no siren. The ride had taken less than five minutes. The three men piled out of the car, seeing Henderson in the doorway. Spotting the huddled group of adults and children, all obviously terrified and hysterical, Spencer sent Chuck Hodges over to give them as much comfort as possible. Hodges was a young man, in his mid-twenties, who had just a few years experience on the force. But he had a sensitive demeanor, and a couple of children of his own. Spencer figured he was the best man of the three to handle the horrified group of adults.

Meanwhile Spencer and Jim Barrett followed Henderson's lead to the back of the house. No words were spoken as the three policemen scanned the crime scene. Barrett was a thirty-five year old black man who had been on the force for fifteen years, much of it spent in the poorer areas of LA, downtown and East side. He was quiet, but his manner radiated strength.

All three men instinctively donned plastic gloves and booties before entering the room. No speech was necessary as they looked over the horrific sight. Five headless bodies, small children at one time, were strewn across the blood covered room. In one corner five small heads were piled up, a bloody note tacked to one. Before going any further, Spencer spoke into his collar mic, "That ambulance on the way? Get hold of the coroner too. Going to need five, make it ten body bags."

"Ten body bags?" the desk sergeant asked incredulously.

"And tell them pronto, on the double, is that clear?"

"Roger, sir, ambulance ought to be there by now."

They could hear the sirens approaching as the men cautiously scanned the room. An open window at the side of the house caught everyone's attention. Bloody footprints and handprints were all over the frame and sill. Plenty of evidence. The perps clearly didn't care who knew what they had done. It was only then that Spencer caught sight of the crude note on top of the stack of children's heads. Without touching it, he peered at the scrawled writing:

سوف أكثر أو أراضينا عن بعيدا البقاء :تحذر الإسلامية الدولة إيموت!

"What the hell do you suppose this is?" he said, almost to himself. The other two policemen examined the note querulously.

"Looks like a bunch of hen scratching," Hodges offered. "Maybe some kind of Oriental or Middle Eastern writing," Spencer muttered. "The guys downtown will know what to do with it."

The sirens outside screeched to a halt, doors slammed, and the sound of several men rushing up the stairs into the house stopped further discussion. Spencer went out into the hall to meet them. He saw Bill Ackerman, one of the coroner's assistants, and two men he didn't know from the Medical Emergency Team. They saw Spencer's gloves and booties, as well as his grim expression, and immediately donned their own protective gear.

Captain Mike Scanlon was head of the Homicide Special Section of the downtown LAPD's Robbery-Homicide Division. Scanlon had been with the LAPD over twenty years and had seen more homicides than he cared to remember.

The impact of all that experience showed in the deep lines on his face making him look ten years older than his true age. His thick head of hair had turned prematurely white.

He looked at the report and the photographs that were on his desk; he sighed as he realized this must indeed be what was called a "hate crime." His section of the homicide division had been assigned hate crimes a few years ago, a designation that automatically brought with it overwhelming press coverage. Having the media look over his shoulder every step of the way was something Scanlon had trouble getting used to. This was going to be a bad one, no doubt about it. Three things about the case struck him right away: multiple homicide, small children, and the hate note in Arabic.

The note had been translated by two of the Arab speakers in the department. According to them it read roughly, *"the Islamic State warns: stay out of our land or more will die!"* There was no doubt they were serious, and seriously deranged as well. The coroner's report stated that on initial inspection, all five children had been beheaded roughly, apparently with a knife. Rags had been stuffed in their mouths to muffle their screams. Of course, all of them were Jewish: Michael Levy, Jerry Stein, and Joey Blanks: age four. Noah Steinberg and Benjamin Rifkin: age five. All came from upper-middle-class families in Beverly Hills.

Judging from the initial inspection on the scene, there appeared to be three sets of footprints and handprints, all bloody of course, left by the perpetrators. They had made no effort to cover their tracks. Entry had been gained from the window, which, according to the teachers, had been left open because of the unusually warm weather. The alarm system had been disabled intentionally to permit the window to be open. The bloody footprints led into an alley behind Elm Drive, then disappeared. Tire tracks were found, their imprint a standard one for medium-sized SUVs.

Chapter 2

Imam Ali Muhammad gazed upon his successful warriors. "How wonderful you have been, my pupils, my friends!" He scanned the five upturned faces, noting whether they indicated pleasure or pain. Killing children, especially the first time, could be difficult. But these young men had proven themselves admirably. He noticed one of them, the youth known as Abbas, looked briefly away. To the keen eye of the imam, this indicated a troubled conscience. He directed his next remarks specifically to him.

"The first Imam, Ali ibn Abu Talib, taught that all nonbelievers, whether Jew or Christian, must be converted or destroyed. But beyond that, Imam Mussa Ibn Jafar, has taught us that the Jew is especially dangerous." He glanced over at Abbas, noting that he had his full attention. "The Qu'ran also teaches us that evil must be nipped in the bud, so to speak. Thus, it is our duty to remove the Jew from existence at any age, young or old." He glanced at the five spellbound faces again, detecting slight nods from all, including Abbas.

The tall, thin imam paused for effect. His piercing gaze, that of a predator, reached every soldier in the room. They were silent and attentive as the imam stroked his long, grey beard. His hair had turned prematurely grey; he was not yet fifty years old. This pleased him; he projected the wisdom of age along with the grace of a youthful middle age. They all respected and admired him.

This was important. These young men were to become the nucleus of the religious leaders' pledge to remove Jewish influence from the holy land, Palestine. They were to begin here, in Los Angeles, where so much money from the rich Jews found its way to the Zionist scum. Their influence on the American government was disgraceful. True, there were Jews, even very rich ones, who aided the Muslim cause. Some Jewish billionaires, investors and entertainment moguls publicly denounced the Zionist state. Further, even Jewish Supreme Court justices voiced opinions that gave aid to the Palestinian quest for Al Quds, or, as the Zionists called it, "Jerusalem."

Knowing he had his minions' attention, he now had to relieve them of any feeling of guilt for the great deed they had accomplished. "You must feel very proud of what you have done. You are shining examples for the rest of our warriors. Further, you have removed Jewish blight before it had a chance to reproduce; much as one has to destroy roaches in their nest."

Looking around his audience again, their gazes had now turned to pride and admiration. They were his.

The imam's demeanor now relaxed. He smiled, stroked his beard again, and implored each of them to describe their glorious achievement.

Abdul-Khaliq, the eldest, born of Syrian parents, spoke first. "It was simple, Reverence. The stupid women teachers left the window open, just as you had predicted. It was an easy matter for me, Hakim and Khalil, dressed as circus clowns, to encircle the five nonbelievers, and quickly silence them. The loud fan in the room helped conceal any noise. After Hakim and Khalil slit their throats, I separated the heads from their bodies, in the manner shown to us on the films. The whole thing took less than three minutes. Wajid and Mukhtar were waiting in the van, just as we had practiced. We heard the women's screams as we were driving off. "

"And did you leave our manifesto as I had told you? Our demands? I saw no mention of it on the news."

"It was there all right! I left it myself, right on the pile of heads," Abdul-Khaliq proudly replied. "The stupid police probably haven't figured it out yet."

"Oh, they have it translated by now," the imam replied. "They probably just don't want to make it public yet."

"Why would that be?" Wajid queried.

"They like to keep the details quiet as long as possible; see who might take responsibility, give them a lead," said the imam with a smile. "You know the U.S. courts have decided the government cannot say anything that might offend Muslims. Their so-called 9th circuit court out here on the West Coast will not allow the FBI or other agencies to publicly advertise pictures or descriptions of suspects; freedom of religion, they call it," he said, laughing. "This gives us a tremendous advantage; we can place the blame wherever we like." His audience beamed with admiration.

Chapter 3

The call came in to the New York office of the Israeli consulate from Los Angeles at 11 a.m. Barely a day had passed since the brutal mass murder. The whole nation, of course, had been left in shock by the vicious assault. Reports had gone all over the world, and messages of condolence poured in from everywhere, including most Muslim countries.

"We condemn these acts of terror most vehemently. True followers of the Prophet would never commit such crimes." This was typical of the response from the Arab countries, as well as Iran. Others, including religious leaders from the region, were more diffident in their reaction: *"We do not condone violence like this in any form. However, one must look at the true cause of this sort of action. Without the support of the United States for the Zionist transgressors, these kinds of acts would never occur..."*

David Peretz, head of the Israeli consulate in New York, took the call. He had been expecting it. His office was overwhelmed with questions and irate suggestions for response to the brutal crime.

"David, how are you?" came the voice in Hebrew over the phone. Peretz immediately recognized Yehudi Gold, the consul in Los Angeles, even without looking at the caller display.

"Shalom, Yehudi," he responded. "You must be under some pressure there; this unspeakable crime."

"That's why I'm calling, David," getting right to business. "The LAPD has been working with us right from the start.

We helped them translate the Arab note, for starters. But they don't want to make the relationship public."

"Yes, I can understand that," David replied. He hoped the telephone line was as secure as it was supposed to be. "They also ask you to help identify the perps?"

"Yes, of course. But it wasn't really necessary; they left their prints all over the place—in blood. They are all here on legitimate visas, but they're not living where they're supposed to be. Not surprisingly, they haven't found any of them. I'm faxing you their names and what we know about them. The LAPD has not made the names public yet."

"Well, I'd like to see the list, but I don't see how I can help. I wish I could."

"The case is being handled by a Captain Mike Scanlon of the homicide-crime section. He remembered there was a woman from the FBI who led the team that got those guys after the nuclear attack here a few years ago. Wondered if you could get hold of her?"

"Sure, Lara Edmond. She's still here in New York, but with the JTTF now. She also helped break up that terrorist attack on Israel a few years ago, you know."

"Yes, of course," Gold replied, "you think Scanlon might be able to get her down here, without making it official?"

"I'll make a call immediately. By the way, you remember that Mossad guy, the Kidon, Uri Levin?"

"I was getting to that. We'd like him here, too."

Chapter 4

Lara got the call from Hadley Parkinson, chief of section. He told her that the Israeli consul general, David Peretz, had asked her to get in touch with him as soon as possible. Peretz, always following procedure, had phoned Parkinson first; making sure he didn't step on any toes at the Joint Terrorism Task Force. Lara knew what it must be about, so she headed by cab while she speed-dialed his office. He must have spotted her name on his display, because he picked up the call himself.

"Lara," he said, "can you make it over here right away?"

"I'm in a taxi already, this about the..."

"That's right," he said, cutting her off. "We'll talk about it when you get here."

She understood, muttered something in return, then realized he had already cut the connection.

The ride down to the consulate at 800 Second Avenue took less than ten minutes. Lara, a trim, blond woman in her mid-thirties, was dressed as usual, in a conservative blue suit and low heels. She had known Peretz for several years now, having worked with him during the last, aborted Arab invasion of Israel. David was a pleasant, no-nonsense man about fifty years of age, who had been extremely helpful to her and her Israeli colleague, Uri Levin. The sudden recollection of her Mossad partner, and sometime lover, gave her a jolt. It had been three years now since their last adventure that had taken them from Waco, Texas to a brief war in Israel. The partnership, short though it was, became some of the most exciting days of her life. She had fallen in love with him, and, she realized, still was.

Lara was not one to dwell on lost opportunities; her lingering feeling for Uri was an anomaly. She had wanted to become an FBI agent since her teen-age years. Coming from a family who saw virtually all its males go off to some sort of active government service, she was the first female to do so. She grew up in a farming community in Ohio, learning the ins and outs of firearms along with other means of defending herself. She was quickly accepted by the FBI, mainly for her enviable talents with computer-based communications.

Lara had quickly modernized and streamlined the many independent efforts that were generating hopelessly useless reams of data. She was able to reconfigure the programs into a single one that could scan the intercepted emails and phone calls from a plethora of sources, searching through them for keywords and phrases in a multitude of languages. Properly programmed, computers were infinitely more successful and efficient than the best of human teams. They did, however, need to be properly programmed, and that task was what brought Lara to the top of the FBI's success in tracking down the most serious of the threats to national security.

Of course, their successes were now at risk of being totally lost. Liberal elements in society had pushed through legislation that brought much of the data-gathering to a close, tying the hands of the FBI and the Joint Terrorism Task Force, the JTTF, while doing little to maintain privacy and security within the general population.

Lara, along with her Israeli partner, Uri, had brought to a successful close the most dangerous radical Muslim threats to the country and the world. After their tearful parting, Lara had been even more single-minded about her career. While she had a few relationships with male FBI and JTTF coworkers, a vicious rumor mill had terminated even that social outlet.

It was only natural that her male counterparts sought her out. She was so delightfully attractive; seemingly frail and approachable, in reality she was the opposite. Fiercely independent and capable in every way, both physical and mental, she was more than a match for any man, as they soon found out. Her lovely blue eyes would turn into fiery caldrons of golden radiance when she felt threatened. Armed and ready for any encounter with both gunplay and the most modern of personal combat, she put down many men twice her size. Her fellow agents in training, and terrorists in action, had fallen victim to her wrath.

Uri left her in New York at the conclusion of the last case, returning to Israel. She had not heard from him since, though she had learned he was still single; well, divorced. Mossad carefully guarded the personal lives and activities of their operatives, so she had no idea where he was or what he was doing.

The taxi stopped in front of the Israeli Embassy, jarring her back into the present. She paid the driver and entered the building. There was only a brief stop at the desk where she showed her credentials and went through security. They allowed her to keep her small Walther PPS 9mm pistol. She took the elevator to Peretz's office. His secretary was expecting her and showed her right in. David gave her a quick embrace and gestured to the chair in front of his desk.

"How are you, my good friend?" he asked, sitting on his desk.

"Busy, as usual," she answered with a smile, crossing her legs and straightening her skirt. "This is about Los Angeles, isn't it?"

"Yes, of course," he replied at once. "Our consulate there asked me to try and get your help. Fortunately, your boss agreed."

Lara had a mental picture of her boss, Hadley Parkinson, and smiled inwardly. The old guy was probably happy to have her on this case and not in his charge.

"You know most of the gory details, I suppose," he said. Lara nodded.

"Pre-school children," he said shaking his head sadly. "This is disgusting even for them."

"I read there was a note, in Arabic. You have it translated?" she asked.

"Yes, we think so. Our Arab speakers seem to agree. Do you want to see it?" It seemed to her an open invitation to check out her knowledge of Arabic. He knew she had been studying it ever since the last episode. She nodded.

"All right, here it is." He showed her the fax transmission of the original:

سوف أكثر أو أراضينا عن بعيدا البقاء :تحذر الإسلامية الدولة إيموت!

Lara was able to translate it in a matter of seconds.

"So the Islamic State is threatening us," she said flatly.

"Exactly!" David replied. "They want to show us they can do the same thing here that they're doing to their own people over there."

"What does the president say?" she asked. "I assume he knows all the details by now."

"You mean the U.S. president," he replied. "We, that is the Israelis, haven't heard yet. I suppose nothing has filtered down through your organization?" He looked at her quizzically.

"Nothing official," she answered. "Though unofficially, I understand he's meeting with his cabinet and the Joint Chiefs to see if a military response is justified."

"I doubt anything like that is in the cards," he said. "After all, no government, or even organization, has taken credit, at least yet."

"You think al Nusra is behind it?"

"Seems reasonable, since we've been bombing the crap out of them. And they call themselves 'The Islamic State'."

"But it could be somebody else, just wildcatters, using the name to justify random killing, right?" she asked.

"It's possible," he replied. "But our Arab speakers seem to feel that the syntax in the note resembles closely other threats we've seen from them."

"Really!" she said with a start. "I hadn't read anything about that."

"That's right. Israeli military intelligence, 'AMAN', has picked it up and supplied it to the NSA."

"Well," she said, sitting back and straightening her skirt. "What do you have in mind for me?"

"Our government would be very pleased if you were to go to Los Angeles, kind of be our liaison. We've already got approval from your boss."

After a moment of thought, Lara responded, "I have a feeling there's a bit more that you haven't told me."

Peretz smiled. "You're too smart for me. Yes, of course, your old partner, Uri Levin, will be there too."

Chapter 5

Meir Rosenblum was well known in Los Angeles; in fact, he was well known all over the United States, and perhaps further. He was a fiery advocate of Israel as a Jewish state; the Zionist through and through. His father, Yossi, had been a member of the Palmach, the military branch of the Hagganah that successfully fought off the Arab attempts to destroy Israel in the 1940's. Yossi had remained in Israel with his family until 1975, when his wife, Rebecca, convinced him to move to California, where life for the young children would be simpler and safer.

Meir grew up in Los Angeles, never tiring of hearing of his father's feats of daring. He became a rabbi, totally dedicated to bringing the truth of Zionism to the somewhat indifferent Americans. His oratory became legendary, as he appeared on talk shows and maintained columns in the Jewish press. His views were so strong that they alienated much of the left-wing press, especially on the West Coast. For example, he denied the existence of the so-called "occupied West Bank," preferring the traditional nomenclature of Samaria and Judea, where the true Eastern boundaries of the promised Jewish State had been set nearly a century ago. He argued strongly for the incorporation of Samaria and Judea within the final, recognized boundaries of the state of Israel. The Arabs, he argued, had relinquished any claim to the lands west of the Jordan River by their constant aggression since 1948.

Rabbi Rosenblum's frequent appearances in front of hostile audiences generated a lot of press. He often attracted more vindictive, young Arab students who were in the United States on temporary visas. They were a constant source of turmoil, and were frequently violent in their denouncement of his right to speak in favor of Israel.

The danger to his life became a concern for law enforcement authorities, and they recommended he hire a contingent of bodyguards. But Meir Rosenblum's self image had a strong "John Wayne" component, one of macho self-reliance. It actually was part of his appeal. In desperation, the Los Angeles Sheriff allowed him to become one of the very few civilians to have a "conceal/carry" permit. Only a hundred or so non-law-enforcement personnel were allowed this privilege. Rabbi Rosenblum was very public about his personal weapon, a nickel-plated SIG-Sauer 9mm semi-automatic pistol.

The LAPD, in particular the robbery–homicide division, were not pleased with Rabbi Rosenblum's cowboy persona, but there was little they could do. He had a right to speak, and he had a right to protection. They warned him however, that he might be pushing the limits.

One night, after a particularly hateful demonstration by Muslim students at UCLA, his talk was terminated, contrary to his wishes. There was a highly public melee, with shots being fired. Then the rabbi disappeared in a crowd of supporters and demonstrators. A widespread manhunt ensued for three days without result. Suddenly a package unexpectedly appeared at his office in Century City. Suspicious immediately, his staff called police, without opening it.

Detectives Joe Randall and Pete Anderson of the RHD were called in to take charge. They raced over to the rabbi's office, where one of his staff immediately pointed to the package.

"Has anyone touched this?" Anderson asked the frightened secretary.

"No," she replied. "It was sitting right there when we got here this morning."

"Good. We'll take it from here." He glanced over at Randall, who nodded in the affirmative.

"We need a squad from hazardous material, immediately!" he shouted into his collar mic. He knew their location was indicated on the board at headquarters.

"Can you give me approximate size of item?" came the calm reply.

"3 x 6 x 10," Randall estimated. Anderson nodded his agreement.

"They'll be there in fifteen max. Secure the area."

The two detectives calmly and politely asked the three staff members to vacate the outer office until the item could be cleared. The staff complied, with obvious concern.

The squad car arrived in exactly thirteen minutes. Two men wearing protective outfits first scanned the suspicious package for explosives. None was detected. They then checked for metal and got a positive response. The parcel, wrapped in simple brown paper, was dusted for prints, yielding nothing of value. After checking with the detectives, they carefully removed the item to the squad car.

The detectives calmly told the rabbi's staff they could return to their desks, and that they would be notified as soon as information was available. The staff members were clearly anything but calm; ashen-faced, they returned to their desks.

Randall and Anderson sped back to headquarters. The package had been taken downtown to the "suspicious item" room in the basement at 100 W. First St.

After radar inspection showed the contents to include a firearm, the package was disassembled remotely. It was in fact, a SIG Sauer P223, nickel-plated. Along with it, was a bloody human finger.

As the robot arm removed the two objects from the package, the detectives saw a hand-written letter underneath. The robot arm plucked up the note so that its contents could be clearly seen:

! فقدت من كل أو الآن الإسلام اعتناق الله كلام إلى الاستماع

The two detectives looked at each other. The conclusion was all too obvious: this was tied up with the school massacre. The Arabic note, or at least a photograph of it, would go immediately to the Arab speakers in the department. The translation came back to them in less than fifteen minutes:

"*Listen to the words of God; embrace Islam now or all is lost for you!*"

DNA testing showed that the finger belonged to none other than Rabbi Meir Rosenblum. The Sig Sauer was indeed registered to the rabbi also.

It wasn't long until the mutilated body of the rabbi was found in the dumpster behind his main congregation in the Valley.

* * *

Lara rapidly packed her belongings into her carry-on suitcase. She hadn't been traveling all that much lately, as there was plenty of work in New York for all the FBI agents attached to the JTTF. The continuous wave of Mideast immigrants had caused the Force no end of difficulty. It had become nearly impossible to identify individuals as "risk" without crossing that vague barrier called "profiling."

She looked around her small midtown Manhattan apartment without much emotion; it was not like she was going to miss being here. Her life had become totally consumed with work; her social life was almost a void. That was the way she wanted it. She dated a few men, but no one seriously since...well, since Uri. And the thought of him brought those emotions back to the surface. *Well*, she thought to herself, *no point in going into that now.* She finished packing, took another quick glance around, and turned out the lights. She was on her way to the airport and to Los Angeles.

Lara was consumed with all the busywork connected with getting to the airport and on the plane. It wasn't until she was settled into her seat on the nonstop flight to LAX that she allowed herself to consider the assignment. As she did, she broke out into a cold sweat. The choice, after all, had been hers. She knew the risks, considered them carefully, and decided to go ahead. Had she been truly objective, she realized, the answer would have been different. For example, had she been assigning this mission to another agent she would not have been able to accept the responsibility. For herself, though, it came down to a matter of personal pride and the need to carry on her family's tradition of extreme courage. Every generation of males in her family had served gallantly in the armed forces.

She thought of her uncle who had been killed in Vietnam back in 1967, and two of her father's uncles who had died on the beaches of Normandy in 1944. The days of women working only in the background were long since passed; she had been trained as a combat operative alongside men. Lara had already proven herself in the nuclear attack on Los Angeles a few years earlier, and in the Arab sneak attack on Israel a couple of years later. If she could handle those situations, she could certainly handle this one. Of course, she thought ruefully, she had welcomed the help and companionship of a certain Uri Levin. The enigmatic and resourceful Mossad assassin remained in her thoughts; did she really expect him to come to her aid in this situation? The rational answer was of course, no; but it was hard to dismiss the eventuality entirely. Uri was, she knew, assigned to the case in some capacity, and most likely in Los Angeles.

Her boss, Hadley Parkinson, had been more than reluctant at her brazen plan: Lara presented the idea of answering an advertisement, made by Muslim clerics, looking for attractive, young American or European women to become "brides." Homeland Security was eager to exploit any and all avenues available toward breaking into the ISIS gang that had carried out the horrific murders in Los Angeles. But their attempts to infiltrate with male agents, even Arabs, had come to naught.

Such horrific murders of innocent children, carried out with wanton contempt, were unheard of in the United States. Reaction around the globe was nearly uniform; even many of the Muslim nations voiced horror and disgust. Only in some of the most radical pockets of Islamic extremism was there even a small measure of pleasure at the torture of American Jews.

Lara's idea of an attractive, blond American offering herself to a possible accomplice in the brutal murders had been rejected out of hand by most of the elite at the FBI-JTTF as well as Homeland Security. But her idea was not without history; several young European women had found husbands by responding to online advertisements from Muslim men. It was easy to see why the men were using this device. They had seen photographs and movies with attractive young European and American women and were eager to make contact. What surprised Lara was the fact that any women would respond. But there were, apparently, a small number of women who were attracted to the adventure of romance with a jihadi. After all, outlaws have appealed to a certain type of young women throughout history; Bonnie and Clyde, for example. The latest version of this phenomenon was called "ride or die chicks." Girls would actually go to courtrooms to find gangster types to hook up with.

At any rate, the jihadi would ask for a video of the "applicant." In it, she must prove both her "blondness" and her consent to move to North Africa or wherever, and become the wife, or one of the wives, of this terrorist. The more notorious, the better. If approved, she would get a one-way ticket to join her mate, and be actively involved in his terror schemes, often aimed at her native country.

Lara was, of course, initially astonished and appalled when she learned of this commerce. But it seemed to her a short-cut into the terror network. Dangerous, of course, but she had already proven herself capable of dealing with these jihadis; but never alone. Would the FBI be willing to provide some sort of back-up for her? So far, the answer had been a resounding "No!" But she was determined to keep after it. She would approach the Los Angeles office with a more detailed plan and see if she could push it through.

She had worked with the agents in Los Angeles against the Hezbollah operatives who threatened the entire country with nuclear devastation. Lara's success in that case was no doubt the reason she had been called in this time. But there was little likelihood that they would readily accept her idea of becoming a radical Islamic bride. She would have to show them she had researched the plan carefully and considered every angle. Lara was nothing if not tenacious. That's the only way she got far as she had in the men's club called the FBI.

Chapter 6

Lara decided to do some preparation before meeting with the Los Angeles FBI. She had taken an early flight from New York, arriving a day ahead of her scheduled meet-and-greet at FBI headquarters in Westwood near the Veteran's Center and the UCLA campus. Realizing there was no direct public transport from the airport, she took a taxi from LAX to the area where she had a room reserved already. It was a small, inconspicuous hotel not far from Wilshire Boulevard in Beverly Hills. She had the driver, who seemed Middle Eastern in origin, both in speech and appearance, drop her off about a block away. It was common practice not to advertise your location. As it was not yet noon, she decided to make the most of her first day in preparation for the FBI meeting.

Checking into her hotel, she changed clothes into the garb of a typical Angeleno: blue jeans, sweat shirt, denim jacket and a small backpack. She wore a Dodgers cap to cover most of her blond hair. Grabbing a quick snack at the little restaurant on the main floor, she paid for the meal with cash. She did not like to leave any paper trail. For the same reason she had paid upfront for the room in cash, signing in as Linda Blakely from New York City; sorry, no valid credit card.

She noted the meager contents of her backpack: her wallet, complete with true ID and credentials, a spare pair of socks, a map of Los Angeles, including the metro lines, meager as they were. And her trusty small Walther: as a Federal officer she had the right to carry the concealed weapon. This privilege was afforded to only a few not in the law-enforcement community. She grimly noted that this benefit had been of no use to the rabbi who had been recently murdered, his weapon and finger sent to the police.

Lara never had a chance, on her other visits to Los Angeles, to scout the area. If she was to get approval for her undercover operation, she needed to have at least an idea of the nature of the city; especially the predominantly Muslim neighborhoods. The internet had been useful in giving her an idea where the greatest concentrations of Muslims resided. This was revealed by the list of locations of the mosques, both Sunni and Shia.

As she suspected, there was no rapid transit line near her hotel. She had become so used to navigating her way around the D.C. area on their Metro, that being without it here was an inconvenience. But there was a bus line that ran east on Wilshire to the downtown area, where, she had seen on the map, there were quite a few mosques. It was only ten minutes before the bus arrived. Being without tokens, the driver was quite agreeable in taking cash. Even with stops seemingly every two blocks, after just twenty minutes or so, she exited at the edge of the downtown area, and started off on foot.

She quickly found Union Station, the famous city landmark seen in innumerable films. Within a few blocks she discovered a bustling Chinatown, a historical Mexican area, and a variety of fashion industry buildings, warehouses, and renovated old buildings that now served as everything from chic boutiques to small restaurants and tiny theaters. Of course, there was also the well-known skid row, very near to the large arts complex and major hotels. There seemed to be quite a lot of traffic, this now being mid-afternoon. She had read that the downtown area transformed at night into not such a hospitable environment.

Even in daylight the skid row was alive with men and women down on their luck, living in tent cities and large cardboard boxes. Still, she had no problem with the panhandlers as she continued her brisk walk around the downtown area, bounded by freeways and the storm canal known as the "Los Angeles River."

She did notice a number of women dressed in traditional Muslim costume: abaya and hijab. A few even had their faces hidden under veils. Many were pushing strollers with young children in tow. The mosques she noted on her map were not, for the most part, distinctive structures. They were mainly converted old buildings, identified only with crudely-lettered signs, in Arabic, Farsi and English. At night, she realized, many of them would be near indistinguishable.

It was now nearing four o'clock, and Lara had yet to check out another mosque-rich area just to the west of downtown. She found a real-life Metro station, where she was able to buy a "TAP" transit pass and head to the end of the line on Wilshire just west of her starting point. Here she was greeted by a sign announcing "Koreatown." It was an incredibly busy area, with both foot and vehicle traffic. Many, if not most of the storefronts were written in Korean or some other Asian language. It was a densely packed neighborhood, with multi-family apartment buildings and condos, loud music blaring continuously, and traffic backed up at every corner. Again, she was able to locate most of the mosques, even though they were not anywhere near as visible as the churches or synagogues. As in downtown, they were mainly housed in converted stores.

Lara now first felt the chill of the ocean breeze and realized dusk was approaching. She did not want to be far from Beverly Hills at night, or even twilight. At no point in her reconnaissance did she feel in any danger to her person, and it was just now that she even remembered that she was armed. Returning to Wilshire Boulevard, she boarded the bus, used her transit pass, and headed to Beverly Hills and her safe little hotel room.

Chapter 7

The following morning, Lara entered the Federal Building at 11000 Wilshire Boulevard with some trepidation. She had already been told by her boss in New York, Hadley Parkinson, that her idea of a marriage proposal to a radical Arab religious leader, was null and void. But she'd skirted around his directives before; she had some positive dealings with the Los Angeles Division of the FBI, now part of the Joint Terrorism Task Force, and hoped for their help.

Mary Robley, Special Agent, had been Lara's contact years ago when Los Angeles was hit by a nuclear strike carried out by Hezbollah. Their relationship had turned out well, as they cooperated in the destruction of the terrorist cell responsible.

Lara was escorted up to the 17th floor, where Mary was waiting for her. After a friendly greeting, she introduced Lara to the agent in charge of the Los Angeles section of the investigation into the killings of children and the rabbi. Mike Scanlon was a fifty something, lifetime cop who had made his mark breaking up Colombian drug rings in South L.A. When they had talked on the phone, Mary had said that Mike was considered best for the job at hand, skilled both in operations and handling of the press. The latter was considered extremely important, as the community was rightfully enraged, especially over the murder of innocent children.

Lara was immediately impressed with his physical appearance and demeanor. He was about six-two, and well put together, similar to the FBI field agents. She figured he spent most of his spare time in the gym. But he was friendly and courteous as he smiled and led her into his work space.

He had been temporarily lent an office at FBI headquarters; a grand area by FBI standards, no doubt to impress members of the media he dealt with daily. His view stretched northward over Wilshire and the veterans' cemetery. In addition to his finely-polished, and totally clear desk and swivel chair, there was seating for five visitors, and another table set up for viewing slides and television. A deep blue carpet, wall-to-wall, completed the picture.

Once they were seated, Mike got right down to business. "Well," he said, "as you know, this case is top priority, and we're grateful for any help we can get, but," he added, "I have a note here from your boss in New York, Hadley Parkinson, that says he vetoed your idea of a marriage proposal to an Arab terrorist."

He sat there, alert, waiting for her reaction. She had been ready for this and had steeled herself up for it. "Yes, that's correct," she replied. "But Hadley tends toward the conservative and Mary tells me that you are more the ready-for-action type."

Mike saw immediately that this indeed what was on her mind. "I see. So you still think you could carry this off?"

Lara's heart leapt at this hint of an opportunity. "Yes, I do! I've dealt with these guys before. I speak and read Arabic, and I'm pretty good with physical defense."

"Well," he said after a brief pause and a deep breath, "Hadley did say that I could at least hear your plans and give you my input. If I felt you had at least an even chance of success, I could forward my okay to him."

Before Lara could continue her presentation, Mike stood up from his chair and said, "But first I want to show you something." He headed off to the viewing screen, Lara immediately following. He motioned for her to sit in the

"captain's chair," directly in front of the screen, while he
went over to the video equipment.

"I want you to see some recordings we've gotten from ISIS
and Boko Haram, who is now affiliated. They haven't been
released to the general public. You'll see why in just a
minute." He turned on the projector and searched through an
immense library until he got where he wanted. The screen lit
up a brushy scenery, filled with wildly grinning men in all
sorts of desert garb, most carrying automatic weapons.

The camera jerked forward to a horrific scene. On the
ground, bound hand and foot, lay six young women, some
barely teenagers, all bruised, cut and bleeding. They were
obviously terrified, unsure what was in store. Their garments
had been torn, exposing them completely.

As Lara gasped unintentionally, the gang was seen to
crowd around the helpless women and impatiently waited
their turn, as the men proceeded to violently rape the women
in full view of the crowd and the camera. Mike kept the
recording going as the scene switched from the Nigerian base
of the Boko Haram to a more Arabic, desert setting in Syria
or Iraq. After ten minutes or so of this grisly presentation,
Lara buried her head in her hands and waved to Mike that
she'd seen enough.

Mike stopped the video immediately. He said, "You can
see why we have not distributed this to the media."

Lara regained her composure. "Absolutely. That is
probably the most disgusting thing I've ever seen. But, Mike,
if anything, it makes me more determined than ever to do
what I can to clean these animals out of our country, at least."

This was not what Scanlon had expected, and he showed it.
He sat down opposite her, his face full of admiration. "Well,"
he added, "I've got to tell you that's not what I expected to
hear. Most folks are violently sick by this time."

"Mike, I can imagine that. But, I was here for the cleanup after the Hezbollah attack, and have seen my share of some pretty hideous serial killer scenes. So, yes my initial reaction was one of total revulsion, my next was the need to do something about it."

He sat there for a moment, ran his hand across his already-grey buzz cut, and said, "You really think you could handle yourself with savages like those?"

"I don't think we're talking about a comparable situation," she replied. "These imams who advertise for a blond wife aren't going to be interested in attacking someone who seems genuine."

"Well," he said, "I can see you're not easily dissuaded. Why don't we meet again when you feel you have some actual leads. I'll contact Hadley and tell him we've not come to a consensus yet." He stood, indicating the meeting was over for now.

Lara followed his lead, rose and shook his hand briskly. At least she hadn't been turned down. She headed back down to street level, and to the parking garage. She sat in the lobby and opened her briefcase. Opening her small laptop, she quickly read in the notes from the meeting before she could forget anything. What Mike hadn't asked her, and she was glad of it, was whether she already had some prospects. In fact, she had already done quite a bit of computer searching at the New York Public Library, on one of their free computers. She didn't want to leave a trail on the FBI equipment with her name attached to it.

She found over fifty websites advertising for Muslim men seeking wives. One particular site held her interest more than the others. It was essentially a dating service that permitted Muslim men to post their photograph and basic information about themselves. Specifically, it had space for personal data such as age, occupation, marital status, number of children, and what kind of woman was desired. In that category was included age range and nationality.

There were over a hundred entries on this site alone, most with blurry photographs showing bearded men, with or without Arab headdress, but not much in the way of identification. Searching through the site over several hours, Lara came upon one entry that grabbed her attention. A serious looking, dark-complexioned man *(what else?),* claiming to be forty years of age, and a cleric, was looking for a woman between the ages of eighteen and forty, of American or Scandinavian descent. This last was what especially caught her eye. Almost all of the other entries had no nationality preference. This guy was looking for a blonde.

He listed his location as "the Los Angeles area." Although he said he was a cleric, he didn't specify whether he was Sunni or Shia. Of course, neither did most of the other wife-seekers. Without a name, she didn't have much to go on unless she responded to the advertisement. She decided to go ahead and do so, using a fake identity, of course, hoping to get approval from Mike afterwards. One thing she would do was to include a grainy photograph of herself from a few years ago, her blond hair on proud display.

Lara took a taxi back to her hotel in Beverly Hills, went to her room, and quickly filled out the application necessary for the response, including the photograph. She had already set up a fake gmail account through a discount server under the name of Lisa Johnson. She said she was thirty-two years of age, unmarried, with no children, and that her occupation was "office clerk." She said she was willing to relocate to the Los Angeles area, but she didn't say where she currently resided. Oh yes, and that she was a devout Muslim, but did not specify what branch of the faith. In describing herself, she said that she was an Ohio native who had moved to Minneapolis some years ago. She had been introduced to Islam by some young Somali men in her night classes at community college. She was impressed by the politeness with which they welcomed her at the local masjid. Over a five-year period she had turned completely to Islam.

That should certainly garner his interest, she decided, sent the email, packed up and locked her things, and set off on foot to find something to eat.

She didn't have far to look; appealing sandwich restaurants were abundant. She found a small deli where she could sit at a table by herself, read the local newspaper, and devour a pastrami sandwich and diet soda. Paying her bill with cash, she walked with luxurious slowness, in the gathering twilight, back to her hotel. Lara realized she was within just a few miles of where that terrible child massacre had occurred; a shiver ran down her spine. She picked up her pace in the last few blocks to the hotel.

Once in her room, she kicked off her shoes and flopped on the bed, not turning on the TV. Then, she remembered her computer, and decided to see if she had any messages from the office. They tended to use secure e-mail rather than phone, unless the matter was extremely urgent. Unlocking her briefcase, she opened her laptop and perused the few standard messages on her government site. There was already a note from her boss, Hadley, saying that he had heard from Mike in Los Angeles, and that she should keep him in the loop at all times.

Before turning off the computer and relaxing for the evening, on a whim, she checked out her fake gmail account. To her surprise, if not astonishment, there was already a response from the "cleric." He addressed her simply as "Lisa," identified himself as "Ali," the imam at the Sunni Masjid al-Fatir, and gave her the address. He invited her to come for a visit at their expense. If interested, she should book a flight to LAX at her convenience, and allow them to meet her at the airport.

Lara quickly checked out this congregation on the Internet. Sure enough, Ali Abdul-Baki was the imam of the largest Sunni masjid in the city. This was her shot. Even if he were, most unlikely, in charge of the ISIS operation in Los Angeles, she could at least observe and report on his actions. It is possible he knew the imam or imams who were in charge of the terrorists.

Chapter 8

Uri Levin, one of the most famous of Mossad's assassins, known for many years as Kidon, was growing restless. He had been kept off active-duty the past few years; ever since the aborted war between Israel and the combined forces of al Nusra and other radical Arabs. He was lonely, no question about that. His marriage had dissolved, and the other great love in his life, Lara Edmond, was thousands of miles away in America.

His meetings with her had been short, but intense. Together they had foiled two attacks, both in the U.S. and Israel; she with the FBI, he with Mossad. Somehow they never managed to get together again or to make any long-term arrangements. He would have loved for her to come live in Israel; she would certainly be welcomed by Mossad. But it was a lot to ask of her: it would mean leaving the country of her birth, where her family lived, the only country she had ever called home.

He had been invited by the authorities to come to the States and join their Joint Terrorism Task Force. His command of English was superb, albeit with an Israeli accent he couldn't seem to lose. But he had an overreaching loyalty to Israel, the country his father had given his life for. The land called to him, seemingly from the centuries his ancestors had been banished. He struggled with his decision daily, but could come to no firm resolution. Now he'd lost touch with Lara and the answer seemed to have been made for him.

He was getting older, too, no question about that. He had been asked, of course, to join the ongoing battles against the seemingly endless skirmishes with the religiously-motivated

Arab states that surrounded his country. But this would be as a desk-bound administrator, not a field operative. The reasons were clear: as a middle-aged man, he could no longer be expected to survive the physical abuse field action demanded. Also, his experience would be more valuable as a leader. He had survived all that one in combat could ever be expected to encounter. He was a legend with whom any active-duty soldier would be proud to serve.

Finally, there was his physical handicap: he had lost an eye in hand-to-hand battle with an Arab terrorist. Although he had proven himself capable since, the fact remained that, at least to the higher administrators, his value as a desk-bound coordinator outweighed his need for further active duty.

To convince himself, as well as his superiors, that he was still capable of combat operations, he kept himself in enviable physical condition. He had a daily regimen of running, weight-training, swimming and cycling. He stood as tall and straight as ever, able to meet the speed, endurance and strength tests required of any operative. His body was as taut and strong as that of a twenty-five year old. His arms and legs, fit and bronzed by Mediterranean sun, appeared to belong to a man twenty years his junior. Only the grey streaks in his thick, curly hair gave him away; and this, he told himself, could be taken care of easily enough, should it be necessary.

Further, to assure his ability to handle life-and-death situations, he maintained his proficiency with his chosen firearm: the deadly and accurate Desert Eagle. It was a matter of pride, if nothing else, that kept him qualified, passing with flying colors the mandatory monthly tests on the range.

He had, at first reluctantly, switched to the new 9mm "Baby Eagle" with polymer grip for lighter weight. This new weapon held a magazine of 16 rounds that could be replaced, seemingly without pause. The lighter weight, he found, was especially effective for him, with only one usable eye. He discovered, as he proved over and over to the range officers, that he could cluster a full magazine in the "bull" at twenty feet, and do nearly as well at thirty feet.

The new commander of Mossad, Yitzhak (Isaac) Har-Lavi, had chosen Uri and a few other veteran assassins to learn to impersonate Palestinian Arabs. The objective was clear: there would be other incursions into the homeland. The next time Israel would be ready with actively-trained fifth columnists. Israelis with Arab or Arab language backgrounds would be held in reserve, ready to dress, speak, and act like Palestinian terrorists or soldiers.

For Uri, who was already fluent in the Arabic used in Lebanon and Jordan, this meant he would have to grow some Arabic-looking facial hair. After a few months, he had a scraggly mustache and beard that would make Yasser Arafat proud. It was half grey, in keeping with Uri's advancing age. He had now passed forty.

Then came the question of what to do about his missing left eye; the one he had lost under the streets of Chicago in a battle to the death with a Hezbollah fanatic. Up until now, he had been alternately using either a prosthetic eye or an eye patch. The patch was more comfortable for him, but it made him clearly identifiable to almost all Israelis and most Arabs.

Fortunately, a couple of years ago, a new surgical technique had become available: Uri had the operation at the Hadassah University Medical Facility in Jerusalem. The surgeons implanted a new "scleral shell" device developed at the Weizmann Institute in Rehovot. After repairing the damaged muscles in the orbit that had surrounded his left eye, they were able to fit him with a new prosthesis. Amazingly, this new prosthetic eye not only looked identical to his right one, but also moved with the natural action of the eye muscles. Those who did not know he had lost his own left eye were unaware of his handicap.

To augment the disguise, he wore a desert *Shemagh*-type *keffiyeh*, wound around his head, that put his eyes in shadow. Worn along with a dusty white "*thobe*" and sandals, he could pass easily through the streets of Ramallah or Hebron. He had, in fact, participated in several missions to break up small bands of counterfeiters and drug dealers who preyed upon the poorer Arabs in those towns.

These missions began rather straightforward. Uri had teamed up with an actual Israeli-Arab named Nizar. Nizar had been born in Syria, but when his parents were arrested and tortured by the ruling family, he escaped to the South into Israel. He was taken in by a family of Bedouins in the small farming village of Aramisha, in the Northwest. When Hezbollah rockets, randomly fired from Lebanon, killed his adoptive parents, he fled to Haifa and turned himself in to the Israeli Defense Forces, the IDF. He was eager to make amends for the loss of two sets of parents. The young man, now eighteen years old, made an apt pupil in Mossad's special Arab Section. Like the other Arabs and Bedouins, he was helpful teaching colloquialisms to those who had never lived outside Israel.

In their first assignment, Uri and Nizar entered a small village near Bethlehem at daybreak, posing as distraught Arabs seeking cheap drugs. After only a couple of hours of inquiry, they were led to a small café. In the backroom, hidden from the main area by some hanging sheets, the disguised agents were introduced to two merchants. Uri's camouflage was clearly successful, as the merchants were eager to display their wares. He and Nizar haggled over the price of hashish and more potent drugs for about twenty minutes. Uri, meanwhile, pressed an alert button in his pocket, bringing an Israeli Home Guard "Shin Bet" squad car racing across the border. The two merchants were taken completely by surprise as the Israeli SUV ground to a halt outside. While two policemen guarded the café, another pushed aside the sheets and entered the backroom.

Uri and Nizar quickly cuffed the two bewildered Arabs and handed them over to the Shin Bet officers. They then collected the array of drugs on display and tossed them all into an evidence bag. The strange-looking group left in the plain, olive-green SUV, leaving behind nothing but a cloud of dust. About ten Arabs had gathered to watch the spectacle; the whole raid took less than five minutes.

Other similar assignments had gone equally well for Uri. In his first year as an undercover agent he had brought in over a dozen small-time gangsters and drug dealers. So it was no real surprise that he was called in by Har-Lavi after the second terrorism incident in California, the hideous murder of Rabbi Rosenblum.

Uri knew as soon as he heard about the child massacre at the Los Angeles Jewish day school, that he would be involved. It stood to reason, since he was immediately recruited the last time there was an Arab-linked disaster in Los Angeles. In the back of his mind, even though he refused to actively consider it, was the knowledge that Lara would be involved also.

"Sit down," said the powerfully-built Har-Lavi. "I hear you make a real good Arab," he joked to Uri. He smiled jovially as he puffed on a large cigar, his feet up on his desk. His sleeves were rolled up, exposing thick, hairy forearms. Smoking had been against the rules in the IDF for some time now, but the ban was very loosely enforced. "Now we've got something really important for you. You know what's been going on in Los Angeles, of course." Uri nodded, his body tensing.

"Well, the Americans want somebody to infiltrate the organization there, someone they know and trust, and who can get the job done. They asked about you, remembering what you did for them with that Hezbollah nuclear bomb business. I told them what you've been doing lately, your new 'eye'...well, they were convinced." He looked Uri over carefully, especially noticing the amazing prosthesis. There was a pregnant pause as he waited for Uri to respond.

"What can I say," Uri finally stated. "I have no family here. Might as well make myself useful." Uri had always been self-deprecating. "When do I leave?"

It was clear to Har-Lavi that Uri had been expecting this. The big man also knew about his involvement with Lara, the lovely young FBI agent. "By the way," he added. "Your old partner, Ms. Edmond, has been assigned over there too."

Uri nodded, his mind full of conflicted feelings. He had no idea of her situation, whether she was married, whether she still had feelings for him. After all, he hadn't spoken with her in the years since they last worked together. And slept together.

"But, first things first," Har-Lavi said, interrupting Uri's thoughts. "Our idea is to put you in place over there as an escaped terrorist."

Uri looked up, somewhat confused.

"We've got lots of really bad guys in prison for life for the attacks they carried out against our civilians during the second intifada. If it were up to me, we'd have hanged all those bastards. But we don't have the death penalty; too bad. Anyway, now we can make use of our treasure trove of worthless trash."

"You're not planning on releasing one of those guys?" Uri asked.

"No, one of those guys is going to 'break out'. At least, that's what the press will report. We've got one guy with a life sentence who's been in since 2003. A real sweetheart.

Mohammed Azizi. Involved with the Kfar Darom massacre, the attack on the settlement at Shilo, Brit Horon in the year 2000, Tulkarem in 2001, and finally Kfar Ba'aneh in the Galilee a couple years later. That's where we caught him. By that time he had murdered seventeen women and children, in addition to eight male settlers. Most of them had their throats slit; others had been bound and tortured before being slaughtered."

"And how is this 'breakout' supposed to occur?" Uri queried, trying to change the subject before his stomach heaved.

"Azizi has been held in solitary confinement in Rimonim prison since it opened over twenty years ago. He was only nineteen or twenty at the time. The story will be the following: he was found by a guard one night, having deathly spasms. The prison hospital staff couldn't help him, had no idea what was wrong, so they have an ambulance take him to Hadassah hospital."

Uri sat there spellbound, wondering where this was going.

"It was in the middle of the night, on a dark spot in the road. The ambulance was supposedly stopped by what they thought was a repair crew. But then, the story goes, the 'road crew' turns out to be, in fact, a team of jihadis, armed with Kalashnikovs. The unconscious prisoner is whisked away into the night. Fortunately the ambulance crew was not harmed."

"And that's the story that Ha'aretz will publish?"

"Not only that; Al Jazeera will pick it up, giving credit to Islamic Jihad!"

"How in the world will you get them to do that?" Uri asked.

Har-Lavi paused and smiled. "We have paid agents everywhere. To give a little added credibility to the story, a vial containing traces of a spasm-inducing drug is to be found in his cell. Investigation into the perpetrators is, ah, ongoing."

"And, I take it, I am to take his identity, is that right?"

"Exactly. We have a complete set of papers for you in the name of Farid Refai. Your picture will be blurry enough to resemble a 40-year-old Azizi. However, you will first shave off that awful beard, and take on the appearance of an Israeli-Jewish businessman. You will depart for Los Angeles on an El Al flight, the tourist returning home."

Chapter 9

Uri arrived in Los Angeles onboard an El Al flight from Tel Aviv, stopping once in New York. He presented his Israeli passport identifying him as one Uri Cohen, businessman. The photo on this passport was taken just a few days ago at Mossad headquarters, showing him clean-shaven and respectable-looking.

Hidden away in his luggage was his false passport with a photo of one Farid Refai, a Jordanian from Amman. The photograph, taken of him earlier, before he had shaved, showed a 40-ish, bearded Middle Eastern man. It contained an authentic U.S. visa.

His luggage consisted only of a traditional travel suitcase. He was wearing a European-style suit, allowing him to blend in with the dozens of other, mostly American travelers returning to New York from a visit to Israel. His gaze was fixed forward as he passed harmlessly through customs. His luggage had of course been examined, but with his government-issued ID, caused him no difficulty.

This entry into the United States had been carefully coordinated between Tel Aviv, Washington, and the Israeli consul in Los Angeles. Concurrent with his trip was a story placed in *Ha'aretz*, an Israeli newspaper, about the escape and disappearance of a convicted terrorist named Mohammed Azizi. A blurry picture of Azizi, purportedly taken on his arrest in 2003, was barely recognizable as Refai. This photo, of course, resembled closely the one on Uri's fake Jordanian passport. According to the story, Azizi had been arrested in 2003; the lone gunman in an assault on Orthodox Jews praying at the Western Wall. The story went on to say that the shooter had succeeded in killing one and wounding three before being subdued.

Uri Cohen (aka Farid Refai, aka Mohammed Azizi, aka Uri Levin) stepped aboard the commuter bus outside the Los Angeles International Airport around 3 p.m. From here he made his way to the small hotel the Los Angeles consulate had reserved for him in the Wilshire district. He would meet with the local FBI folks tomorrow; now he needed some well-deserved sleep.

Chapter 10

Uri stumbled into FBI headquarters on Wilshire Boulevard at ten o'clock the next morning, as pre-arranged. He was still groggy from the long flight. He was to meet Mary Robley, the Chief of Operations there. After registering his credentials at the front desk, a courier took him up to her office. Mary greeted him with a smile; they recognized each other from the last episode he had been involved in Los Angeles: a foiled Hezbollah plot to terrorize the U.S. with nuclear destruction. He shook hands with her, she apparently taken aback just a bit by his business-like attire. She was accustomed to seeing him in the typical Israeli clothing of open-neck sport shirt and casual slacks. It was only then that he noticed the other person in the room: Lara Edmond.

He couldn't control the shock to his system as he saw her there. He knew she was on the case, of course. He just had not been prepared to see her yet. There she sat, as beautiful as he remembered: trim, blond, and attired in a well-fitting, blue business suit. There was no doubt in his mind that she could see the immediate effect on him; and she seemed pleased at it. The fog of the long plane trip cleared as he gazed at her, somewhat oblivious to the reason for the meeting.

"You remember Lara, of course," Mary said tauntingly. She was well aware of the brief romance between them, and seemed amused at his discomfiture.

"Yes, excuse me, my head is still somewhere over the Atlantic," Uri said haltingly, his eyes still fixed on Lara. It was she who finally stood up and grasped his hand, obviously trying to ease his embarrassment; but at the same time flattered by at his reaction. And, she realized, pleased by it as well. There had been no diminishment of the mutual attraction over the past few years.

"Sit down please, folks," Mary finally interjected. "Let me get some fresh coffee while you two get re-acquainted." Mary was discreet enough to recognize the awkwardness of the situation. She knew the two agents had not been in contact for some time; it was the Bureau's business to know these things. Under other circumstances, they might not have linked these two, given their history. But the extreme seriousness of the current situation, and the fact that they, as a team, had performed so well on two equally daunting assignments, made the teaming a necessity.

After Mary left, it was Lara who broke the silence again. "I hardly recognized you, in that fancy getup," she teased. She was surprised to see Uri clean-shaven, in a business suit instead of his usual open-neck sport shirt and slacks.

"An official order, from the boss in Tel Aviv," Uri replied blushing just slightly. He was still somewhat disoriented by her presence. He cleared his throat, trying to come up with something close to intelligent to say. "How are you?" he finally muttered.

Lara laughed, breaking the tension. "All right," she said lightly. "I like my new posting in New York. It's a nice change from D.C." She shifted slightly in her chair and ran her fingers through her hair as she waited for his reaction. When he didn't say anything she added, "...and you?" and folded her hands in her lap.

"I've been alright too, I guess," he offered after an awkward silence. "Been running around the West Bank playing Arab."

"Your eye," Lara said straightaway, "it seems so..."

"Natural?" Uri responded. The last time she had seen him, he had only a crude glass prosthesis to fill the void left by his

45

tussle with a Hezbollah terrorist under the streets of Chicago. Relaxed by her casual demeanor, he added: "leave it to those surgeons in Israel. They came up with this new gadget that moves in concert with the real, right one, see?" He gave her a demonstration, much to her amusement, as he moved his gaze from left to right.

"Terrific," she said, agreeing. Then, after a brief pause, she added, "we really need to coordinate our activities...soon." She waited for his reaction. His heartbeat quickened at this proposal; it was more than he had even hoped. But first he had to get oriented and decide how to proceed. He didn't want to let his heart overrule his head...not yet, at least.

"Yes, I'd like that, I mean, we need to..."

Lara laughed charmingly at his unease. "Let's have lunch and talk it over." She touched his arm and it sent electric shocks through him. He struggled to regain his composure.

Mary returned with coffee on a small tray and got back to business. "As you know, Uri,...uh, we can be on 'first names', right?" Uri nodded, smiling. "Right, well, as you probably know, we're dealing with a brutal gang here. No doubt connected with ISIS, or ISIL, anyway, Islamic State folks. I guess you've seen the markers they've left at the scenes. It appears the school massacre and the rabbi's murder are both the responsibility of the same group. We, of course, have been teaming up with the local police to check out all the immigrants here from the Middle East. But it's a big job, as you can imagine. Plus, there's the 'political correctness' aspect to consider. Please don't quote me. But it's quite a chore trying to find out who is here in the whole county, Los Angeles, on expired visas. What we're hoping you can do is utilize the resources available to you..." She nodded knowingly at Uri, indicating he would surely have Mossad's help.

"We can't just interrogate every Muslim in the county, or even the city without cause," she continued. "You, I'm sure, know about our limitations regarding 'profiling'." She grimaced, wishing she had the sensical laws the Israelis had at their disposal; laws that had kept their citizens relatively safe from terrorist attacks. "In any event, I have gotten permission for you to see all the information we have been able to gather so far. I'm afraid it's quite a massive bundle, but we'll give you time to work through it before we get together again. Basically, it's everything our ICE people— that's our Immigration and Customs Enforcement office— have on refugees from target countries who have arrived in the last ten years."

Instead of the pile of folders he had feared, Mary showed Uri three DVD's in protective cases. "Lara here has already gotten a head start; she has a proposal we're still mulling over. As you may know, she has an idea of scoping out Muslim clerics who are reaching out to try to find American wives. That operation, I should add, is not as yet approved." She glanced pointedly at Lara as she said this. "Well, I guess that should do it until you both reach the next level. Let's hope the bad guys give us enough time to come up with some ideas. Be sure to keep in contact! Oh, by the way, Uri, these DVD's have to stay on the premises; you'll be able to get them from the desk officer. They're locked so they can only be viewed on our computers on the fifth floor. You can get them tomorrow." With that, she rose, shook hands with both agents and left the room.

Chapter 11

Lara and Uri left the meeting at FBI headquarters with mixed emotions, both hiding their true fears and feelings. Lara suggested, and Uri quickly accepted, the plan of going to the small restaurant in her chic hotel in Beverly Hills. With Uri looking every bit the part of the Los Angeles lawyer or businessman, they would attract no attention. They hailed a cab outside the building on Wilshire, and arrived at her hotel in less than twenty minutes.

The restaurant was perfect for an intimate conversation; they sat in a small booth at the back, where they could watch the door. Both were clearly uneasy at this encounter. They had not seen each other, or even communicated in several years; still their brief, but electric romantic involvement in the past was obvious. They were like two magnets held apart by tenuous restraints. Both knew, from talking to their associates, that neither was currently involved in a relationship.

Uri, who had deliberately avoided looking directly at her during the meeting, knowing full well that their prior involvement was common knowledge among everyone at the Los Angeles FBI, now could scarcely take his eyes off her. She was incredibly attractive in her tailored blue suit, her neatly-cropped, blond hair reaching just to her shoulders. She had not changed, he thought to himself, if anything, even more alluring than when he last saw her. As they glanced at the menu, he caught her looking at him, too. She laughed cautiously and said, "You look so different in civilian clothes, I hardly recognized you." She paused and looked him over, dapper in his tan business suit.

"And the new eye," he interjected, "you saw how nicely it moves, almost like a real one." He was smiling as he said that; it was obvious to her that he was comfortable with it. He realized he had already demonstrated the prosthesis to her, and blushed self-consciously.

"Yes," she said, laughing brightly, happy he was willing to talk about it. The waiter showed up, and they hurriedly ordered some sandwiches and iced tea. As they were passing the menus, their hands briefly touched. An electric shock passed through Uri's entire being; there was no denying it, he was still crazy about her.

She must have felt it too, Uri thought, as a moment of silence passed between them. Then she added, "you look so different, all dressed up, like you just came from the financial district." She rubbed her hands nervously together as though wishing for physical contact as much as he.

It's mutual, Uri thought, as he looked directly into her strikingly-blue eyes. Her pupils dilated clearly as they gazed at each other, a sign that he had long learned was one of trust and desire. He was filled with internal conflict as her nearness almost overwhelmed him with emotion. In their previous two encounters, he had been the one to break it off. The first time, after they had foiled a Hezbollah plot to place nuclear devices in several U.S. cities, he had decided to return to his estranged wife. The second time had been more difficult; he had been in too much internal conflict over the need to decide between life with Lara in the U.S. or a return to Israel. He often regretted his decision; his marriage had ended and he realized how much he cared for Lara, how sweet life would be with her. He couldn't expect her to pick up things a third time, yet...

He decided to change the subject; even though this was a relatively insecure environment, there was enough background noise to allow them to have a brief, though important, conversation. "Your plan, as I understand it, to make a match..."

"I know," she interrupted, "it sounds dangerous..."

Uri looked up, more than startled. He had been briefed already about her idea of replying to advertisements for American wives. "An understatement, if I ever heard one," he replied, a little more sharply than he intended. It was clear to both of them how strong his feelings for her still were.

Lara was pleased with his reaction, yet that feeling was tempered with the thought that he might not be totally comfortable with her ability to confront dangerous situations on her own. "Let's just say that it's a 'proposal' in progress. I'll keep you updated on any progress." Her eyes told him much; she was delighted he cared, and would not act without consulting him. At that moment it seemed to her that no time at all had passed since their last contact.

They quickly dispatched their light meal, and Uri reached for the check, ready to leave the restaurant. Impulsively, she suddenly reached out and touched his arm, looking at him with a clear answer on her face; an answer to a question that hadn't been spoken. It didn't have to be, as he left cash for the meal along with a hefty tip. Rising together without touching, a couple of customers finishing a business lunch, they headed to the lobby of the hotel without exchanging a word. What was happening next had already been decided without speaking.

He shook her hand, continuing the charade, as he quietly asked her room number. "504," she replied, smiling, then turned toward the elevator. Uri went over to the newspaper stand, and after a brief perusal, bought a copy of Business Week. He sat in a lobby chair and appeared to glance through the magazine for a few minutes. He was actually studying the few new arrivals to the hotel; the other patrons gave him no more than a cursory look. When he was convinced he was not being watched, he went over to a different elevator and took it to the seventh floor.

It was a small hotel, and on exiting the elevator, he quickly spotted the access to the stairs. Fortunately, the door was not one of those that locked from the inside. Checking the hallway for curious eyes, he ducked into the stairwell and made the quick trip down to the fifth floor. With his heart beating wildly, he tried the door and found it unlocked. As quietly as possible, he let it close behind him and searched out room 504. It was just two doors away. She'd had about ten minutes head start. After a last cautious look around the hallway, he tapped lightly on the door. It opened silently, and he found himself staring into those beautiful blue eyes. Everything else on his mind, the child murders, the threat to Israel and the U.S.—disappeared as he swept her into his arms and closed the door behind them.

She was already in a bathrobe, one of those shorty-style hotel garments that allowed him a quick look at her lovely legs. She reached up and undid his tie, smiling at his clear arousal. "This is probably not a great idea," he said hoarsely.

"No kidding," she giggled playfully. "Certainly not in the FBI playbook," she said helping him off with his jacket, and loosening his belt. They crashed onto the king-size bed, his shoes and trousers kicked loose. They kissed each other lightly at first, Uri struggling to remove his shirt without ruining it. His kisses got more frenzied as she ran her hands across his well-muscled back and chest, not caring at all about the thick curls of hair. Their ardor became more urgent as their tongues intertwined in a passion renewed as though no time had passed at all since they had last been together.

He opened her robe and was thrilled to the renewed sight of her glorious shape. She, meanwhile, added to his ardor by sliding down his underwear. He was, by this time, fully aroused. He had not spoken a word as he continued to explore her body with his hands and mouth. She purred like a kitten as she gently reached for him, stroking him with tantalizing lightness. Meanwhile, he found her to be completely ready for him. They plunged together in a locked embrace, her legs wrapping themselves around his waist. She moaned as he thrust himself in completely, a gasp coming from his own throat.

Afterward, they lay there in each other's arms, deep in thought. Finally, Uri spoke softly, running his fingers through her hair. "Seriously," he said imploringly, "you really intend to go through with this 'marriage proposal'?"

"Like I said, it's still in the initial stages," she replied, not wanting to alarm him too much, at least not yet. "Now, you better get going." He realized she was right. Both of them had plenty of things to accomplish, and not much time. Furthermore, they could not afford to be seen together. The FBI would no doubt find their intimate association a distraction, at least, and a dangerous bit of information for the hidden enemy.

Chapter 12

The next morning, Uri showed up at the FBI building bright and early at 8 a.m., ready to examine the DVDs containing the data on the Muslim immigrants. He figured he needed to start by catching up with whatever information the U.S. agents had to work with. He showed his pass to the desk agent, who retrieved the discs and procured an escort for him to the secure computer room. Here he was locked inside with a dedicated desk-top PC, but no printer. There was a small washroom and table with coffee, water, doughnuts and paper towels. He supposed he could take notes; at least, he hadn't been warned against it.

He got right to work; he was eager to see what had been collected. From the start he was disappointed. There was a huge listing, arranged by date of entry into the States, with the names, country of origin, passport ID number, and destination within the U.S. That was it. There was a way to cross check using the name of the person; but there were so many near-identical names it seemed a hopeless task. Another tool allowed him to access persons through country of origin or passport number, but that also seemed an unachievable goal.

He was dismayed to find that there appeared to be no record of those persons who had overstayed their visa dates. As long as they stayed out of legal trouble, they could move around the country with relative ease. The "students" were free to transfer from one school to another, get employment, and move freely among all the states. They could even visit other countries, as long as those countries weren't on the "no travel" list; countries like North Korea and Syria.

After about two hours, Uri rang for the clerk, handed him the discs and left the building. He was disappointed, but realized he hadn't expected to find a treasure trove. If useful information was there, the JTTF would have already been out on the hunt.

He did, however, have a more promising destination, one that was close by. He took a taxi, eschewing the bus system for the time being, and headed to Beverly Hills. He had the driver let him out a few blocks from his destination, as was customary. The area was a thriving, upscale part of Los Angeles, known worldwide for its glitz and glamour. He was in one of the expensive business areas, actually not far from the school where the massacre had occurred. That thought lay close to surface as he perused the busy crowd of shoppers and sight-seers. He was headed for a meeting with one of Israel's hidden friends, a civilian who acted as an agent while maintaining a normal life and career. These people, known as "*sayanim*", were typically Jewish professionals, citizens of their country of residence, but willing and able to offer assistance when called upon. They could be counted upon to provide money, shelter, and information vital to the operation of Mossad.

Uri walked the last couple of blocks down Wilshire Boulevard to the man's office. Dr. David Emelkies was a well-known and respected dentist—oral surgeon, actually—who had a modern, attractive set of offices on the first floor of one of the many high-rise office buildings in this part of Beverly Hills.

Dr. Emelkies was one of the tens of thousands of Persian-Jewish émigrés from Iran in the late seventies, who settled in Los Angeles. His father had managed to escape the Islamist revolution with much of his wealth, and, of course, his training as an eye surgeon. The son, David, Uri knew, had received his education and training as an oral surgeon here in Los Angeles, at the University of Southern California.

Uri entered a spacious waiting area, empty of patients. Behind a shimmering granite counter, devoid of anything except a huge model of a tooth, sat a stunning young woman who smiled at him in greeting. She had Middle Eastern features, long, straight dark hair and amazingly blue eyes. No doubt Persian, he thought to himself.

"You would be Mr. Cohen," she said brightly. Uri had dressed for this meeting with the dentist in normal attire, but with his prosthetic eye in place. "Dr. Emelkies is expecting you," she said before he had a chance to speak.

"You are correct," he replied, "Uri Cohen."

"And I am Dr. Emelkies," came a strong voice from behind Uri. He turned to find a broadly smiling man in a shirt, tie and blue smock, his hand extended. "David."

Uri took his hand, smiling in return, taking in all the features of this strongly-built, fifty-ish man with a short, full beard. He was clearly of Persian origin, but he wore a tiny Star of David around his neck. "Come with me and we'll take a look at that number 14 of yours."

Uri looked at him for a second, not quite understanding. He glanced back at the young receptionist, who was looking at him admiringly with her beautiful blue eyes.

"That upper left molar, let's take a look at it," Emelkies said, his hand on Uri's shoulder guiding him into a room with a huge chair, lights, and all sorts of electronic gadgetry. As he entered the room behind Uri, he said, "don't pay any attention to Sarah," indicating the young girl. "My daughter, she's at that age, very flirtatious, I don't know what to do with her," he said, smiling.

"*You've got a job ahead of you,*" Uri thought to himself, as the doctor closed the door. He noticed that Emelkies switched on a small white-noise machine.

Following Uri's glance, Emelkies said, "For privacy; I do it with all my patients. Now let's get a picture of that number 14." He sat Uri down, put a paper napkin around his neck, and laid a lead-filled blanket across his lap. "Here, just bite down easily on this," he said, placing something inside Uri's mouth.

Uri followed the doctor's instructions, figuring he had to complete the charade. The oral surgeon stepped behind a protective shield, pressing a button. "All right, let's have a look." An image of the left side of Uri's mouth appeared instantly on a digital display. "I've got to have this with the records," he said quietly, as Uri nodded his understanding. "Well," Emelkies said as he looked at the x-ray. "I can see why you're having trouble with that tooth. It's out of line with its neighbors, 13 and 15."

Uri had indeed been bothered with that tooth for some time, but had no intention of doing anything about it now. He was encouraged by the elegant cover story this doctor was producing, however. It showed he was no amateur at this *sayanim* business.

"What we can do, what I recommend, is that we extract it and put in an implant. Do it all the time. Couple of visits, that's all."

Uri gave him a look that was intended to say, "*I like your attitude, doctor, but we both know that's not what I'm here for.*"

David Emelkies smiled in return, made some notes in a manila folder, and removed the napkin and lead apron. He moved Uri's chair to an upright position and rolled his chair directly opposite. "Alright," he said quietly, "now we can get down to business. How exactly can I be of service?"

"The things that have been going on here, we need to know who's responsible. Do you have any leads for me at all?"

Realizing he was asking an impossible question, Uri backed off a little. "I mean do you know of any specific mosques or imams who have been especially anti-Semitic? Especially Sunni mosques, since we're looking for ISIS affiliation."

Emelkies sighed and rubbed his temples. "I have something for you; I don't know how much it will help." He brought out from his inside breast pocket a single piece of paper on which there was a handwritten list of names of mosques and imams. Handing it to Uri, he said "for what it's worth…"

* * *

Uri glanced quickly at the list before he slipped it into his pocket. He recognized many of the large Sunni congregations. A few others on first glance didn't ring a bell. No matter, he decided; he would make an initial attempt at his Muslim disguise at one of them. His facial hair had not grown back to the extent necessary for him to use the fake Refai passport photo, so his plan was to merely pass himself off as one of the congregants at a large mosque during midday prayers. This would give him the confidence he needed to "expose" himself first as Farid Refai, then later, hopefully, as Mohammed Azizi. He chose a mosque at random from the list, one near the downtown area, and took a couple of Los Angeles buses from Beverly Hills into the metro center, near Union Station.

He didn't talk to anyone on the way, but he did see a few poorly-dressed people, most of whom just nodded at him. He politely returned their nods. Although he had been in Los Angeles before, he was not familiar with the downtown area. But he knew what he was looking for: The Sunni mosque called the Masjid El Tahid. It was now about time for the post-sunset, or Maghrib, prayers, so this would be his first test.

He found the Masjid readily from the map, a prominent, white-tiled structure, its name boldly displayed in gold lettering, both in Arabic and English. Opening the door, he found himself in front of two smiling Middle-Eastern men, dressed in full white robes and headdress. They greeted him in English, not unreasonable, considering his dress and appearance, and he correctly returned their greeting, but in Arabic.

"You're just in time for Maghrib," said the first man in heavily-accented English. He was a tall, light-skinned Arab, perhaps a Saudi. "You speak Arabic, but I have not seen you at our Masjid before, is that not right?"

"You are quite correct, I am new to the area," Uri replied, again in Arabic. The tall Arab politely pointed to the obligatory shoe depository. "Thank you," replied Uri, slipping off his shoes and placing them neatly next to more than fifty sets of various footwear.

Uri had managed everything alright so far, he felt, but it was with some unease that he entered the prayer room. He had practiced various prayers, or "sulaat," but never had to perform under these conditions. He knew he would be observed closely, but he was confident his hours of practice would pay off.

Pulling a knitted, white *kufi* from his pocket, Uri placed it on his head as he found a convenient place at the side of the prayer room, next to a grizzled, old Arab. Most of the congregation was dressed formally, in white robes. There were however, several men in casual street dress, much to his relief. From there on things went smoothly. He followed along the lead of the other men in the room, as they went through their prayers; standing, kneeling and prostrating himself appropriately.

He noticed only three or four women, who had found places to pray to the rear of the men. They were inconspicuous, being covered completely and arranging themselves in such a way as to not reveal any aspect of their physical makeup. Thankfully, the Maghrib ended in about half an hour. He rose, bowed in greeting to his fellow supplicants, and found his shoes right where he had left them. As he made his way to the exit to the street, he noticed the two Arabs who had met him. They watched as he headed out toward the bus stop, but said nothing to him; they simply bowed. He returned the bow and said to them, "*as salaam alaykum*." They broke into broad smiles and replied to him in unison: "*wa alaykum salaam*." He had passed his first real test.

Chapter 13

The newly appointed Iranian Prime Minister, Feroze Abbasi, sat comfortably in his huge armchair, sipping strong, sweet coffee from a dainty cup. His counterpart, Dmitri Kazakov, Foreign Minister of Russia, sat with equal comfort in his lounge chair next to Abbasi, noisily drinking his equally strong tea. It would be evident to anyone watching the scene that each of the two was trying to assume a position of superiority.

"Well," said Abbasi finally, "I suppose it's time to get down to business." He spoke in Farsi, a language with which Kazakov was fairly fluent, having grown up in Azerbaijan, on Iran's northern border.

"Yes," replied Dmitri, pleased that it was the Persian who was forced to initiate the business part of this meeting. He took one more slurp of his tea, plopped the cup and saucer sharply down on the small table in front of them, and rearranged himself to a more businesslike posture.

Abbasi was, he knew, at a distinct disadvantage, being younger and considerably less experienced than his Russian guest. Abbasi was the one who had requested this meeting, arranging for the highest ranking Russian official to come to Tehran for this semi-official conference.

News media were not only absent, they were totally unaware that this face-to-face was occurring. Satellite surveillance had alerted the Western powers that a Russian Sukhoi MC-21 passenger jet, probably governmental, had landed at the Tehran military airport. Some sort of official delegation departed the plane and was whisked off in limousines. Apart from that, they were in the dark as to what was occurring.

"Dmitri," Abbasi said finally, "I'm sure you have an idea why I requested this meeting."

"I think so," the Russian replied. "Why don't you go ahead and speak frankly. We are, after all, friends and allies."

Abbasi nodded, smiling, knowing that the Russian was referring to the secret and not-so-secret arms shipments Iran had received in defiance of the West. Iran was able to beef up its intermediate range and intercontinental range ballistic missile supply, much to the chagrin of the United States and its allies. But the Western allies appeared helpless, or at least unwilling, to do anything about it. Their attempts at economic sanctions had proven unable to dissuade the Iranians from arms buildup, not to mention their advances in nuclear capability. All this improved Iran's ability to instill fear in their primary objective, Israel, which had been designated over and over again by the Ayatollah, as an entity doomed to destruction.

After a brief pause, Abbasi once again shifted his posture and became more serious. "Nuclear weapons," he said finally. "Ones we can place on our missiles and demonstrate to the world that we have not only the will, but the power to destroy our enemies."

"Let's be clear about this," the Russian said, "we're just talking about demonstrations, not actual warfare?" There was a pause in the conversation. "We don't want to start World War III just on account of the Jews."

"You know as well as I do that it was the Jews who started World Wars I and II." He paused for a moment. Then he continued, "and who profited from them, I might add. Just look at what they stole from our country during our revolution. Half of our wealth now resides in Beverly Hills."

The Russian smiled in agreement. "You have no argument from me, my friend. They did the same to our country. With all their false claims of genocide, they looted our treasuries and ran off to Israel."

Of course, neither man believed what he was saying; it was just reassuring to hear each other repeat the lies they liked to spread among the populace.

"Let me first tell you our ambitious scheme for you," Kazakov said to Abbasi, with a deliberate alteration in posture and attitude. He had the Iranian's full attention. "Our nations both wish to destroy both the DAESH 'ISIS' Caliphate and the Zionist State, correct?" The Iranian bolted to full attention, nodding eagerly. "What we, the Russians, propose is for your allies, the Hezbollah fighters, to attack not just the Jews in the United States, but also the Sunni Muslims." Kazakov was, of course, well aware of the Hezbollah terrorism against the Jews in Southern California.

Abbasi started to interrupt, but the Russian motioned for him to be silent. "You see, if we can increase the hostility between America and DAESH, it will help our cause here, in the land of the Caliphate; the U.S. will increase their bombing campaign against them." The Iranian nodded for him to continue. "Then we build animosity against the Jews by casting blame on them for some outrageous acts of vengeance against innocent American Sunni Muslims." He waited for the impact of this bold strategy to sink in.

"You mean, I take it," probed an uncertain Abbasi, "that we get our Hezbollah allies to create internal havoc in the U.S. by finding Jews to kill Sunnis?"

"Not quite. You must disguise the Hezbollah forces in the U.S., preferably Southern California, where your operatives have already conducted successful missions. Get them to appear to be angry Jews. It should not be that difficult. After all, we are both Semitic people; Americans cannot easily tell the difference between Muslim and Jew. The Anti-Israel sentiment will build, as there are many in the U.S. who feel the Jews have too much power and influence. These kinds of acts will feed a growing movement. We both get what we want: U.S. force focused against our common enemies, DAESH *and* the Zionists!"

Abbasi smiled broadly as the creativity of this plan crystallized in his mind. Indeed, a coup for both the Shia and the Russians! "Yes," he declared, "yes, a brilliant strategy."

"Fine," the Russian replied. "We will continue to supply you with weaponry and other assistance that you can use to demonstrate your strength against the U.S. But let's again be clear: demonstration only."

Abbasi eagerly nodded. "So, I can tell the Ayatollah that we have an agreement?" the Iranian asked hopefully.

"Well, my friend, of course I must take this to our Russian prime minister and president for final approval; but I think, in principle, they would enjoy this twisting of the American's nose. Their president has shown himself to be so weak that there is little likelihood of any retribution." Kazakov sat back and waited for the Iranian's response.

"Exactly so," the jubilant Abbasi concurred. "Look at what the North Koreans and the Pakistanis have gotten away with. The American public has shown it has no stomach for any kind of military action, no matter what happens to its allies."

"I presume you're talking about a *non*-nuclear demonstration in the Persian Gulf." Abbasi smiled in reply. "But may I tell our leaders that your engineers would be *capable* of attaching some small nuclear payloads to your existing intermediate range missiles?" the Russian asked, knowing what the response would be.

"Precisely! We want to show that we have missiles ready to strike the Jew where he lives."

Seeing they were in near total agreement, Abbasi leaned back into his comfortable cushion and enjoyed his beverage. He was very pleased. His Russian protégé was also.

Chapter 14

Sheikh Hassan Nasrallah lowered his bulky frame gingerly into the soft cushions provide by his host. He had long since acknowledged that his Shia group in Lebanon was fighting across all of Syria in support of its dictator-president's government. But this was the first time he had actually met directly with his prime supporter, the newly appointed prime minister of Iran.

Hezbollah was the western arm of the Shia battle against DAESH, which the West called ISIS or ISIL, in their fight to maintain control of the Levant. Stopping DAESH, and their planned Sunni Caliphate, was a necessary step in converting all Islam into the true religion. The world would then follow, as their multitudes migrated to the West to destroy their decadent democracies.

The Ayatollah ruling Iran had been pleased to see the Americans fight against DAESH; they aided the Syrian government, and with it the advance of the true religion. And so the invitation to Nasrallah had been logical. Arms and other logistical support had been flowing from Iran to Hezbollah for some years already. But now they could formally set up a dedicated military alliance.

Sheikh Nasrallah appeared quite different from the posters the Hezbollah supporters brandished gleefully around Lebanon. The once young, trim fighter with dark hair had become a soft, grey-bearded, sickly man well up in years. The constant fight against both Israel and the Sunni rebels had taken its toll. That is why he welcomed the invitation to come to Iran. Perhaps now he would learn what the Shia leaders had in store for the evil West.

The two men sipped their strong Persian coffee from small cups and sized each other up. The Hezbollah leader was eager, and even somewhat desperate, to please the prime minister. He was in fact ready to do anything to solidify his position and help drive the Sunni apostates from Syria and Western Iraq. He was delighted to have apparently reached a position of equality with his Iranian Shia allies. Together, and with the unwitting support of the Americans, they would drive the Sunni Arabs into submission, if not total conversion. Arabs, after all, he reasoned, would gravitate toward the most power. He wondered what specifically the Iranians had planned. "How can we be of assistance?"

The prime minister, Abbasi, still sat deep in apparent thought. Finally he stated bluntly, "I suppose you are aware of the current turmoil in America, most specifically in California."

Nasrallah immediately recognized the prime minister was referring to the recent slayings of children and prominent Jews in Los Angeles. "Yes," he said, "DAESH is making quite a bold statement, showing how they can attack Americans with impunity right in their own backyard."

The prime minister smiled, almost laughing, confiding to his Hezbollah ally, "Yes, that is precisely what we wish them to think!"

The aging sheikh bolted upright. "Are you telling me that these glorious beheadings are *not* the action of DAESH!?" He was both astonished with the boldness of the Iranians and delighted that the prime minister would share this information with him. It meant that Hezbollah was now in high standing with the fight against the West.

The Iranian prime minister smiled again, allowing his moment of triumph to sink in. "That is what we want the Americans to think; in fact, what we want the *whole* western world to think. So they will use their vast resources against the growing DAESH Caliphate, and in so doing, aid our effort in obliterating it."

Sheikh Nasrallah could only gape in wonderment as he realized the clever workings of the Iranian Shia ministers. By sending Shia troops to Iraq to help blunt the Sunni DAESH invaders, they were ingratiating themselves with the Americans. This, along with the heinous attacks on civilians in the United States, supposedly by DAESH operatives, made the Americans and their Western allies less prone to see the Shia as their real enemies.

"*'Taqiyya'*," my friend. "When has it been more appropriate to use the Arabs' own invention?" The Shia leader was clearly referring to the ancient, well-recognized custom of the Arabs: *Lying and cheating in the Arab world is not really a moral matter but a method of safeguarding honor and status, avoiding shame, and at all times exploiting possibilities, for those with the wits for it, deftly and expeditiously to convert shame into honor on their own account and vice versa for their opponents. If honor so demands, lies and cheating may become absolute imperatives.*

Sheikh Nasrallah nodded thoughtfully. Their Persian allies had been one step ahead: committing atrocities on the Americans and at the same time blaming them on their Sunni enemies. How better to split the forces of the Western apostates than to focus their attention on the so-called "Islamic State." With the United States and its ally Saudi Arabia intent on destroying the fanatic Sunni forces, whether in Syria, Iraq, or Yemen, they would eagerly accept the savage killings in California as the work of DAESH.

The acceptance of Iranian forces in the battle against DAESH in the remnants of Iraq was even more an example of the usefulness of *taqiyya.* When the successes of the Shia against the West became known, Arabs from all parts of the world would flock to join with the victors.

The Hezbollah leader from Lebanon shook his head in wonderment at the audacity and cleverness of his Iranian benefactor. "So how can we be of assistance to you?" he again inquired.

Abbasi smiled warmly. "We must do everything possible to prevent the Americans from discovering the true source of the sword of Allah. As of now, they are throwing all their considerable forces against the Arabs of DAESH. We have shown ourselves to be their allies. As long as we can maintain this pretense, we are free to work our will against the crusaders. And the Americans have no idea what we have in store for them."

"But what of this new pact you have signed with the Americans?" Nasrallah asked. "I understood it to mean that in exchange for more than one hundred billion U.S. dollars, you have agreed to abandon your nuclear arms development and will allow them access to your military establishment."

The prime minister shook with laughter, slapping both hands against his ample thighs. "This 'pact', as you call it, merely releases monies the United States has illegally held back from Iran, to whom it belongs. Assets that were 'frozen' years ago."

"Yes, I understand," the sheikh acknowledged, "but doesn't this mean that you must abandon your nuclear weapons and other advanced military programs?"

The Iranian grinned at his co-conspirator, leaned across the low coffee table, and clapped him on the shoulder. "Taqiyya, my friend, taqiyya. The weak American president has no conception at all of how the Muslim world works."

Rising slowly to his feet with the aid of a high-back chair, the prime minister walked unhurriedly into the next room, gesturing for the sheikh to follow. There on a well-lit wall had been placed a large map of the nation of Iran.

The sheikh gazed in wonderment, both at the detailed map and the décor of the room itself. A huge, beautiful Persian carpet graced the floor. The windowless room housed a curved table, over twenty feet in length, surrounded by twenty-four chairs. The table itself was a marvel of opulence, created from dark wood, perhaps ebony, covered with a seamless layer of thick glass. The chairs, constructed of the same exquisite wood, were comfortably upholstered in padded velvet. The table and chairs were magnificently trimmed with ivory, illicitly obtained from poachers. It was truly a room fit for a king.

The prime minister announced with a sweep of his hand: "This, my friend, is our war preparations room." He strode over to the map on the wall. "We, as you can see, are a very large country. Small perhaps in comparison with our neighbors, the Russias, but much larger than the typical American would ever imagine. When convinced by their president that we would be bound by this so-called 'pact', the American people think of us as some small Middle Eastern country, perhaps the size of Lebanon. Their knowledge of geography is as pitiful as their knowledge of taqıyya."

The sheikh was struck with the detail exhibited on the large, colored, topographical map. "Let me show you a few things," Abbasi proclaimed as he used a baton to point out some features. "These buildings, shown in red, are schools; the blue buildings are hospitals, the green are pedestrian malls."

The sheikh merely nodded, not quite getting the idea. "You see, my friend," the prime minister said patiently, as though talking to a schoolboy, "this is what we present to the Americans. What they don't see are the fortified, underground bunkers that house our burgeoning nuclear weapons program." With a flourish, he flipped a switch on the wall, displaying an otherwise invisible network of complex buildings.

"The whole world knows of our Bushehr reactor here," he said, pointing to the map, "near the Persian Gulf, built with the help of the Russians. But it is considered relatively harmless, capable only of producing power and not weapons-grade material. What the rest of the world does *not* know is that the Russians have helped transform this reactor, and others like it hidden in the mountains in our East and North, into a type that can produce plutonium. Weapons-grade plutonium!"

The sheikh collapsed in wonderment as he gazed at the panoramic spectacle in front of him. "But the Russians, aren't they afraid of retaliation from the West if this were ever to become known?"

"My friend, the Russian president can see full well how unprepared the Americans are for any attack. Furthermore, we have assured the Russians that our new weapons will be used only for demonstration purposes; to convince our enemies that we have the capability of massive retaliation against any attack they might consider."

"If, for example, Israel should…," the sheikh began.

"Precisely," the prime minister continued. "To prevent any interference by Israel or the Western powers, Russia has agreed to provide us with the means necessary to demonstrate our readiness. We will be able to fire a test missile with a nuclear warhead far down into the Persian Gulf."

"But," the sheikh implored, "will not the Americans react violently to such a show of disdain for them?"

Abbasi laughed heartily again. "They will react precisely as they have against North Korea and Pakistan. They will do nothing, except perhaps complain. But they are not about to start a World War; the Americans and Europeans have had their fill of interference in the Middle East."

Nasrallah sat pensively for a moment. Then, clearly in submission to his Persian colleague, he once again asked, "I must repeat, what do you wish from us, the Hezbollah?"

"Very simple. We want your help in furthering our attack against the Americans in California. We want to multiply the destruction of the Jews, blaming it entirely on DAESH. I know you, the Hezbollah, have agents in Los Angeles, as do we. Let us work together to create further havoc."

The sheikh was impressed at the Iranian's knowledge of the Hezbollah influence in America. They did, in fact, have many "public information" agencies there with labels such as: "Truth in the Middle East" and "Council on Islamic-American Relations."

"We have two main strategies in mind," the prime minister continued. "First, we want to strike the Jew with a multi-pronged attack on one of their festival days. It is to be a massacre similar to those perpetrated in Paris and other places."

"But, have those been the work of DAESH...?" the sheik implored.

Abbasi just smiled once again, but said nothing in reply. "We would like you, with your agents, to carry out such a scheme on the next Jewish holiday. We will provide whatever aid we can through our imams in Los Angeles. I will provide you with a list."

The sheikh remained motionless for a moment, filled with wonder and awe at the magnitude of the delicious scheme, and the magnificence of Hezbollah's part in it. "And the other stratagem...?"

"We have good information that an Israeli Mossad agent has infiltrated the Muslim society in Los Angeles. You may know him—Uri Levin."

Nasrallah jerked upright in astonishment. "You mean that Kidon bastard who helped the FBI against our bomb threat years ago!?"

"The very same," the Iranian replied, "not to mention the assassination of our great leader, Imad Mughniyah in 2008. To add insult, he then killed 'The Ghost', a few years later—one of the most successful of our fighters in the Middle East!"

The sheikh's mouth flew open. "You know this for a fact? I thought this Uri Levin had gone into retirement or was killed. He already lost an eye in the fight against our operatives in the United States. How can he possibly..."

"We're pretty sure. But not only that, his Jew whore has been recruited as well."

The sheikh was dumbfounded. He sat upright in his chair with open mouth and stared at his host. "The two of them, in Los Angeles!?"

"At this moment they are trying to infiltrate the DAESH organization there!"

There was a long silence as Nasrallah tried to put all this together. Several things bothered him. First, how could the Iranians, nearly all Shia, know that the Israeli and his American mistress were trying to access DAESH, a fully Sunni organization? DAESH, after all, was trying to rid the world of the Shia. Second, how did the Iranians plan to arrange a massive strike in Los Angeles? And finally, what could Hezbollah offer, when they had practically no organization in the U.S.?

It was Prime Minister Abbasi who finally broke the extended silence: "You are wondering, no doubt, what role you can play in our scheme."

"Yes," the sheikh replied weakly, "that, among other things."

"Everything will become clear, in time. But first, tell me, are you willing to join with us?"

"Of course, but how have you managed to carry out this charade, right under the very noses of the Americans *and* Mossad!?"

"We have our agents, too, you know," the Iranian retorted, looking at his new associate with a knowing smile.

Nasrallah could see that he must agree with the Iranian without knowing any more details. He realized he would be similarly secretive if he were in the same position. "All right, you have my word—and the blessing of Allah! You shall have all the resources at my disposal!" Standing, he grasped the prime minister's hand firmly in both of his, as they kissed each other on both cheeks.

"*Allahu Akhbar*," they exhorted in unison. "And death to the Jew!" the sheikh added with a flourish.

"*Insha'Allah,*" they declared in unison.

Chapter 15

Sheikh Nasrallah finished up his fruitful meeting with the Iranian with the usual congratulatory hugs and kisses. They had set up a master plan, as well as the avenue for communication between them. They both had the latest satellite phones, ones designed by two engineers working for a new Qatari start-up firm. The engineers in charge, Amir and Izad, had graduated from a fine school in America, the esteemed Massachusetts Institute of Technology, with degrees in electronics miniaturization and satellite communications. They found employment involving the Department of Defense (DOD). While they did not have the top-secret clearances needed to work specifically on the DOD contracts held by their employers, the work allowed them to discover the use for the modules they were in charge of developing. They would, they correctly reasoned, likely be used in any electronics communication modules, especially covert satellite communications.

After two years, and the failed plot attempted by other Hezbollah operatives in Southern California, Amir and Izad were sought out by Nasrallah's head of operations in the U.S., one Javad Abdouleh. Javad had charge of a small team of young Iranian and Pakistani engineers with faultless academic records from other U.S. technical universities. His twelve "apostles," as he jokingly called them, were recruited at a friendly Shia mosque in California's Muslim-rich Orange County.

Both Amir and Izad were sought out by high-tech start-ups and met Javad at the social gatherings that often followed services at the mosque. After the near-success in Los Angeles, carried out by another Hezbollah team, Javad had kept a very low profile for two years. But, by then, Orange County had grown in Shia population with no overt threats against the local Anglo population. So the mosques, dress, and customs were very well accepted in the area.

New members were carefully vetted by Javad and his second-in-command, Basir Kashani. Both had lived in Southern California for over ten years; although not skilled in technical matters, they had shrewd eyes for likely recruits to the Hezbollah cause. Sipping hot, strong, Persian coffee in the meeting area in the rear of the mosque, discussions often crept into the areas of politics and religion. It became clear to Javad and Basir, over time, which young recruits were thoroughly anti-Shah "a curse on all his family" and devoted to the Islamic Revolution. Amir and Izad, recruited shortly after the failed, Hezbollah-devised, nuclear-bomb scheme, had both the skills and temperament needed for the work Javad had been instructed by Sheikh Nasrallah to conduct.

Other young members of the cabal were relegated to less technical duties. The group carried out demonstrations against Israel and pro-Israel organizations. They also handed out circulars and petitions on the many college campuses in the area, and attempted, often successfully, to harass pro-Israel speakers at college and neighborhood events.

It was, in fact, Javad's small band of operatives who identified Rabbi Meir Rosenblum as a target for assassination. They found out, through a local gun merchant, that Rabbi Rosenblum had a license to carry a concealed hand gun. That would add a slice of glamour to the discovery of his body, Javad reasoned correctly. The assassination itself was carried out, of course, by Imam Ali's band in Los Angeles. The lack of direct connection between the two terrorist groups helped deflect the LAPD's efforts at solving the crime.

The success of the rabbi's elimination was what led Nasrallah to assign the next tasks to Javad's gang. After getting the blessings of the Iranians, Nasrallah quickly decided that Javad's men were the appropriate contractors for the next outrageous attack on the Southern California Jewish Community: The Purim Assault.

"Purim" was a festival celebrated by Jews the world over, one that was enjoyed by adults and children alike. It involved costumes and feasting; a happy time, indeed. It was of special significance to Javad and his followers because it purported to recognize a victory of Persian Jews over their masters.

Javad and his followers were all immigrants to the U.S. under student visas. He and his recruits had all come from Pakistan or Iran, with the stated intent of studying engineering or computer science, and then returning to their native countries. They all had, indeed, enrolled in mid-rank schools all across the country, with varying degrees of success. Javad, himself, was a Pakistani, devoutly Shia, with enough Qu'ranic study to justify calling himself "Imam." Nasrallah himself had allowed him this privilege.

Javad was a distinct physical presence. He had a strong hawk-like face with sharply defined features. He was tall, lean and strong, notably different from the portly sheikh. But he was deeply devoted to the blessed sheikh. After all, it was Sheikh Nasrallah who had led all the havoc against the cursed Zionists, killing scores of their offspring in the villages along the southern borders of Lebanon.

Javad was also instrumental in maintaining the public pressure against the Zionists, by bringing the weight of "human rights" groups to bear against the United Nations. That had been relatively easy, certainly, given the bias already present. But having the added pressure of the naïve, liberal elements of the Western press had certainly made their task easier. True, Hezbollah had to sacrifice some of their own children to martyrdom in order to convince the press that Israel was responsible for the continued violence. But, after all, wasn't martyrdom preferable to living under the constant threat posed by the enemy?

Javad and his men had found employment in various small companies requiring relatively low levels of skill. The job market was rich in Orange County, California, with the many small start-up firms needing just the skills these men possessed. The wages were meager, as were the responsibilities, but these were the perfect conditions for them. They were used to living in multi-dwelling apartments with slim amenities.

English was, of course, the second language for all the men, the first usually being Farsi. All spoke some Arabic, as well. The U.S. government soon lost track of all these immigrants on student visas. The companies that hired them had no problem filling out the simple paperwork to keep them employed as "part-time students." As with most of the foreign students on campuses, they tended to socialize with others from their home countries. Those from Pakistan and Iran, speaking mainly Farsi, soon found Shia mosques in which to pray and congregate. Javad, being in the country the longest, and a natural-born leader, brought many to his mosque, Ah-Bayt, in a small community near Santa Ana. In just a few years he had assembled more than thirty acolytes.

The assembly of his team began with after-service meetings on Friday evenings. Here Javad had first brought forth invective against Israel and the Zionists; this had met with universal approval. Over the next weeks and months, the antagonism increased in scope to include America and Western Europe. It was not a difficult sell; many, if not all of his listeners had already been introduced to the anti-West rhetoric in their home countries. They had seen the suffering of their peoples brought on by the oppressive nature of the Judeo-Christian cabal. In a short time he had assembled a core group of hardened jihadis ready to do their part in whatever havoc Javad had in store.

Communication among his team had, at first, been an issue. That was soon allayed by the computer whizzes at his disposal. They instigated a clever means of email notices using the school computer system, delivered through a network of interlinked servers. The path was near unbreakable once the key to the code, based on Shia Qu'ran passages, was distributed among the most trusted of the operatives.

Javad got word of his assignment through an emissary, close to Sheikh Nasrallah, who made periodic trips to Turkey under the guise of a salesman. His jihadis, under orders from the sheikh, were to link up with the team in Los Angeles that had carried out the now-famous beheadings at the Jewish school. Javad would meet with the imam, Ali Muhammad, who had directed the celebrated massacre. First, though, he had to make doubly sure of the veracity of the sheikh's command. Unknown to his first emissary, he maintained contact with another, based in Lebanon, who could be contacted only on the most urgent matters. This certainly was one. Through a complex code, he did indeed get confirmation from this secondary source, that the coordinated attack was authorized: on the next Jewish festival of Purim, the celebration of the imaginary triumph of a Jewess traitor over the great and gracious Persian King Xerxes in the 5th century B.C.

Of course, as with the other executions of the Jews, the blame would be laid at the doorstep of the Sunnis. Banners of "DAESH", the group known in the West as ISIS or ISIL, would be left at the scene. While Sheikh Nasrallah would, of course, prefer to take credit for the massacre in the name of Hezbollah and their backers, the Iranians, it made sense to deflect the wrath of the Americans, allowing time for even more destruction.

Chapter 16

Javad Abdouleh looked over his ardent group of jihadis. He had been given his orders, and he was thrilled to be able to share them with his troops. Sheikh Hassan Nasrallah, blessed be he, had graced his, Javad's, humble gathering with the task of aiding the efforts of Ali Muhammad, the Los Angeles imam. What could be a greater assignment than to join forces with the courageous men who had carried out the delicious slaughter of the young Jews!? How grateful his minions would be when they learn of their assignment! It remained only for him to decide which of his warriors were to perform the necessary tasks.

Certainly, Basir Kashani, his second in command and most experienced, should be granted the glory of leading one of the attacks to be made on the coming spring night.

Basir, at age twenty-seven, had the intelligence and maturity required of such a mighty raid. They were to remove from the earth more spawn of the accursed Jew. On the night when the Jews had the effrontery of celebrating the treachery of the whore, Esther, against the great Persian King, Xerxes! "Ahasuerus," they called the great Xerxes, mocking his supremacy.

Every year at this time, the Jews ridiculed the King in their feast of "Purim," as they called it. Their children dressed in grotesque costumes, feasting while they derided the great King and his lieutenants. Well, this year the feast would have a different and bloody ending, one to be felt around the globe!

Javad continued the perusal of his devotees, knowing that his choices would end up in the martyrdom of several, but glory for all! He had already explained the basics of the plan to the gathering, reveling in their appreciative applause. Now, as he nodded first to Basir, denoting his choice for the leader, the others were rapt in attention, each hoping that he, too, would be chosen for the glorious martyrdom. In every mind there danced visions of Paradise, with its fruits of eternal life, filled with scores of nubile young virgins ready to accede to their every desire!

Yousef, the young engineer, received the next nod from Javad. Twenty years of age, he had already received enough education, courtesy of the U.S. government, to aid instrumentally in the planning and execution of the raids. Javad was pleased to see him glow with pride at being selected.

Kazem, the youngest, but among the most ferocious, was the next recipient of a nod. The dark-skinned, slightly-built Pakistani made up for what he lacked in skill with his fierce devotion to the cause. Mahmoud, Reza, and Sajad, the bold jihadis he knew would unflinchingly carry out their assignment were then added to the swelling group. Looking over his choices, Javad knew the Los Angeles imam would be pleased indeed at the strength his warriors would add to the attacks.

There were to be two simultaneous assaults on Jewish congregations that glorious night. He had promised Ali ten dedicated soldiers of Allah, blessed be his name forever, to merge with an equal number from the Los Angeles masjid. Javad, of course, would have joined the marauders himself, but the blessed Sheikh Nasrallah had ordered him to refrain from the fray, in order to be available for upcoming duties. Well, his martyrdom would just have to wait a while. Actually, at his mature age of forty, Javad was looking forward to some more years of earthly pleasures before he entered the kingdom of Paradise.

The chosen group of ten brave warriors congratulated each other at the glory that now awaited them. Javad then met with each individually and told them how important this mission was, and what its success would mean to the Shia world. They would truly be heralded as champions of justice; perhaps martyrs for the world to envy. He then sent them on their way to Imam Ali in Los Angeles.

Chapter 17

Imam Ali Muhammad gazed at his eager, young acolytes. They had been assembled at his mosque in Los Angeles to hear their latest assignment. "Well, my friends," Ali said, "it is again time for action. The Jew has become complacent and we need to put an end to that. I can tell you now that our organization has grown in size and strength. We have collaborators all through the holy lands as well as the countries inhabited by infidels. I guarantee you everything we do here is viewed by our brothers all over the world as examples of our growing strength!"

The imam was pleased to see that his words had their intended effect. Thirty pairs of eyes gazed at him with love, respect and adoration. "We now must strike again at the Jews' soft underbelly, their children. As they celebrate their ancient ritual of what they call 'Purim', their joyous moment of proof of what they have taken from us, the true descendents of Abraham, we will show them once again our strength!" He noticed that some of the group seemed not to recognize the word 'Purim', so he paused to explain:

"Purim, for those of you not acquainted with the lies of the Hebrew bible, is the mythical victory of the Persian, I repeat Persian, Jews over our glorious King Xerxes, by the treachery of a Jewess. One they call 'Esther'. According to their account, the Persians were so stupid as to take the word of this lying Jewess over that of their own good officers. And every year Jews all over the world celebrate this treachery over our gracious King by having their children sing, dance and feast, while mocking King Xerxes and his faithful lieutenants."

The imam's gaze fastened on his five most trusted warriors: Khalil, Hakim, and Abdul, who had slit the throats of the children in Beverly Hills; and Wajid and Mukhtar, who had helped carry out the raid. They smiled at him, knowing that the others in the room were envious of their status. This included the ten neophytes recently sent him by Javad.

"Now, as the Jew usurpers all over the world gather in their houses of evil to rejoice in the treason they committed against our people, we will show them there is no safety for them, anywhere or anytime." A spontaneous burst of applause sprang forth from the enthralled audience. Each of the young fighters felt his blood rise with the prospect of glorious combat. The fact that the enemy consisted mainly of unarmed children and elderly made no difference; they were carrying out the will of Allah, praised be he!! Shouts of "*Allahu Akhbar*" rang through the hall.

The imam raised his hands, smiling, as he urged the crowd to quiet. "Here now is the plan, my friends. We shall strike the Jew at two of his places of devil-worship, simultaneously. This time, as our brothers in Paris, London, and Madrid have done, we will use automatic weapons to magnify the fruits of our labors. Khalil and Hakim will organize the two attacks. We will hit them on the first night of their festival. Timing is critical; we will wait until the services are well underway, at 7:30 p.m. There will be police presence, of course. Four members of each team will nullify them with tear gas and mace. The police are not to be harmed unless necessary, so as to show the public our only goal is to destroy our enemy. Once the police are subdued, five members of each team will force their way into the main hall, firing indiscriminately into the crowd."

Excitement rolled through the assembled group as each member tried to visualize his assignment. "We have provided complete diagrams of each of the temples. The leaders,

Khalil and Basir, have already visited the sites and are ready to assign duties to each of the team members."

Basir, of course, was one from the new group brought in by Javad Abdouleh from Orange County. He had proven to be every bit as intelligent, resourceful and devoted as Javad had assured Imam Ali. He, and his comrades, had assimilated well into the imam's gang of marauders. Their zeal for the mission was infectious, and gave added fuel to the importance of their goal.

"The whole business should be completed in less than five minutes," the imam added. "Your escape routes are planned out, and the speed of execution should blunt any but the weakest of response from the authorities. To all of you, I say, 'Allah is with you' and to those who are martyred in the process, glory and everlasting life lies before you!"

After a brief, stunned silence, the crowd broke into extended applause and back-slapping. Khalil and Basir each went through the group, touching the already-chosen members of their team on their shoulders. They then each led their squad into separate rooms to begin the detailed planning.

Khalil's team of ten men was assigned to hit congregation Beth Sholem in West Los Angeles. Basir and his men were to strike Temple Mitzpah in Santa Monica. All the arms, ammunition, and gas canisters were already stored in the hidden second-level of the garage. Twenty-five Kalashnikovs with 1000 rounds of ammunition had been purchased over the past year at various gun shows. Teargas and mace had been acquired over the internet. The purchases had been made so secretly that none of the young assailants-to-be had been aware of what was occurring. The preparations had taken more than six months and no apparent alarm had been raised in the Los Angeles area. After all, the populace had been arming itself in an effort to prevent just what was about to happen.

Chapter 18

The day was another typical spring day in Los Angeles, flowers blooming everywhere, and a cool breeze off the ocean abating the heat of the sun. Jewish families were preparing for the feast of Purim with children in costume and hearty meals planned. While the holiday was often celebrated on a Sunday, it had become a custom lately to keep to the traditional date on the Hebrew calendar, in the evening, instead.

The attacks began right on schedule. Basir and his men drove through the foggy streets of Santa Monica, staying well within the speed limit. They had stolen an innocuous-looking black van the previous day from a quiet side street in the Valley. The dirty windshield indicated that the van had not been driven in several days. It was a simple matter for one of the young members of the team, Hassan, to unlock the car with a coat hanger, and then start it by short-circuiting the wires leading to the engine. He learned this trick while spending a few days in the County jail for shoplifting. The license plates were then replaced with a pair stolen from another car in the LAX airport long-term parking lot. Hassan was, in fact, a recruit from Orange County, one of the devotees of Javad Abdouleh.

At 7:25 p.m. they made a cautious pass by Temple Mitzpah. As expected, four uniformed police officers were standing on the sidewalk outside the main entrance, talking with each other, and looking casually around for any suspicious activity. *This was going to be easy,* Basir thought. One teargas canister should disable all four of the guards, without necessitating any gunfire. Hassan drove slowly around the block, and at exactly 7:30, stopped at the corner, where the streetlights were effectively dimmed by the fog. Four members of the attack team, led by Basir, slipped silently out of the two side doors. All were wearing black hoodies, black jeans and black sneakers. Their faces were also covered with black masks. All were carrying Kalashnikov AKMS semi-automatic rifles with four extra magazines, each containing thirty 7.62 mm rounds.

They knew, from the imam, that the children, celebrating the festival of Purim, would be wearing the traditional masks and costumes, made to resemble both the saintly Jews and the "evil" Persians. The attackers in their black costumes could easily be mistaken, if only for a few moments, by the guards, for late-coming congregants. This should give the attackers a crucial advantage.

The van continued by the Temple, around the other corner, where another five terrorists slipped out and crept along the dark buildings leading towards the Temple. This left Hassan alone, driving the vehicle. He had been instructed to circle the block for four minutes, observe the activity around the Temple, then pick up the successful jihadis.

The two teams could see each other as they approached their target from either direction. They waited until Basir gave the signal, then threw two gas canisters against the wall close to where the policemen were idly conversing. Unfortunately for Basir and his men, they hadn't tested the canisters beforehand. They watched in disbelief as the cans struck the wall, fizzled a bit, then spun crazily around on the sidewalk in front of the startled policemen.

All the participants, the nine attackers and the four police, stared for a few seconds at the spinning dervishes. Then, seeing his plan dissolving in front of him, Basir unshouldered his weapon, and ran toward the policemen, screaming "*Allahu Akhbar.*" His men, following his lead, did the same. The guards, taken unawares by the costumed men, thinking them part of the celebration, could do nothing more than draw their pistols before they were drowned in a sea of their own blood.

Basir realized that one of the goals of the mission, that of sparing the police, had already been lost. But, seemingly unfazed, he pushed open the doors of the Temple, and led his gang into the lobby. Somehow one of the ushers witnessed what transpired outside and managed to call 911. Another had enough wits about him to break open the fire alarm and set off a loud clanging that reverberated inside the auditorium. The startled rabbi, Dr. Edith Rosenbaum, reacted as best she could, screaming to her flock to take cover. Just then the doors to the auditorium were flung open and eight terrorists began to fire their weapons indiscriminately. One of the first to be hit was the rabbi herself, who was cut down instantly to the stage. Others in the congregation dropped, screaming, under the cover of their padded seats. The terrorists, not seeing many clear targets, fired into the backs of the chairs.

What they had not been prepared for were the security guards stationed *inside* the Temple. Within less than a minute of the commotion outside and the alarm being struck, the four guards emerged from the cover of curtains along the walls, and engaged the attackers with their long-barreled .44 magnum Smith and Wesson revolvers. Four of the terrorists, easy targets in their black costumes, were dropped quickly in their tracks. Basir and the others, seeing their plan go wildly awry, raced back out of the open auditorium doors. Rather than chase them, the guards searched around to see what they could do to aid the victims.

Outside, sirens were racing towards the Temple from all directions. Hassan, in the van, was waiting immediately outside to collect the triumphant warriors. Instead, he saw Basir and the other surviving jihadis staggering blindly out onto the sidewalk. He honked his horn to get their attention.

Casting their weapons aside, they attempted to clamber into the side doors of the van. The arriving police, however, recognized the attackers for who they were, and immediately shouted brief warnings to them. The surviving team members disregarded the commands of the police and attempted to flee, leaving poor, young Hassan alone in the van.

Seeing the carnage on the sidewalk, the police did not hesitate before commencing fire with their pistols and shotguns. Unfortunately, the situation became confused as passersby and escaping congregants wandered, dazedly, into the fray. The congregants, many the parents of the costumed children in the Purim festivities, were screaming in terror, trying desperately to find their offspring.

Lieutenant Frank O'Connor of the Santa Monica Police shouted into his bullhorn for his squad to hold fire. The fight scene had become dangerously confused. But the identity of the assailants was now clear. O'Connor got the attention of three of his men, pointing out the conspicuous terrorists in their black costumes. "Bring your fire only on them," he commanded.

Hassan was the first to receive mortal wounding. Seeing all escape routes now blocked by police and their vehicles, he jumped out of the van and searched for one of the discarded weapons. Just as he found a Kalashnikov, Patrolman Jim Snyder found him. Armed with a powerful, short-barreled police shotgun, he was within ten feet of Hassan, who reached for the assault rifle on the pavement. One round from the shotgun hit Hassan in his mid-section, spewing blood and other bodily fluids onto the sidewalk. The spectators gasped in shock and horror as Hassan stood there looking down at his life ebbing away, his fate now clear. "*Allahu Akhbar*," he shrieked, as he collapsed.

If anyone present had any doubts about what was occurring, they now dissolved into the fear that had gripped the city for months. Muslim jihadis had struck, right here in Santa Monica.

Basir, the ersatz commander of the terrorists, shouted orders to his remaining men in a fearful fit of Farsi, then dropped to the cover of a parked car. The surviving members of the team had, by now, run for cover or escape. "Pick up your weapons and fire on anyone in range!" he ordered. Three of the police shot at him simultaneously, blowing away most of his skull, as blood spouted from his chest. His cry of vengeance never made it out of his mouth. Basir, seeing none of his troops surviving, and sensing the end, decided to deny the police the pleasure of his execution. He rose from his cover, put his Kalashnikov under his chin, and, with his left thumb on the trigger, blew his brains out. His attempt at *"Allahu Akhbar"* never made it to his lips.

Lieutenant O'Connor cautiously surveyed the scene, both inside and outside the Temple, and radioed the Santa Monica station. The officer in charge that evening, Captain Jack Morgan, had already been apprised of the ongoing battle. The LAPD headquarters downtown had been notified at the onset of the assault and had dispatched their terrorism team. Word had gone out immediately to the JTTF and FBI at the Wilshire station. All had access to the report coming in from O'Connor. Fewer than ten minutes had transpired since the attack had begun.

"Hostilities terminated," O'Connor reported. Although he tried to keep a professional demeanor, his voice was trembling, his pulse racing. Never in his twenty-plus years at the SMPD had he encountered anything approaching the carnage he had just witnessed. "We have twenty victims inside the Temple, request all ambulances available, all Westside of LA," he reported, his voice shaking. "Several fatalities, many critical, all with multiple gunshot wounds. At least half the victims, children," he added, his voice now reduced to a sob. After a short pause, he added, in a more professional tone, "All perpetrators terminated. We count nine, no, ten, dead at the scene, some at their own hands."

Regaining his composure, even as he heard the sounds of police and ambulance sirens approaching, O'Connor added, "Our personnel scouring Temple and vicinity for more victims or assailants. None reported, so far. Over and out."

* * *

Mike Scanlon, head of the Homicide Special Section of the downtown LAPD's Robbery-Homicide Division, and the FBI liaison for the slayings of the Jewish children and rabbi, left his desk at 6:30 that evening. It was time for his weekly haircut; a trim actually. He maintained his military-style buzz cut scrupulously. On his way back to his office to make a last check of any incidents that required his attention, he stopped off at the local deli for a corned beef sandwich and root beer, his favorite snack.

He had just finished and was checking the log on his computer when reports of the attack at Santa Monica Temple came over the hot line. He immediately called the desk sergeant at Santa Monica and verified the terrible news. That done, he ordered a contingent of his men, six officers in three cars, over to assist the Santa Monica police in what appeared to be another hate crime. He then made sure that the Los Angeles instant response team, under his direct command, was prepared for coincident attacks.

Although all the local synagogues had been warned of an event such as this, there was no way to assure they had all taken adequate precautions. Scanlon then apprised all squads currently on patrol of the Santa Monica attack, ordering them to make an immediate check on all Jewish congregations within their neighborhoods.

* * *

The attack at Beth Sholem, in West Los Angeles, went no better for the attackers than the one in Santa Monica. Mahmoud, the driver of the assault vehicle, a small dark, skinny man with a scruffy beard, had trouble finding a suitable car to steal. They wanted the theft to be as close as possible to the day of the attack, to avoid immediate capture by the police. So the day before, Mahmoud and his friend, Yusuf, cruised through the East Los Angeles neighborhoods looking for appropriate vehicles. Yusuf, in contrast to Mahmoud, was a pudgy little fellow with no beard at all to cover his acne scars.

In a highly Muslim neighborhood they finally happened on a broken-down looking old van that actually looked abandoned. But Yusuf was able to hot-wire the old Chevy into a coughing start. After putting five dollars worth of gasoline into the old junker, paying with cash of course, they nursed it back to the mosque, not even bothering to replace the license plates.

The next night, that of the attack, Mahmoud and Yusuf drove eight of their colleagues, including the leader, Khalil, into the West Los Angeles neighborhood where Beth Sholem was located. The old van was hesitant from the very start, coughing and sputtering as they approached the synagogue. Then, a half mile from their destination, it gasped and died, like an old horse that had been overworked for too many years. The attackers decided, after a brief argument, to go the remaining few blocks on foot. By this time however, they were already ten minutes late for their 7:30 p.m. date with destiny. They had no way of knowing that, after the shootings at the Santa Monica Temple, the police all over Los Angeles and Orange Counties had been put on high alert. The hundred or so largest Jewish congregations were warned of the possibility of simultaneous assaults and asked to halt their services and move their audiences to safety.

By 7:45 p.m., when the strange group of Arab-looking warriors arrived in their black costumes, they were met by a phalanx of the LAPD's finest. They had heard and responded to Captain Scanlon's alert. Having no warning, the ten attackers saw the squad cars and heavily-armored police vans, just as they turned the corner by the synagogue.

Kazem, the young jihadi from the Orange County assembly sent by Javad, saw the situation for what it was and steeled himself for the inevitable. He was not going to allow the obvious slaughter that awaited them to go on without a brave, though doomed, assault. If they were about to die they would take some usurpers with them. He had been assured by Javad that the whole neighborhood, congregants as well as police, were Jews.

Kazem, not awaiting orders from Khalil, commanded the ragged assembly to continue their mission. Kazem never had been certain of the strength of Khalil, and was not about to lose this opportunity to murder the enemy, no matter the cost.

Realizing they were about to enter Paradise and defile a multitude of beautiful virgins, Khalil took back the flag of command from Kazem. He rejected the order leveled at them over a police bullhorn. Instead of throwing down their arms and surrendering, the team spread out and began wildly firing their Kalashnikovs in the direction of the police vehicles.

Only Kazem, Mahmoud, and Khalil were aware enough to find the relative safety of the surrounding parked cars before bringing their Kalashnikovs to bear on the riot police. A pitched battle ensued, as the commander of the LA police detail, Lieutenant Michael Preston, alerted headquarters downtown of the situation. He asked for backup and ambulances, as he, a veteran of eighteen years, and survivor of war in Afghanistan, was immediately aware of the intensity of the upcoming gunfire.

It was all over in less than a minute. The police, dressed in riot gear and wearing body armor, overwhelmed the jihadis with a flurry of semi-automatic gunfire. Most of the attackers, easy targets in their black garb, fell to the ground in pools of blood and gore, their weapons thrown askew.

Khalil and Kazem, determined to die bravely, screamed "*Allahu Akhbar*" almost simultaneously from their cover under parked cars. They fired indiscriminately at the attacking police. Both were hit in the face and chest by shotgun blasts. They had been jumping for safety when observed by Preston and his men, and clearly were not going to surrender. Their remains scattered around the curb, even as their cries for vengeance hung in the air.

Mahmoud, from the Orange County group, was the last to die. Sergeant David Green, carrying his shotgun, saw some slight movement behind a car. He spotted the crazed-looking assailant kneeling next to a shiny, new Lexus and ordered him to drop his weapon; but Green knew full well he would refuse. As Mahmoud aimed his weapon at the officer, his head exploded into fragments, the slug finishing its task by blowing out the car's left front tire. The last thing Mahmoud saw before the shotgun blast hit him square in the mouth, was the gold Star of David hanging around Green's neck.

Chapter 19

"Take seats everyone," Mary Robley offered, actually more like ordered. "You all know each other?" she asked. Seeing some nods, but no actual confirmation, she continued, "this is Mike Scanlon, our lead officer and liaison at LAPD homicide," she said tilting her head to a man who looked like he came off a TV cop show, complete with crisp blue uniform replete with insignias. He seemed fifty-odd years old, sporting a buzz-cut. He stood quietly and never blinked his icy blue eyes.

"And this is Mark Higgins, from the LAPD Counterterrorism and Criminal Intelligence Bureau," she said, indicating a beefy, red-faced man in a tight blue suit. It looked as though he had purchased the suit when he was twenty pounds lighter. Higgins appeared as if he were ready to burst into action, twisting his hands together with nervous energy.

"And finally, from Homeland Security, Los Angeles, meet Bret Williams," she said, nodding toward an anchorman-type in a perfectly-tailored expensive suit. The four Los Angeles agents all stood behind chairs on one side of a gleaming walnut table, protected with a pristine glass cover. In front of each chair was a fresh yellow pad and set of four sharpened pencils.

"I think some of you may know Uri Levin and Lara Edmond already; Uri has been kindly lent to us by Mossad, and Lara is based in New York, formerly with the FBI but now with the JTTF." Uri stood stiffly, somewhat uncomfortable in his business suit, white shirt and tie, but with thick, black, partially-grown-in facial hair. It had been over two weeks since he arrived in Los Angeles, and his naturally curly beard had given him a distinct Middle-Eastern appearance.

He knew Mark from the terrorism incident in Los Angeles several years ago, but still felt somewhat out of place. Lara, on the other hand, was dressed in business attire, a dark blue business suit, crisp white blouse buttoned to the neck, and low pumps. She knew all the people and was quite comfortable with them. Uri, however, was a surprise to her; his appearance was quite different from when she had last seen him just a couple of weeks ago.

"As you all probably know," Mary continued, "Lara and Uri helped us tremendously with the Hezbollah nuclear attack nearly ten years ago. Without them, a bad situation might have gotten many times worse." The Los Angeles contingent was, of course, well aware of the help the two outsiders provided in the termination of the terror cell responsible for the bomb that devastated Marina del Rey.

With that introduction, they all sat down at the table, Los Angeles people on one side, Lara and Uri on the other. "Lara and Uri are here specifically to aid in the investigation of the attack on the Jewish school last month, and the killing of the rabbi shortly afterward. Before they could even get started on the case, there was this tragedy last night." She looked around the table; she clearly had everyone's attention. "Well, let's get down to business," Mary stated bluntly, picking up a pencil and tapping it sharply on her pad.

"We suffered a serious setback last night, with these attacks on the synagogues. We lost four of our own, and twenty-seven innocent civilians, many of them children, in a savage, Islamist terror attack. We're calling it what it is, and I think even the most liberal of the politicians will do the same, if they haven't already."

Actually, only the most liberal politicians, including the president, had so far withheld any public judgment on the motivation for the brutal killings. The Fox network already labeled it "part of Islam's War on America." Al Jazeera reported the incidents simply as another of America's "ongoing battle against senseless gun violence."

"We terminated twenty terrorists, all of Mideast origin, though some appear to be U.S. citizens. They all carried the flag of ISIL, or ISIS, on their persons, indicating they were connected to the gang that carried out the Beverly Hills school massacre," Mary continued grimly. She paused, looking around the table, to see if there were any questions. The Los Angeles police members were clearly aware of all these details, and showed no shock or surprise.

Lara, however, was obviously upset by the cold nature of Mary's description of the massacre of the Jewish Purim worshipers. She deliberately avoided looking directly at Uri. She need not have worried; Uri had seen these sorts of attacks in Tel Aviv and Jerusalem.

Mary's next remarks, however, caused both Lara and Uri to sit up in alarm. "We were quite ready to classify this case as an attack by Arab extremists, but we found something very strange on one of the terrorists. He was carrying a Qu'ran of obvious Shia origin, written, not in Arabic, but in Farsi."

Uri bolted upright, causing his chair to slide backwards into the wall. "Are you quite sure!?" he asked in disbelief.

"Quite sure," she countered. She had been ready for his reaction. "We've had it analyzed by both our Arab-speakers and our Persians. The kid, and that's what he was, only seventeen or so, probably forgot he had it on him. But our conclusion is that this was a 'false-flag' operation. It may well be that the school killings were too." Uri ran his fingers through his hair as he pulled back his chair and slumped into it.

"We've got to rethink our whole strategy," Mary stated to the shocked attendees. She stood and said to her Los Angeles constituents, "I'll get back with you folks in an hour or so. I need to reconfigure the operations of our colleagues." Scanlon, Higgins and Williams caught her drift immediately and left the room. They had taken no notes.

Mary, now alone with Lara and Uri, said, first to Lara, "you can forget looking for Arab 'husbands', obviously. And start checking out Iranian and Pakistani types." Lara had been keeping her informed of her internet husband search. "And I guess *you* can start looking at Shia mosques, and forget the Sunni variety, at least for now," she said to Uri with a flat smile. "Do you think your Persian dentist can give you some leads?"

Uri, still in a bit of shock from the news, could only nod in reply. It was clear he and Lara were back at square one.

"Well, I'll leave you to it," Mary said, checking her buzzing cell phone. She packed up her notes and exited the room.

Chapter 20

Lara and Uri stayed in the FBI meeting room after Mary Robley was called away. They remained in the same chairs they had been in for the briefing about the Purim attacks on the synagogues. This was the first time they had been alone together since their romantic encounter when he first arrived in Los Angeles. They sat close, but not touching. "So, how have you been?" Uri began, nervously. Something was bothering her, he was sure. He stroked his awful-looking facial hair in a self-deprecating manner, "Do you think we could...meet somewhere, unofficially I mean?" He reached over and touched her hand tentatively.

She immediately withdrew. "I don't think that's a good idea. For one thing we might compromise our assignment. Who knows who might see us? Besides..." Her physicality told him she still felt something. But it would have to wait, he felt instinctively, until the business part of this operation reached a stable point. "Yes, of course, you are right." he said, closing that discussion, but not the conflict in his own mind. "Well, look," he added in a more business-like manner, "we both need to re-design our strategies. This new information, this Shia business, changes everything."

She lightened up at this change of direction in their conversation. "Well," she started, "I'm glad I didn't agree to marry a Sunni!" She laughed brightly.

"So, you've actually made some connections; I mean, through the online advertisements?"

"Yes, believe it or not, there are quite a few Arabs out there quite eager to recruit a blond American who wants to become a jihadi."

"I'll bet that's right. Have you actually sent pictures out?"

"Oh, yes! And got lots of offers to meet. But I'd been waiting for some connected to one of the suspect Sunni mosques, and now I'm glad that never happened. I mean, now that we have every reason to think the perps are Shia."

Uri shifted in his chair uncomfortably. "Do you really feel safe doing this?" He asked, with more than a little fear in his voice and his mind. He could see now what was the cause of her reluctant behavior.

"They've got me well covered, Uri. They can track me wherever I go, and break up any situation."

"And just how, exactly, are they able to do that? Can you tell me?"

"Tracking device, in my hair. Look how tiny it is, I'm wearing it right now." She bent her head down and parted her hair. All Uri could see was something that looked like a tiny mole on her scalp, almost entirely invisible.

"And what if they discover it?" Uri had always felt very uneasy about her planned operation.

"If I squeeze it, an automatic silent alarm goes off, and the cavalry comes to the rescue. That's what they've assured me." Uri looked unconvinced. "So tell me what you've been up to?"

"Like you, I've been focused on the wrong targets—Sunni mosques. I got the names from our *sayan*, the Persian dentist in Beverly Hills. Gone to prayers at several, no problem. I haven't exposed myself as Azizi, the escaped terrorist, yet, or even Refai, the name on my passport. A good thing, too. There are a lot fewer Shia mosques in town, so my chances of hitting our target are a lot better. And I figure there's got to be some communication going on among them, so once word gets out that Mohammed Azizi is in town, I'll be getting some visitors."

"And what's your plan from there?"

"I'll have to go by the seat of my pants, as you say here in the U.S. If I'm accepted as Azizi, I figure, once the right people get in touch, they'll want my help with their next ops. The sloppy operation at the synagogues shows they need experienced help. And I'll offer it. We could smash the whole gang!" Uri felt a surge of excitement just talking about it. He hadn't been involved in an operation of this magnitude in years.

There was a pause as Lara considered his plans. "You're not thinking of going at it alone, are you?" she said, worried about his pent-up emotions. He could hardly believe his ears. After hearing what she was up to, his assignment seemed like child's play.

Uri laughed. "Hardly. I'll be in constant contact with Mary. We'll set up a coordinated attack, once I know the players and their plans."

"I'd like to be part of it, Uri," she responded, touching him lightly on the arm. Her touch left a warm reminder of their passionate encounter just weeks earlier. He looked at her, hoping for some sign, but she glanced away.

"So what is your plan, now we have a new target to work?" he asked.

"Same as before. I'll just cruise the internet, looking for Shia imams interested in a blond wife." She smiled engagingly, teasing him. "Now that I know specifically what I'm looking for, I think I'll score pretty quick."

Uri winced at her choice of words, images of what she might be in for racing through his head. "I sure hope that

101

little beacon you've got in your hair works perfectly. Do you have an alternate escape plan?"

"I'm not totally helpless, if you remember," she reminded him. He recalled her use of martial arts in their previous battles with terrorists, and smiled, despite himself.

"Alright," he said finally, "but I'd like to be part of your operation, too. Can we agree on that? Will you keep me up to date?"

"It's a deal," she said, standing and grasping his hand like a partner, rather than hugging him like a lover. He smiled and shook her hand, wincing inwardly at the pain of lost romance.

"*We'll see how this goes*," he thought to himself as they headed for the elevator.

Chapter 21

Farid Refai (aka Uri Levin) stepped aboard the commuter bus that would take him to the Shia mosque he had chosen. Though he had expected the dentist, Emelkies, to lead him solely to Sunni mosques, he was pleased to notice a few Shia houses of worship at the bottom of the list.

In contrast to the large Sunni mosque he had visited just a few weeks ago, he found this inconspicuous Masjid in a converted warehouse, just as he had researched it. Opening the door, he suddenly found he had two companions. They greeted him in Arabic, and he correctly returned their greeting.

"Welcome to our humble Masjid," said the first man, a dark, hirsute man with glowing eyes. His appearance gave Uri the impression he was from Yemen.

"Thank you," replied Uri, slipping off his sandals and placing them neatly next to an assortment of other shoes.

"Please make yourself at home," said the other man, short and overweight, but of unknown origin.

Uri was somewhat uneasy as he entered into the prayer room. True, he had passed his first test, at the Sunni mosque, but now he was masquerading as a Shia, and not as comfortable with their language and customs. He hoped his hours of practice with both Arabic and Farsi would pay off.

The prayer room was rather large, minimally ornamented, with the supplicants, of course facing east, toward Mecca.

He put on his proper headdress, found an empty spot near the back of the room, with a wooden head-block, and went through the ritual as he had rehearsed, in the Shia fashion. They, of course, recited their prayers in Arabic, as did the Sunnis. That was a relief. As in the Sunni mosque, the few women remained almost unseen, in the rear of the prayer room.

After the short service, Uri went out into the anteroom and retrieved his shoes. The two men who escorted him in were there waiting for him: the tall one and his short, dark, stout companion, with the heavy beard. The latter was also dressed in white robe and keffiyah.

"Won't you follow me, my friend?" invited the tall man with a smile. The shorter man just grunted some sort of approval.

"Certainly," Uri replied. "I am Farid Refai," he said, extending his right hand.

"Oh yes," the tall man responded graciously. "You are most welcome here! You are from Jordan, are you not?"

This was tricky, Uri thought to himself. "Yes," he said, "though my family is from Iraq. I was taught both Farsi and Arabic as a child."

The short man said nothing, bowing and gazing at Uri, appearing to size him up.

"Come," said the taller man. "I am Turiq, and this is Munir. Our leader, the blessed Sayed Ali Imam, will surely want to meet you. We don't often have visitors from Jordan."

"I am his servant," said Uri. This was the moment he had feared the most. Would there be some secret test, something he had not learned in his two years of study?

The two men escorted him through a back exit, then a long hallway, which ended in a plain, unmarked door. The man called Turiq knocked lightly on the door.

After a few seconds a light voice answered in Farsi, "Yes, come in, please." The short, stout man known as Munir opened the door and motioned for Uri to enter. The other two followed. Uri found himself in a warm, richly carpeted room lined with floor-to-ceiling bookcases. The imam sat on the floor facing them, cushioned by thick, maroon-colored pillows. He was a rather small man, as far as Uri could tell. But he had those intense eyes so common among clergymen. There was an ornate tea service on the low, glass-covered table directly in front of him. He did not stand, but rather indicated that the three visitors sit on the pillows placed around the table. Uri was impressed with the sharp, steady gaze of the imam. His dark eyes, hooked nose, and non-blinking stare gave him the appearance of an eagle assessing his prey.

Uri was initially taken aback by the lack of surprise shown by the imam. He quickly realized that his appearance at the mosque was not all that unusual. No doubt Muslims entering the country made an early visit to a mosque, to help get situated, if nothing else. After just a moment's hesitation, he sat on the pillows directly across from the imam. His escorts then sat on either side of him, in a collegial manner.

"So, my friend," the imam said in a light, even voice, "What brings you to us today?" Uri took in every detail of his appearance, trying to match him with pictures of the dozens of terrorists he had viewed in the files, back in Tel Aviv. This mosque had, of course, not been on his early list in the search for the child-killers, as well as the murderers of the rabbi. The imam's gaze appeared to chronicle every emotion, stripping him of his disguise. He forced himself to reject these reactions, and respond as the escaped assassin he was supposed to be.

"It is my honor to be here with you, most blessed Imam Sayed Fatima Ali," Uri said smoothly in Farsi. The imam showed no reaction to Uri's knowledge of his full name. His attendants had referred to him only as Sayed Ali. But Uri had taken the time before his visit to check out all he could about this Shia masjid and its imam.

"You know of me, then," the imam said, smiling just slightly.

"You are well-known in my native land." Uri actually only knew the imam's full name from the directory published by the "Muslim-American Friends Committee."

"Most Honored Farid Refai," the imam continued deferentially, "You Jordanians are welcome here, always. You have a difficult life, living as you do, in such close contact with the Zionist usurpers." Uri tried to hide his excitement; he had apparently passed the first level of scrutiny. He bowed down deeply to conceal any possible facial changes. This was, after all, only the first gate.

"Usurpers, indeed!" he declared with as much venom as possible, bringing a flush to his face, his fists clenching.

The imam seemed to take note of the violent reaction from their visitor. He and his two supplicants nodded in deference to him, as if they knew more than he had admitted. Uri's head swam; he hoped he hadn't given away too much. It was as though he had suddenly taken three steps forward, yet he feared he may have placed himself in jeopardy.

"You are most welcome here any time, my friend," the imam said, placing a warm hand on Uri's shoulder. "But now, I must say farewell, as I have other duties." He gave the Farsi version of goodbye to Uri, who replied correctly.

Uri was about to leave the masjid, when suddenly the shorter man, Munir, who had vanished moments earlier, reappeared. With a furtive gesture, he thrust a note, written in Farsi, into Uri's hand. With a conspiratorial look, Munir turned and retreated into the building. Uri left the building quickly, and only when he was certain he was not being followed, glanced at the note. On it was simply the name of another Shia mosque, one unfamiliar to Uri. But its address, scrawled under the name was most intriguing. It was in Orange County, just south of Los Angeles.

He had best let Mary know of his findings right away; this information was of the highest priority.

Chapter 22

Yehudi Gold, the Israeli consul general in Los Angeles, considered the idea of any sort of subterfuge carefully; there was obviously a lot at stake. Mossad had been responsible for some monstrous mistakes in the past. The disaster in Norway, for example, when an innocent Moroccan man had been killed after being mis-identified as one of the Black September Munich assassins. Then the humiliating misadventure in Dubai, when a Hamas leader was eliminated by a comically-clad Mossad team; the whole thing was recorded by hotel cameras and shown around the world.

Mossad came up with a bonanza. The agents they use to infiltrate the surrounding Arab countries' espionage and sabotage networks are most often turncoats. That is, enemy agents who, for whatever reason: money, change of heart or desire for freedom, decide to switch sides. It happens all over the world, as is well known. But Israel's secret services have thrived on the success of their "turned" enemy agents.

This time it happened to be the "son" of a famous Ayatollah who resided in Lebanon. The youngest child of the infamous Grand Ayatollah Mohammad Hussein Fadlallah, spiritual leader of the Hezbollah, disappeared after an assassination attempt in 2003. The Ayatollah himself died in 2012 died at age 75. The remains of the child, Ahmad, were never found. The only known record of Ahmad was a picture of him sitting on his father's knee, a young boy being lovingly stroked by the hand of the terrorist leader. A large, ornate ring can be seen on the fourth finger of the Ayatollah's left hand.

The child is clearly seen in the photograph, which was widely published after the assassination attempt. He had a large, distinct mole above his left eye near the center of his forehead.

The young man who actually slipped across the border from Lebanon a few years after the Ayatollah's death looked remarkably like the boy in the photograph; even including the mole. Of course several years had gone by since the photo was taken; still the resemblance was striking. His name, as given in the ID he showed to the IDF troops guarding the border the night he escaped into Israel, was Ahmed Tschourukdjian, age twenty-two. His father, his story went, was a simple baker, named Noubar, who was falsely accused by the Hezbollah of spying for Israel. Noubar was tortured and killed in front of his family, inflaming the young Ahmed. He vowed then to avenge his father's death.

The young escapee was quickly transferred to Mossad agents in Tel Aviv, who cared for the frightened Ahmed and checked out his story. From all the information they could obtain, his tale was accurate. But what was most interesting to Mossad was the young man's likeness to the Ayatollah's missing son, Ahmad. Even the mole, though not in exactly the same spot on his forehead was remarkably similar. Word of the find went quickly to headquarters. The young man passed all the tests, psychological and physical, and assumed the name change from Ahmed Tschourukdjian to Ahmad Mohammad. His resemblance to the Ayatollah's son, as seen in the Beirut newspapers following the Ayatollah's funeral, was indeed remarkable.

The new Ahmad was intelligent, well-spoken in Lebanese-Arabic, Farsi and some English. He had been schooled in a well-to-do section of East Beirut. But mainly he was driven by a need to retaliate for his father's brutal murder.

The head of Mossad offered "Ahmad Mohammad" the chance, not only to punish the killers of his father, but to make a new life for his mother and two sisters in Israel. He needed, however, to partake in a dangerous assignment in the United States.

To Gold, the idea had all the earmarks of disaster. A Shia Muslim, one "Ahmad Mohammad," had transferred allegiance to Israel for the usual sum of money (classified information, but in excess of one million U.S. dollars) and safety for his Lebanese family. The true story of Ahmad's journey from Lebanon to Mossad, was of course made clear to everyone involved. Ahmad, according to Mossad headquarters, would be willing to undertake a most dangerous mission in California in an attempt to find the cell responsible for the rash of terror. Mossad even went so far as to craft a ring for the young man similar to that worn by the Ayatollah in the photograph so many years ago, seen in the Beirut newspapers.

The real Ahmad Mohammad was, of course, well-known by the Hezbollah to be the son of the famous cleric, Fadlallah, associated with the 1983 bombing of the American Marine barracks in Beirut, killing 241 American military personnel. On his death bed, Fadlallah famously stated his greatest wish was for the "Zionist entity to cease to exist."

The plan, as forwarded to him by David Peretz in the New York embassy, was as follows: their *sayan*, the oral surgeon in Beverly Hills, Dr. Emelkies, would suddenly disappear, leaving a trail of seeming kidnapping and murder. His daughter, Sarah, who worked in his office, would report the crime. Sarah, who lived in the guest house at the Emelkies residence, would say she had been staying at a girlfriend's house the previous evening, and that it was totally unlike her father to miss a day at his office.

Police, of course, would search the residence on Scenic Drive and find a broken window on the side of the house facing the garage. There would be glass on the inside of the house, the library, and they would find evidence of a struggle: broken furniture, spilled glassware, etc. in Emelkies' bedroom. Most significantly, there would be traces of blood on the overturned table in the bedroom. He lived in the main house by himself, his wife having passed away four years previously.

DNA tests performed on the blood found in the bedroom, sadly, would match the DNA from the dentist's hairbrush and toothbrush. The evidence would clearly indicate that the man had been kidnapped, killed, or taken prisoner.

This news would hopefully generate activity within suspect mosques that Ahmad and his accomplices could use in tracking down the terrorists. That part of the scheme was incomplete.

In reality, Gold was assured, the dentist would be safely transferred to another location, still to be determined. The other details of the operation were in review by the Israeli government, with an eye to the previous Mossad disasters. Yehudi would be kept informed of the progress of the situation as it developed.

Gold somewhat reluctantly gave his approval, knowing he had little choice.

Chapter 23

The strange case of the disappearing dentist began, just as envisioned, scarcely one week later. The newspapers reported the apparent kidnapping and ongoing investigation. The daughter, Sarah, was not initially considered a suspect; she had reported the crime, had a viable alibi and no known motive. The case, though, within days, lost front page visibility.

There were no further developments for some time, the dentist having not reappeared and no further evidence found. Then, about a month later, a corpse was discovered in one of the drainage canals leading into Los Angeles harbor. Unusually heavy late spring rains apparently swept down the body of a middle-aged man, badly decomposed and almost completely consumed by marine life.

This occurrence was not particularly uncommon. Homeless people living underneath canal overpasses had occasionally fallen into rushing rainwater during and after storms. Their remains often end up in the screens covering the canal exits into the ocean. As usual in these cases, there was not enough tissue or clothing found for DNA analysis, probably due to the unusually warm water in the canal. There was, however, a single shoe recovered with the remains. That shoe, an athletic running shoe of a particular Asian brand, was compared to those recovered from the closet of Dr. Emelkies. It was found to be the same brand and size worn by the missing dentist. Computer records confirmed that several shoes of this brand and size had been ordered online by the presumed victim…

* * *

Two weeks after the actual disappearance of the dentist, Sarah Emelkies was reported missing. She had not appeared at her night school classes, and her friends said they had not seen nor heard from her in three days. The police suddenly resurrected her as a "person of interest," and began a well-publicized search for her.

These events did not go unnoticed by the criminal Shia gang in Orange County. The disappearance of a wealthy Persian Jewish professional man was also very interesting to Imam Ali and his followers. They knew of no plan in the works of this nature; in fact, since the disaster of the Purim raids in Los Angeles, Ali had not heard of any other ongoing operations.

That same day, the Israeli consulate got word of an anonymous tip received by the FBI. According to Mary Robley, someone had reported that a Shia mosque in Orange County was harboring some very radical elements. The leader there, Imam Zainal Abidin, was believed to have very strong views about the Shia claim to be the "true" religion. The informant claimed to be a devout Muslim, did not want to see these radical elements destroy the faith, and felt he must do his duty and report his suspicions. The phone used to make the call was a disposable cell type, untraceable. However, the call did originate in Orange County.

Mary phoned Yehudi Gold, the Israeli consul general, on their secure line. She told him that the FBI and police could not act because of the sensitive nature of the information. They certainly would be accused of illegal profiling if they showed up at this mosque with nothing other than an anonymous tip. In giving Gold this information, she said she could not advise him on any action, and that he certainly must exercise caution. But, of course, since an American agent, as well as a Mossad operative, was involved in the handling of the terror incidents, this was of the highest interest to the Israelis.

Gold immediately called his embassy in New York and explained the situation to David Peretz. "Could we send an anonymous team down to that suspicious mosque on a purely investigative trip?" he asked David. "It can't be Uri or Lara; they are already fully occupied here in Los Angeles."

David knew whom he had in mind: Ahmad, the turncoat spy, and Sarah Emelkies. "If you're talking about whom I think you are, our two new recruits, the answer is a cautious 'yes', although we must have no official knowledge of the matter, of course. Our government cannot afford another 'black eye'."

Known to only a few, and on a "need to know" basis, Sarah, the dentist's daughter, was also one of the "sayanim"; the Israeli agents working under deep cover in Los Angeles. Under tutelage from her father, a native Persian, she had been taught to read and speak fluent Farsi, as well as the elements of his spycraft.

"Furthermore," David added, "you'd better let Mary, Mike and Uri know about this. We don't want our own folks tripping over each other."

When Ahmad had signed on, Mary and Yehudi set up a plan for the two young people to work together. Both had received training in hand-to-hand combat as well as small-arms firing. Sarah and Ahmad had hit it off immediately; both were eager to use their skill and daring in smashing the terrorist ring.

The next step for Mary was to convince Mike Scanlon, the conservative head of LAPD homicide and FBI liaison. He was averse to using non-LAPD personnel in matters of such importance. But Mary assured him that his troops would be called in as soon as the terrorist plans were unveiled. The armed combat and public disclosure would be left to his forces. After a long discussion, he reluctantly agreed. But he demanded assurance that no ties between the LAPD and Israeli intelligence be revealed as part of the scheme.

Mary contacted Gold, who immediately got the sense of the message. He quickly concluded that they must repay the U.S. government for their efforts in the ongoing case of the murders of American Jews. Yehudi reached Ahmad and Sarah, telling them that their plan, which had been in the works for some time now, "had the go-ahead. Off the record, of course" he demanded of them.

Now Gold must convince David Peretz, in New York, of the viability of the scheme. If anyone could convince Jerusalem, it was David.

Chapter 24

Sheikh Nasrallah was anything but relaxed as he settled his aging frame into the large, soft cushions provided for him by the obsequious male servant. The sheikh looked for a sign, any sign at all of what lay in store. He had been called to this meeting with the Iranian prime minister in the middle of the night. "Come at once" was the order. There was no preamble, no other directive, just that unspoken urgency that left him shaking.

The trip overland in the midst of all the fighting was anything but pleasant; in fact, it was a nightmare. Getting from war-torn Syria through and around Islamic State Caliphate lines in Iraq was nearly impossible. His entourage paid bribes at every checkpoint. Fortunately, many of these were guarded by Iranian militia, supported by Russian air power. To Nasrallah's relief, it was apparent throughout the journey that he had the prime minister's support. Otherwise, he would have been beheaded, or worse, at any of the several border crossings. *"What could be so urgent?"* he asked himself throughout the week-long ordeal. Certainly, there had been some stumbles along the way, but they had successfully caused immeasurable havoc and headaches for the Americans in the past few months. And, as far as he knew, all the responsibility had been placed at the doorstep of the Islamic State, and not the Iranians.

He thought back to the grisly assassinations of the Jewish children in Beverly Hills, and the fatal torture of the gun-carrying rabbi. These were glorious victories for the radical Shia cause, and humiliating losses for the Westerners. Even the "Purim" attacks on the two synagogues had been partial, if not total, successes. The main thing, as he saw it, was that the credit, or blame, had been laid at the feet of their Islamic enemy, "ISIS." As he had numerous times during this arduous trip, he could not conceive what would be of such concern as to place his life in jeopardy. Not to mention discomfort, he thought angrily.

After leaving the elderly sheikh waiting for fully one-half hour, Prime Minister Abbasi finally made his way casually into the ornately furnished room. A manservant, moving with equal languor, followed with a tray of coffee and sweets. Nasrallah did not rise at his benefactor's entrance; he was still petulant at the lack of proper esteem shown him.

"Please give my guest some coffee and pastries," Feroze Abbasi ordered his servant, as he placed himself comfortably into his ornately furnished chair. He made an elaborate show of arranging some papers on the low table in front of him as the servant obligingly offered Sheikh Nasrallah some delicacies. Despite having traveled all this way with minimal food and rest, the sheikh was hardly able to sit back and enjoy himself. He still had no idea what sort of message he was about to receive from his benefactor. While all had not gone exactly as planned, many Jews had been killed, and the blame laid squarely at the feet of the Sunni Arabs. Taken as a whole, it seemed he had more than accomplished his mission. Still, this hardly seemed like a congratulatory meeting…

"So, my friend," Abbasi began enigmatically, "you feel our campaign is going well?" He bit delicately into a large Turkish sweet roll. The sheikh, more nervous than ever, watched his host for any sign of sarcasm. He fidgeted in his cushions, trying to make himself more comfortable, wishing the Iranian would get to the point.

Finally, when it was clear that Abbasi was not about to elaborate, Nasrallah took a cautious approach in reply. "Yes, my Prince, though there have been some minor, let us say, mishaps, I think, on the whole we are succeeding nicely." He was sweating profusely under his robes, his undergarments already soaked.

"And you feel your chosen lieutenant, this 'Javad', is carrying out his duties well?" Abbasi took another large bite of his sweet, following it with a dainty sip of the strong, sweet coffee. He watched as his guest labored for the appropriate reply.

"I think so, yes, he seems quite capable." More perspiration drained down the sheikh's bulky frame. Surely some judgment was about to fall.

"And have you bothered to compare our losses to the enemy's?" The Iranian was staring directly into his guest's eyes now. There could be no mistaking his demeanor. "Do you realize what the world press has done with these 'attacks'?"

"The world press is run by the Jews, as you know," the shaken Nasrallah replied weakly. *How far was this going to go?*

"You fool!" Abbasi roared. "The Jew is being seen as the innocent victim, due to your incomparable ineptitude! Muslims everywhere, both we and the Arabs are seen as monsters, not benefactors."

The sheikh was bewildered. The Iranians must live in a different world. What else could he do? Surely his benefactor must take at least some pleasure in the elimination of these evil-doers?

"Well, never mind that now, we have to look to the future," the Iranian stated, to the sheikh's immediate relief. Perhaps all this was just an introduction to the next steps in the Holy Battle. "You must take full control of things from here on out. You cannot depend on this Javad any longer. Our losses are unacceptable. You have made us look like rank amateurs on the world stage, killing a few heathens, with the loss of an equal or greater number of our own soldiers!" He paused and took another sip of coffee. Then, staring at his clearly stunned guest, he roared judgmentally: "Do you know that the Mossad agent and his American whore are still loose in your territory?"

"Yes, but we have rid the world of one of Israel's American spies, the Jew dentist living in Beverly Hills, an Israeli agent—that is, until he was eliminated!" the sheikh retorted.

Abbasi sat there, apparently unmoved by this news. "Yes, we already know of this; we have had word from our agents in Los Angeles. It is good news, of course, but does not move us forward. We must apprehend the Mossad man, Uri, and his slut, Lara."

He shifted slightly in his opulent chair and stirred his thick coffee with a tiny gold spoon. "But I have another, even more important task for you and your minions in Los Angeles. I hope you, and they, are up to the task."

Sheikh Nasrallah was both relieved and provoked by these words. On the one hand, the Iranian was apparently satisfied enough at the events of the past months to retain the alliance. But what was this new job, he wondered silently. He was about to find out.

The Iranian clapped his hands loudly twice; the manservant appeared immediately. They had a brief discourse that was not audible to the anxious sheikh. "There is something I want you to see," Abbasi finally said to Nasrallah. Seemingly at the same moment the servant reappeared with a television monitor and controls on a movable cart. He set the cart in position where both men could view it, then quietly left, handing the remote control to the Iranian. "This is footage not available in Lebanon, where you are, nor in the United States. In fact, it has been removed from the internet almost everywhere. Fortunately, I have been able to access and store one of the few copies left." He pressed some buttons on the remote and the screen flickered to life.

The scene was in the desert somewhere, with yellow dust blowing in the gusting winds. In the foreground, ten men were seen kneeling on the ground, their hands tied behind their backs. The angry voice of the narrator was heard, yelling curses in Arabic. In the background the black flag of the Islamic State fluttered everywhere. Sunni soldiers stood around in eager anticipation of what was about to occur. Abbasi suddenly paused the action to narrate the proceedings for the sheikh. "What you see are some of our finest Shia fighters, captured by the Sunni 'Caliphate' in northern Iraq, where they were defending their homeland."

The sheikh, sweating profusely again, was transfixed by the events on the screen. He knew this was not going to be pleasant. Abbasi resumed the action on the screen. Two men appeared at either end of the line of captured, kneeling Shia soldiers. Both wore the black headband of the Sunni fighters, and carried large execution-style swords. At an order, shouted in Arabic off-screen, the executioners began slicing the heads off the kneeling men, not even bothering to have them bend over. They simply approached their victims from the rear, and with large, slashing strokes beheaded the prisoners one-by-one, the heads flying off into the air, blood spraying from the men's necks as they collapsed into the dirt. With each decapitation, a loud cry of appreciation billowed from the onlookers. Within two minutes, all ten prisoners lay in pools of their own blood, the executioners dancing victoriously to the glorious shouts from the crowd. The Iranian stopped the action to see his visitor's reaction.

For the sheikh, who had gleefully heard reports and seen videos of his Hezbollah fighters killing Israeli families in the Galilee, this was most discomforting. To see Muslims killing fellow Muslims this way was abhorrent, even to him. He wondered why he was being shown this, and what more was coming. He didn't have long to wait.

The Iranian, seeing the intended effect on his guest, fast-forwarded the video to a scene with a large steel cage filled with Shia prisoners. The location looked similar to that in the last scene. The prisoners, about fifteen in all, of all ages, but most quite young, were not shackled. They moved about the cage, shivering in dread for what lay in store. As before, a large ring of Sunni soldiers, all wearing the black Islamic State headband shouted curses in Arabic at the frightened captives. Suddenly, a man wearing a black hood, with only small eyeholes, appeared at the right, carrying a hose. He began spraying the men with what appeared to be a high-intensity stream of water. He continued until all the prisoners were completely soaked.

Only then did it become clear to the sheikh that this was not water they were being sprayed with; the men shrieked and vainly tried to wipe the liquid from their eyes and mouths. They scrambled around the cage, desperately searching for an exit. None was to be found. Meanwhile, the onlookers cheered the proceedings, eager to see the climax.

The sheikh twisted nervously in his now-drenched cushions. He had a feeling about what was coming, but hoped he was wrong. He frantically wished this spectacle to conclude, but sat helpless, afraid to look away for fear of displeasing his host.

To the cheers of the crowd, another hooded man appeared from the left with a blazing torch. The sheikh feared he might soil himself as the action proceeded to its ghastly conclusion. The torch was thrown into the cage, the prisoners frenziedly trying to evade the flames that now devoured them. Their screams were drowned out by the shouts of encouragement from the surrounding crowd. The video continued until all that remained in the cage were charred, smoldering corpses, indistinguishable as human remains. Abbasi stopped the video and looked at his guest. "You see who we are fighting? The Arabs will stop at nothing! They are no better than the Jews."

Nasrallah sat numbly, unable to fully comprehend what he had witnessed. He had heard news reports, of course, but to see his co-religionists slaughtered like animals in this manner was almost too much for him. "Disgraceful," he finally mumbled, realizing even as he uttered the words how inadequate they were. "They are no better than beasts. But why have you shown me this?"

The Iranian, pleased with the reaction, nodded and stated simply: "To prepare you for your next task, my friend. I hope you are capable of carrying it out." The sheikh nodded silently, waiting for the rest of the lecture. He frankly could not imagine what was in store. "I have a marvelous plan for you and your men in Los Angeles. You must meet with this Javad and whomever else you deem necessary for the successful achievement of our goals." The sheikh was motionless, his attention fully focused on his master and patron.

Before continuing, Abbasi paused to refresh himself further, with coffee and sweets. His next pronouncement would shake the sheikh, he was certain. "Your team, or *teams*, will carry out an unforeseen attack meant to cripple both our enemies at one time; both the Arabs and the Jews will suffer." He paused, waiting for reaction from his guest. Seeing none, he continued. "There will be an attack on a Sunni mosque in Los Angeles, carried out by radical Zionist American Jews, in apparent retaliation for your bumbled 'Purim' attacks." Now he got the reaction he had been hoping for. The sheikh dropped his pastry into his lap, his mouth open in shock.

122

"And I am supposed to find a group of angry Jews to carry out this attack?"

The Iranian laughed. "Of course not. I will give you a copy of the video you have just seen. When your men in California see it they will certainly be motivated to carry out vengeance against our Sunni 'friends', don't you think?" The sheikh nodded, trying to assimilate everything he had seen and heard. "And when the blame for the vengeance is to be placed at the doorstep of the Zionist filth, your men will be sufficiently motivated to learn to act and speak like heathen Jews as they carry out their vengeance! What could be a more apt description than the Western phrase: 'two birds with one stone'?"

Nasrallah sat there stunned, trying to digest what he had just heard. Did he really understand his host to mean his disciples in the U.S. were to masquerade as Jews and then slaughter fellow Muslims? Of course, that was happening in the Middle East all the time, Sunnis killing Shia and vice versa. But in the States? He shivered as he considered the possible consequences...

Chapter 25

Imam Javad Abdouleh, known on his British passport as one Abu Makri, British subject, settled himself in on the Air France flight to Beirut. He had successfully completed the long American Airlines flight from Los Angeles International Airport through Charles de Gaulle Airport in Paris. Now this second and last leg on his flight schedule would bring him to the Rafic Hariri Airport in Beirut. He once again smiled to himself at the names of these airports. Both were significant in the seventy-odd year struggle for Islam against the West.

Charles de Gaulle, the French "hero" of World War II, had been instrumental in the radicalization of North Africa, giving needed strength to the spread of Islam to France and the rest of Europe. Were it not for his efforts, the conquest of Europe and the rest of the Western World might have been delayed for scores of years, if not centuries.

Rafic Hariri had likewise been a feather in the cap of radical Islam, though not in the way he intended. The Lebanese puppet of the West had been eliminated by the loyal members of the Hezbollah, led by the very man he was about to see: Sheikh Hassan Nasrallah, blessed be he! A thrill ran through Javad as he thought of his own role in the destruction of the Zionists. He had been chosen by the sheikh himself to lead the raids that had created so much carnage and welcome press in Los Angeles. No doubt the sheikh had requested his presence to congratulate him! He had time for just the shortest of pleasant naps before his audience with the great man.

The noisy Beirut airport was filled with a mixture of Middle-Eastern and Western men. Judging by his clothing,

Javad could have easily been mistaken for one of the latter. But the man sent to meet him had no trouble identifying him. Waiting outside the gate that separated the arriving passengers already cleared through customs and immigration, from the throngs outside, were scores of eager of taxi drivers, souvenir vendors and food purveyors. Among these was Nasrallah's driver, one Bijan Tahiri.

Bijan was a small, wiry young man, highly devoted to the sheikh and the cause of Hezbollah. He sported a short, well-trimmed beard, western clothes and no headdress. Otherwise unremarkable among the crowd, he had dazzling bright blue eyes, unusual among the mostly-Arab crowd, but not unheard of. In fact, those blue eyes had been found quite charming among the few young women who had the pleasure of seeing him. That had made no difference to the devout Bijan, who was bound to celibacy until his entrance to Paradise. As a martyr, he would then have access to all the beautiful virgins he could ask for.

Bijan and Javad spotted each other almost immediately upon the latter's exit from the terminal. No words were spoken; none were necessary. Javad, with his simple carry-on bag, followed Bijan to the dirt-covered Nissan van sitting in the short-term parking area just outside the policed area to the right of the terminal. The two sat in silence as they drove the short distance from the airport to the Hezbollah hidcout in the Haret Hreik neighborhood of southern Beirut.

Bijan was immediately recognized by the guards at the hidden compound. Not that secrecy was needed. The residents of this area of Lebanon were well aware of the presence of the Hezbollah, and pleased that this militant arm of resistance to the Zionists had chosen to grace their neighborhood.

Javad was shown into the underground enclosure that housed the leaders of the glorious soldiers of Allah. These were the warriors and martyrs who were at the forefront of the battle against the Jew usurpers, and would be those who uprooted them.

Javad did not have to wait long before being greeted with hugs and kisses from the smiling Sheikh Nasrallah. "Sit down, my friend," he said to Javad, as if they were long-lost family members. "Congratulations on your successes!" Javad relaxed a bit; he had feared the loss of so many of his patriots would have angered the sheikh.

"Thank you, most revered Sheikh," Javad supplicated himself and kissed the sheikh's plump hand. "I regret losing so many martyrs, but…"

"That is all part of the battle, I'm afraid. But they are all now in Paradise, enjoying the fruits we all yearn for."

Javad relaxed even more at this word from his mentor. Now he wondered what the sheikh had in store for him; surely he did not bring him all the way here just to congratulate him.

The sheikh got right to business. "We have a new, and even more outrageous, plan set out for you and your men."

Javad leaned forward to absorb this news. He was eager, yet a bit apprehensive as to what might be in store.

"First, my friend, you must watch something. I warn you, it is quite disturbing."

Javad said nothing, but watched in nervous anticipation as two of the sheikh's men set up the visual equipment necessary to view the awful scene Nasrallah had seen at the Iranian prime minister's headquarters. As the scene unfolded, the effect on Javad was even more dramatic than it had been on the sheikh. He trembled, wishing for an end to this dreadful slaughter of his fellow Shia by other Muslims.

Allowing his guest a few moments to collect himself, the sheikh waited as his men packed up the screening equipment. The DVD itself, Javad noticed, was placed in a foam-lined box and secreted away by Nasrallah. "Well, my good friend, what do you think of that?" the corpulent sheikh finally said to his astonished guest.

"The DAESH are truly apostate brutes!" Javad finally responded.

"Precisely. And that is why I have chosen you and your men to carry out an act of vengeance that will deal a crushing blow both to our Sunni enemies, and the Zionist filth!"

Javad listened intently as the sheikh laid out his, and the Iranian Prime Minister Abbasi's, bold plan. Javad's mind whirled as he tried to envision how he could mastermind this brilliant act of retribution.

"You will meet with our blessed Imam Ali Muhammad, who has carried out, with your help of course, our successful attacks in Los Angeles." Javad knew he was referring to the massacre of the Jewish children in Beverly Hills, as well as the execution of the rabbi, who had been dispensing anti-Islamic propaganda.

"You will again combine some of your warriors with his to make this new attack," Nasrallah continued. "However, this time we must be more careful. There are to be no martyrs left at the scene." He saw Javad sit up as if to protest, but held out his hand to calm his protégé. "On your last assignment, the 'Purim' attack, we lost all of our men for the police and FBI scum to find and desecrate." The fleshy sheikh wrinkled his nose at this recollection. Javad nodded in recognition of this loss.

"But," the sheikh continued, "The U.S. authorities have no way to know the identities of the martyrs. They carried no papers, no identification. They undoubtedly thought them

agents of Islamic State, Arabs, as with the other...events."
Javad nodded, not knowing exactly where this was headed.

"Now we need to perform an act that will shock the world
both Muslim *and* non-Muslim." The sheikh sat forward to
emphasize his next disclosure. "The world is to see an act of
vengeance performed upon Sunni-American Muslims,
carried out by...American Jews!"

"American Jews!" the astonished Javad cried out. "How
would we get American Jews to do such a thing!?"

"You haven't been following me, I can see," the sheikh
replied patiently. "The 'Jews' are going to be *your* men
disguised as Jews. That is why they must not be caught, alive
or...otherwise. It is not a mission for some inexperienced
martyrdom-seeking neophytes. No, this will require seasoned
professionals. We will need a relatively small number of your
best men to properly carry this out."

Javad mulled over this audacious request from the sheikh.
Nasrallah knew what he was doing. The blessed sheikh, after
all, had survived many assassination attempts by the Israelis
over the years...the cursed Israelis, who had, without a
doubt, murdered the former leader of Hezbollah forces in
Lebanon, Sheikh Imad Mughniyah in Damascus several
years ago. Though never "officially" admitting it, there was
never a denial. It was a blow to the cause that still burned
hatefully in the hearts of all the Hezbollah.

Javad was ready to do Sheikh Nasrallah's bidding,
whatever it would require. "What, then, is the plan?" he
asked resolutely.

The sheikh took a sip of his strong, syrupy coffee and
relaxed. He laid out his plan: "On a Friday evening service, a
well-known Sunni mosque, but one that is not guarded, will
be attacked by a select group of your men...well, yours and
the Los Angeles Sheikh Ali Muhammad's...appearing to be

vengeant Jews. They will randomly kill and maim as many Sunni worshipers as possible in as little time as possible. Then they must escape. It is essential we leave no martyrs behind. The police must not have any surviving attackers or martyrs to identify. It must appear to be an act of retribution for the killing of the children and the rabbi, as well as the synagogue attacks in Los Angeles."

"How is it they will think it is Jews who have carried this out?" Javad queried.

"Your warriors will be appropriately dressed, in black, shouting in Hebrew, and leaving behind this sign." He held up a crudely lettered sign, written with a bold black marker on white paper.

Javad looked at the sign and smiled appreciatively. This indeed would appear the work of retribution-minded Jews. "It will be done, Holy One, I assure you."

"I have the utmost confidence in you," the sheikh replied, a satisfied smile on his round face. "And I should add that it is you yourself who will have the honor of leading this raid; after all, who better to trust with this important mission?"

Javad was somewhat taken aback by this last pronouncement, but then considered: who better to be responsible for this audacious assignment. He smiled at the sheikh in silent acceptance.

The pleased sheikh smiled in return and, rising, clapped him on the back, kissing him on both cheeks. "*Allahu Akhbar!*" he cried out.

"*Allahu Akhbar!*" Javad shouted in return. A daring mission; just like he always wished for. What could be better: vengeance against the Sunni usurpers of Islam, as well as the Zionist transgressors. A supreme achievement!

Chapter 26

Throughout the long flight back to Los Angeles, Javad considered the details of this bold new plan. He ran through, in his mind, all the possible members of his believers who might be trusted to bring with him. There were several among his own men, of course. Men with years of experience and complete faith in their leader, that was who he needed. The first to come to mind was his devoted assistant for the past ten years, known only by his first name, as was custom: Jabaar.

While not overly bright, he was quintessentially loyal and a strong fighter. An older jihadi, Jabaar was in his mid-thirties. He brought with him to the States extensive terrorist training in Afghanistan against the Americans, a fact never discovered by the immigration authorities. He was tall, strong and frightening to look at; scars crossed his face and neck as well as his chest, which he seldom showed. He had told the U.S. immigration officers that he had been wounded fighting the Taliban.

Next on Javad's list was little Kabir, from Pakistan. Kabir was younger, in his late twenties, but swift and clever. He extricated himself and his comrades from several scrapes during the American campaigns in his native land. His dark, innocent-looking eyes made him look even younger than his age in years. His smile was infectious, and made him a favorite among the troops.

Then there were Malik and Razzaq, who always seemed inseparable. They were similar in appearance, too, almost like brothers. Both were about twenty-five years old, dark, lean and lithe. Both could be counted on in vicious hand-to-hand combat. They were veterans of the U.S. occupation of Afghanistan, but that fact never appeared in their immigration papers.

The tall, quiet Sabur was a loner, but a fierce fighter. He had lost his parents in the fighting at the Afghan-Pakistan border, but readily accepted the chance to emigrate to the U.S. as a "student." Finally, there was Akeem, a leader if there ever was one. Javad knew he could always count on the strong, slender Akeem if anything ever happened to himself. He would be designated second-in-command of his forces in the upcoming campaign.

Javad was somewhat familiar with Imam Ali Muhammad's men in Los Angeles, based on his limited meetings with them prior to the "Purim" campaign. Unfortunately, many had been lost in the bloody exchanges with the Los Angeles and Santa Monica police. Yet he remembered the clever, young Faraj, from northern Iran, near the Caspian. The light-skinned, blue-eyed Faraj could easily pass as a native-born American, something that could be very useful. Imam Ali also had at his disposal, the burly young Hanai, from southern Iran. This man was feared, even among his compatriots, for his strength and quickness, despite his massive bulk.

Javad remembered one more of Ali's men who had not participated in the Purim attacks, and so had survived. The unassuming Jahiz was considered by Imam Ali, as Javad recalled, one of his most dependable men. It was no doubt for this reason that Jahiz was not chosen for the dangerous raids on the synagogues, but saved for more important assignments. Jahiz was unassuming in appearance. He would likely never be recognized at a later time; that is, after the upcoming raid on the Sunni mosque.

This was crucial. That is, the survivors, and they *all* must survive, of course, would not be easily recognized as

Muslim. In fact, they must appear to be, at least passably, as Jews. This made the blue-eyed Faraj especially valuable. If any surviving Sunnis at the mosque, after the attack, happened to see and remember his blue eyes, they would not immediately associate him with your average Iranian.

After the several hours it had taken him to reflect on these likely choices for his warriors—none written down of course—Javad settled back and prepared for his arrival in Los Angeles and his meeting with Imam Ali Muhammad. He had little doubt that Imam Ali would agree with the plan. After the rather disastrous Purim attacks, Imam Ali should be grateful to participate in the upcoming campaign. Especially once he saw the brutal scenes on the DVDs. Revenge upon the Sunnis—and the Jews—would be a welcome respite from the current state of affairs.

Chapter 27

Javad had already completed his selections when he next met with his team in Orange County. He knew some would be disappointed, so he would be clear how he came to his decisions. It was a hushed group of holy warriors that met in the locked prayer room. The last worshipers had long left the premises; only Javad's loyal troops remained.

"First," he stated boldly, "we are about to undertake a curious but important mission. Those of you not chosen should not be discouraged; there are reasons you'd best not know, for your own safety." Javad had selected six of his finest men for the bold strike at the Sunni mosque. He decided not to tell any of the others, so, if ever questioned, they could honestly claim ignorance. It would be only after the fact that the others could share in the glory.

"Akeem," he told the slender Pakistani, "you shall be my second in command." The quiet man straightened noticeably in his folding chair. "Malik, Razzaq," he continued, "You will be on the front line." The others all strained forward hoping beyond hope to be able to participate in whatever their leader had in store. Perhaps the chance to die brave martyrs for the everlasting glory of their families. "Finally, my little Kabir, you shall be one of the chosen."

With this, there was a pause, as Javad would not divulge anything further for the rest of them. They realized their chance at splendor was not yet to be; they left, disappointed but hopeful for success of whatever fate had in store for their compatriots.

Once the others had gone, Javad wheeled out a small television monitor and played for his chosen four, the DVDs given him by Sheikh Nasrallah. The effect was immediate and electrifying. Their fellow Muslims ravaging imprisoned Shia! They were, to a one, horrified and outraged.

Javad then described the upcoming attack. Their target was to be a Sunni mosque, he told them, and waited for any concern. Seeing none, he then described to them the reason for the strange mission, and how they must now prepare to look, as much as possible, as religious Jews. It became clear to all that one reason for their choice had to do with their physical appearance. The tall and muscular men had been eliminated as too recognizable. They all, Javad noticed, seemed very pleased at their selection.

They would shave their beards to a size and shape more in keeping with the religious Jews; ones who could be seen on the streets of the West Side of Los Angeles. Further, they would learn a little Hebrew, enough to shout "Arabs, go home!"; "Stay out of our Holy Land!"; and "Death to the heathens!"

"That ought to do it," Javad concluded to the laughing, jeering group. They had learned to dislike Jews and Sunnis with near equal venom.

"There is one thing you must pledge," Javad added solemnly. "No one, I mean *no one*, must be caught or killed. It is essential that the image of Jews killing Muslims be impressed by a willing press upon the world! Better to terminate the attack than lose any of our team!"

With that, he gave them a week to prepare. He would let them know the chosen mosque when the time was right. Meanwhile, they must all acquire the proper black clothing and skull caps. A second-hand store was the best place for that, he told them. "And for the sake of Allah, don't go together! One by one."

It was ten days later when the group assembled. In the interim, Javad traveled to meet with Imam Ali Muhammad in Los Angeles. He showed Ali the DVD of the massacre in the compound and was met with the expected outrage. Imam Ali was more than happy to reach out to the selected two warriors from his mosque: Faraj, with his blue eyes, and Jahiz with his slight build. They would meet with Javad's group in one week, here, in Los Angeles, and prepare the attack. Javad would bring the weapons at that time. He reminded Ali that no one was to be taken, dead or alive; this was most important.

* * *

Javad decided it best that he drive the lead car himself. Akeem would follow. The chosen Sunni mosque was situated on a corner in the Wilshire district, not far from the bustling area known as Koreatown. Javad had scoped it out himself, seeing doors on both sides of the corner. This would allow all the attackers to gain entry simultaneously, and two places for rapid exit. The entire proceedings were to take no longer than two minutes, beginning to end.

They would hit the mosque at the start of the evening, Isha prayer, at 8 p.m. The day before the raid, Malik and Razzaq, who had some experience in the matter, were sent out to steal two older, plain cars. They went to the beach cities, where the streets were packed with parked autos, many with windows rolled down in the hot, sunny weather. It was a simple matter to find two older vehicles, a Volkswagen and a Chevrolet, with no sort of alarm system or special locks. The thefts were accomplished in less than an hour. As usual, license plates, stolen from other cars the night before, were used as replacements.

All was made ready at 7 p.m. The assailants went over for the sixth time each of their roles. Speed was essential, Javad reminded them. Each had a watch that would signal them when they must leave. Kabir, Malik, and Razzaq would arrive and leave the mosque via the Chevy, driven by Javad. Faraj and Jahiz would use the VW, driven by Akeem. The first group would enter and exit the building via the Wilshire Avenue entrance, the other by the second door on the side street. They would hit at exactly 8 p.m. and be out no later than 8:02.

Traffic had lightened up by 7:30 when the convoy departed the downtown mosque where they had assembled. It was so light, in fact, that they had to circle the block twice before they could park both vehicles in the passenger loading zones on either side of the corner. At exactly 8:00, the team members pulled on their thin, flesh-colored surgical gloves and exited the cars, Javad and Akeem staying behind the wheels. Little Kabir was the first to reach the Wilshire entrance—only to find the glass-paneled door locked! Jahiz, at the other door found the same situation. Seeing each other through the glass, they simultaneously broke the glass with their pistol butts and then reached the "panic bars" on the inside.

Once inside, the raiders, dressed in black shirts and pants, with hats over skullcaps, instantly shot the two startled attendants and rushed into the prayer room, shouting, in Hebrew, "Death to all Arabs!" and "Go home, camel jockeys!" They sprayed the kneeling parishioners with almost their entire magazines before turning to leave. None of the worshipers had a chance even to rise to their feet. In just over a minute, it was all over. Their guns empty, they sprinted for the two open exits. Faraj was careful to place the signs they had prepared in plain sight at the entrance to the prayer room. The cars were waiting at the curb, as planned, as the victorious gang leaped in, exultant.

It was only when they were driving away, well within the speed limit back toward downtown, that both Kabir and Jahiz noticed their black sleeves were cut, apparently by the broken glass doors. There were also gashes on their arms where they had reached through to grab the panic bars. A few drops of blood stained their shirts.

Back at the assembly area, the triumphant warriors congratulated each other as a very pleased Javad looked on. His, and Imam Ali's, men had done well. It was only after the initial jubilation lessened that he noticed the blood on the two men. "What happened there?" he asked them, pointing to the red stains.

"Oh, it's nothing," they both replied, unconcerned. "Just little cuts from the glass doors."

Javad's mood darkened noticeably as he considered the possible consequences.

Chapter 28

Mary Robley was clearly distraught as she entered the conference room on the top floor of the FBI building on Wilshire. Bret Williams, from Homeland Security, along with Mark Higgins and Mike Scanlon from the LAPD, were already there, as was a very shaken Uri Levin, and an equally upset Lara Edmond. In contrast with how they had last seen him, Uri was now clad in his normal attire of open-neck sport shirt and slacks. Combined with his now fully-grown Muslim beard, he was quite an apparition, especially in view of all that had transpired. He was glad they all knew him already.

"You all know from the news reports, I'm sure, what occurred last night," Mary began. "But let me give you a thumbnail extract of what we have put together. It's a bit more than what we have released to the news bureaus, of course. Although, I must say, the vultures have been unusually persistent in not letting us do our job." She sat at the head of the long walnut table and took a drink of water from the glass in front of her. The others took the opportunity to do likewise.

"There was an attack by a group of what appeared to be Jewish extremists, upon a large Sunni mosque in the midst of evening prayers." She paused as Uri grunted his clear disapproval. "Alright, I'm sorry, I should emphasize the word '*appeared*'. We really have no evidence regarding who they were—well, almost no evidence." This enigmatic statement provoked a reaction from all except Scanlon. He appeared to know something the others did not.

"At any rate," she continued, "the attackers took the assembly completely by surprise. There were a number of fatalities, as they had Uzi submachine guns, similar to the ones used by Israeli shock troops." Noting Uri's discomfiture again, she added, "of course, these arms are available to anyone world-wide." Uri calmed a bit at this disclaimer. "At this point, at least twelve are deceased, with at least two dozen in critical condition. Over fifty others have non-life-threatening injuries."

Everyone at the table, including Uri and Lara, was visibly distressed at this news. No good could possibly come from this apparent vengeance. "There are reports," she added, "of Hebrew shouts of retribution and punishment. Some were actually recorded on cell phones. They are all indistinct, of course, through all the screaming and gunfire. But our language experts agree the language is, in fact, Hebrew. Uri, I have a copy for you, and I have already forwarded the voice data to your consulate."

Uri sat there, dazed, in disbelief; he knew of no Jewish groups that would even consider such outrageous activity. The results would be disastrous for the community and for Israel itself, in the world view.

"Unfortunately, none of the attackers was apprehended," she added, adding to the general despair felt in the room. "However, as I indicated, we do have something to go on, little as it is." She paused to gather everyone's attention. She needn't have bothered; all were in a state of suspended animation. "The police responded almost immediately, as you may have heard on the news reports. There is a local station only a block away, and the calls for help came even as the attack began. Their approach caused the shooters to scatter before they could do even more damage. I can't imagine the carnage had they not been so close to the scene." She nodded at Scanlon who must have been involved in the police response. They all waited for the evidence she had hinted at.

"The attackers broke a couple of windows in their haste to gain entry. In so doing, two of them sustained cuts, we believe, to their hands and forearms. The glass, apparently, cut through the black robes they were wearing, and the LAPD recovered bits of cloth and blood, even bits of skin from the shards. As you can imagine, DNA tests are already ongoing. There appears to be ample material for our forensic teams to determine complete identity."

There was an audible sigh of relief, especially from Uri. Though he had no idea who was responsible for this horror, he was certain the Jewish community would be vindicated.

"There's a little more we haven't yet released to the newshounds." She pulled from her briefcase a plastic envelope containing a crudely lettered paper note. "Several of these were left at the scene, presumably by the perpetrators."

She placed the envelope on the table for all to see. Scrawled on the paper with a broad felt-tipped pen were the words, in English, "**NEVER AGAIN**."

Chapter 29

Uri left the meeting in a state of shock. Things were getting worse. He was now presented with the disturbing suggestion that radical Jews had carried out a horrific attack on Muslim-Americans at prayer. The note left by the attackers could have only one interpretation. "Never Again" was the brief, descriptive slogan of the Jewish people, referring to the Holocaust. Of course, anyone could use it with the goal of blaming Jews for the massacre at the mosque, but it was an attractive handle for the news media.

Still, he had to continue with his plans to visit Shia mosques disguised as the assassin Azizi and see if he could penetrate the enemy's compound.

He and Lara left the meeting, equally distressed by the news. "What now?" he asked her.

Lara was grim, but apparently determined. "I've got to continue my search for an imam looking for a blonde as a potential wife," she declared. "Now he has to be a Shia, that's all."

"Alright, but stay in touch, please, OK?"

"You, too. Be careful." She pecked him on the cheek after peering around to make sure no one was watching. They held each other's hands until the elevator arrived, Lara taking the first one; Uri waiting for the next. When he arrived at the street, she was gone.

He was still gathering together his thoughts when his cell phone buzzed. It was Mary Robley. All she said was..."there is news; see your consulate." He wasted no time in heading down to the Israeli consulate just east on Wilshire from his present location, in West Los Angeles. The taxi dropped him off right in front of the unassuming building, and he rushed in to find the consul general, Yehudi Gold, waiting for him.

"Come into my office, my friend," Gold, a small bald man of about forty-five, said as he grasped Uri's hand in a firm grip. They entered his inner office without a glance at his somewhat astonished secretary. "Sit down, I have some important news." Gold, of course, had been kept up to date regarding Uri's participation in the investigation. He was also in contact with the FBI regarding the latest disaster, the Sunni mosque killings. "The LAPD has been working like crazy on the DNA from the blood on the broken glass doors in that Sunni mosque massacre," he began. Uri jerked to attention. "They haven't been able to make any connections yet...," he began. Uri felt a mixture of emotions at this partial news. "But," the consul continued, "the genetic markers are all consistent with Semitic, Middle Eastern parentage."

Uri's heart sank at this disclosure. "So, it might well have been our people..."

"Not likely," Gold continued, recognizing Uri's concern. "It's true that Arabs, Jews and others from the Middle East all have many of the same markers in their DNA. Jews, especially the Ashkenazi, all have European and Asian markers as well. We typically see Russian and Polish genes in our makeup. On the other hand, the Arabs and other Muslims seldom show these."

"Then who do you suppose?..." Uri began.

"We're guessing, and I mean by we, David Peretz in New York, as well as the JTTF, think this may well be a case of 'false flag' again. The Shia trying to cast blame on the Jews now, by killing Sunnis!"

Chapter 30

Uri hastened back to the FBI building and sought out Mary. "I've spoken with Gold," he said breathlessly. "I've got to get to Orange County as soon as possible."

"You have a lead?"

He quickly reminded her of his adventure in the Los Angeles masjid, the small Shia congregation, including the note given to him, with the name of an Orange County mosque. Gold had confirmed that this mosque, indeed, was one rumored to have radical leanings.

She quickly recalled the warning she had received about Imam Zainal Abidin. "Is he the imam at the mosque you are headed for?"

"Actually, no," he replied. "The note I got referred me to another mosque. One headed by an Imam Ali Al-Naqi. Maybe it's best that I start there, and then find out about this Abidin when I am settled in a bit. It might seem to them a bit odd that an escaped assassin fresh from an Israeli prison would be able to home in on him so easily."

Mary considered his request only briefly. Uri was a cautious man, she realized. That's how he had survived so long, she mused. Her options at this point were limited, but she needed results in a hurry. She decided to go along with Uri's plan, but to remind him of the urgency. "You know your job better than I, but please keep in mind that this may be our best shot at these guys." He nodded gravely. "I can get you a plain sedan and a driver's license," she added immediately. "Do you have a weapon?"

She knows what I have in mind, he realized. "No, but I sure could use one."

"We'll get you taken care of. But you recognize, of course, the U.S. government can have no role in this. I'm sure Yehudi told you."

"I know. This is an Israeli operation taken without the cooperation or knowledge of the U.S. When can I get going?"

Mary got on her phone. "Pardon me a minute, would you?"

Uri ducked into her outer office for just a few minutes; she called him back in.

"Head down to Room 319. They'll take care of everything." She shook his hand with a knowing smile. He hoped he was able to deliver. She hadn't told him of the parallel operation with Sarah and Ahmad. If one team failed, she hoped the other wouldn't. She was having enough trouble already.

By the time Uri left the building some three hours later, he was in possession of a California driver's license, the title and keys to a Ford sedan, and a 9mm Sig Sauer. The lightweight pistol, made of polymer, was a far cry from his beloved Baby Eagle, but he was familiar with it. It carried only 7 rounds, but was small enough to hide easily. He also had a concealed-carry permit, valid for a law-enforcement officer. It was made out in the same name as his driver's license: Farid Refai. Finally, he had been given a tiny tracking device in the form of a pin with a transmitter head to hide on his person. If he were to run into trouble, he only need pinch the transmitter twice. At least he hoped so.

He headed down to the garage, picked up his Ford, and made tracks to his hotel to pick up his essentials. He had no idea how long he'd be gone. It was now 6 p.m. as he headed into the tough traffic down to Orange County.

* * *

Uri found a cheap, weekly rental room in the midst of a predominantly Muslim neighborhood. The neighborhood was crowded and noisy, typical lower-middle-class, but he would be reasonably safe from discovery. It seemed appropriate and was within walking distance from the target mosque, located at the address given to him by the little attendant, Munir. He found an inexpensive long-term parking facility about a mile away, where he could store his car. He purposefully backed the car into the space to allow for a quick getaway. In it he left his secure satellite phone and other items belonging to the Israeli, Uri Levin. There was still time for him to reach the mosque for the evening prayers.

He walked through the crowded neighborhood, passing scores of women wearing hijabs, many also with the traditional abaya. Most were pushing strollers with toddlers in tow. The men paid them little attention as they hurried to their destinations. They did, however, each give Uri a friendly nod. There was a constant stream of chatter, in Arabic or Farsi as the women met their friends and exchanged greetings. It was similar to any predominantly ethnic big-city neighborhood.

Uri, now Farid, passed shops displaying chickens, recently slaughtered, clothing, groceries and sundries. He attracted no attention whatsoever, much to his relief. In just five blocks, he found the mosque he was looking for. It was housed in a nondescript brick building, obviously converted from some other use. A sign above the wooden door displayed the name of the mosque, along with the name of the current imam, Ali Al-Naqi. There was a glass case at the side with a sheet of paper showing "salaat" or prayer times for the current week. He was late for the beginning of the sunset service, he noticed.

He entered the mosque in street clothes, but carrying his kufi head cover and Shia Qu'ran. After removing his shoes and leaving them with a score of others, he quietly entered the prayer room, finding the service already in progress. He was welcomed by two men, who quietly, but politely, pointed him to a space near the rear of the room where there was a Persian prayer rug and head block for him. He purposefully avoided taking a spot near any of the few women, who occupied the last row of those in attendance.

He quickly went through the motions he had learned, making sure not to fold his arms, the way one does in the Sunni services. For the remainder of the service he followed the actions of the other supplicants, mumbling the Arabic prayers.

At the close of the service, the two greeters met him again at the door, politely requesting he wait a moment. As the twenty or so men, clearly regulars, left the mosque, followed meekly by the women, they exchanged simple good wishes or nods as they exited to the street. Finally, the imam, all smiles, arrived and offered his hand to "Farid." "Hello, and welcome," the imam said in Farsi. "I am Imam Ali Al-Naqi."

Like most, if not all, Shia imams, he had taken the name "Ali." Ali was the cousin and son-in-law of the Islamic prophet Muhammad, and a member 0f the "Ahl al Bayt." This means, literally, "People of the House." Ali is considered the "first Imam" by the Shia and is thought, along with his descendants, to be one of the divinely-appointed successors of Muhammad who are considered the only legitimate religious and political leaders of the Muslim community.

Unlike the Shia imam he had met in Los Angeles, this man was quite unassuming in appearance. Ali Al-Naqi was short, rather stout, with a curly, scruffy, black and grey beard that sprung from the sides of his round face like bristles from an old brush. His eyes, unlike those of the Los Angeles imam were warm and friendly. There was no hint of the predator Uri had seen in the other man.

Uri took his hand, bowed politely and replied, "I am honored. I am called Farid Refai."

"You are new here, are you not?"

"I am indeed," Uri responded, "recently arrived from the Kingdom of Jordan."

"Your Farsi is excellent," the imam complimented him.

"Yes, we learned both Arabic and Farsi in my village. We learned both in school, so we could do salaat and also speak with many of our Arab neighbors. My family had migrated from a part of Iraq where there were many displaced Persians...Iranians."

"Well, you are most welcome here anytime, for salaat and our community meals!" the imam offered charmingly. Uri smiled, bowed and left with an Arabic goodbye.

It was now growing quite dark, and Uri was very hungry and tired. He found several Persian-style restaurants on his way back to his small room. He picked one at random; one that looked clean and well attended, and had a light meal of falafel and chicken with hummus. They served him a carafe of mineral water, allowing him to sit as long as he wished. The newly arrived Farid Refai leisurely finished his meal and sipped his water for nearly an hour, without garnering any undue notice. During this time, there was a large turnover of men, women with children, and families. Finally, growing increasingly tired, he paid the modest bill, left a reasonable tip, and left. It was with weary feet that Farid Refai returned to his room and collapsed into bed.

He already decided to assume the manner of a most devout Muslim, and so was up in the morning well in time for sunrise prayers. He reached the mosque along with the small group of obviously regular worshipers before the services began. These were the true believers, Uri surmised. At the close of the short service, the imam spotted Uri again and gave him a very friendly nod. His warm, affable smile revealed an understated intelligence.

For the rest of the day, Uri familiarized himself with the neighborhood, noting where the other Shia mosques were located, as well as the schools, post office and police stations. He already scoped these out on the map, but wanted to make sure he could find them by sight. He decided to skip the noon service at his new mosque and use the time to find a few alternate routes to the long-term parking lot where he had stored his satellite phone and other tools of his trade.

Uri walked, seemingly without purpose, around the neighborhood, getting used to the shops and buildings, so that he could find his way around without recourse to a map. His first trip to the parking garage was purposely aimless in appearance. It took more than an hour as he doubled back, stopping several times to check reflections of the passers-by in the shop windows. He even stopped for a noon meal, sitting in the rear of an open-air restaurant, where he could watch the pedestrian traffic. He was pleased and relieved to see no one he recognized in the busy noon-time throng.

Lazily, he paid his check and sauntered back out into the mass of people and made his way, using a pre-determined primary route to the garage. He stopped often, a man not in a hurry, wiping his nose, fiddling with his shoe laces as he casually made his way to the garage. The structure, on a little-used side street behind some warehouses, was completely devoid of foot traffic as he made his way up to the fourth floor where he had pre-paid for a month's rental. His Ford was covered in yellow dust, no doubt from a mixture of sand and pollen in just one day. He got in the car and started the engine, using the windshield washers to clear his view. Letting the car idle for a few minutes, he watched for any curious visitors. Only when he was sure it was safe did he reach under the seat and retrieve the satellite phone. He kept the phone charging while he thought about whom to call and what to report.

Lara, of course, was first on his mind as he sat there reviewing the last day's events. But they had agreed to avoid direct contact during the most dangerous part of their mission. Instead, each would check in with either Mary Robley at FBI headquarters or Yehudi Gold at the Israeli consulate. It was also agreed that each would make contact at least once a day, making sure their tiny homing devices were working as promised, at least.

After fifteen minutes of review, Uri decided to call Yehudi and tell him of his progress. They could speak in Hebrew, making it even more difficult to intercept their conversation, even though these latest-technology encrypted satellite phones had been vetted to be ultra-secure.

"Yehudi," Uri said as the consul answered almost immediately. "I am safely ensconced in the target neighborhood, have a room, and have showed myself at the mosque!"

"Wow," replied the Israeli consul, "I am glad to hear all that! You meet the imam?"

"Yes, but I don't think he's our man. However, he does seem to accept my story. I will keep on going there, at least twice a day. I'm hoping that news of this stranger suddenly appearing will reach our target. And what of my partner, Lara?"

"Right, I know you two want to keep track of each other. Well, as far as I know, and Mary has been good about keeping in touch, Lara is continuing her search for an acceptable Shia imam-seeking-a-blonde."

Well, there was, apparently, no way she was going to be dissuaded from her plan, he thought with a tinge of disappointment. "And are our little tracking devices working as advertised?"

"I'm glad to report they are," Gold answered brightly. "They are guaranteed to work for at least two months. Be sure to carry yours with you all the time. Mary just told me she sees you on her map every half-hour or so. Are you in the garage now?"

"Indeed I am. No way I can get in trouble with her watching me. Speaking of that, you can spot me at the target mosque most every day for sunrise and sunset prayers."

"Shalom, and good luck, my friend," the consul said before signing off.

Chapter 31

Uri returned to his room and cleaned up for the sunset service at his new mosque. He was met by the same greeters again, and being on time, stayed for the entire service, which included a short sermon on the need for Muslims to practice the good tenets of the faith at all times. There was no mention of any acts against people of other faiths.

At the end of the short service, as he was leaving, the imam stopped him with a smile, saying, in English, "May I have a word with you, brother?"

Farid answered in Farsi, "Yes, of course, Imam Ali."

"Please," the imam responded, "let us speak in English. All the brothers need to communicate with non-Muslims now that we are in the United States. And it is best that we practice our English as much as possible."

"That is an excellent idea, Imam Ali!" Uri replied enthusiastically, hoping his Israeli accent would not be apparent to him.

"Well then. It is my job, as they say, not only to conduct religious services, but to act as a sort of mentor, especially to newcomers like yourself. You seem to be alone here, and I was wondering if I could be of help to you in any way."

Uri thought for a moment, considering his alternatives. It would be good to establish himself in the community. "Well, Imam Ali…"

"Just Ali, please," said the imam. "And may I call you Farid?"

He remembers my name, Uri thought to himself. This mosque to which he had been referred must have relatively few members for him to know all the regulars.

"Yes, of course, Imam...that is, Ali, I should like that."

"Please tell me if I am intruding on your privacy, but are you on your own here in this big city?"

"Yes, I am, Ali, starting a new life here in the States. I was referred here by some friends I met in Los Angeles. They said this was a good community for a Muslim 'fresh off the boat', as it were."

"I am so glad to hear that," Ali responded, beaming. "And did they refer you to our little mosque, as well?"

Uri had to be a little cautious here. To what end was the imam probing? He decided to be bold, hoping the terrorist connection might appear. "Indeed they did, and I am glad! You and your congregation have been so friendly."

The imam took this well, it seemed to Uri, as though he had crossed a significant threshold. "Well then," the imam said, "how may I be of service? You have a place to stay? A job?"

"I do have a very nice place just a few blocks away in a fine rooming house," Uri exaggerated. "But I am looking for employment. I have basic computer skills, but while I look for a permanent position, I would like to support myself with something here in the neighborhood. Perhaps in a shop; I also have some experience in sales and waiting tables."

The imam seemed pleased. "I think I can help you! There are a few opportunities. Some of our congregation own or work in restaurants here, and they are always looking for waiters. At the evening service Friday, I will introduce you to one or two." Because he had shown up for salaat two days in a row, the imam seemed certain Farid would be there for the important Friday service.

Uri was delighted. The next day he repeated his routine of the previous day, scouting the neighborhood after the morning service, then taking another route to his car. Again, he saw no obvious tail as he reported in to Yehudi Gold at the Los Angeles consulate from inside the parking garage.

"And how is it going, Farid?" the consul asked brightly.

Uri detailed the day's activity, to the clear approval of Gold. "Excellent," he proclaimed. "What's next?"

"Well, I hope to get a job and start paying my way."

Yehudi laughed and joked back, "Don't get too comfortable. We still have a tough 'row to hoe' here."

"Indeed. Don't worry, I hope to get in contact with the bad guys soon. But meanwhile what do you hear from Lara?"

"Nothing more, I'm afraid. She's still working on her 'marriage plans'."

"Alright. Tell her hi, and I hope to have more news for you Friday night. But it will be late."

"I shall be pleased to hear from you! Goodbye, my friend, and shalom. We are all with you."

"Shalom," Uri replied and ended the conversation.

Friday morning, Uri repeated his daily schedule, showing up on time for the sunrise service, much to the delight of the imam. "I will see you tonight, then, Farid?" he queried of Uri.

"Indeed, Imam Ali," he responded, reverting to the more formal address here in the mosque in the presence of others. "I am looking forward to it."

Uri spent a restless day, roaming the streets, looking in more shops and restaurants. He hoped his experience in the West Bank would prove useful, even though that was as an Arab, and now he was a Shia. He noticed that the shopkeepers and patrons spoke both Arabic and Farsi, even a little English, though highly accented. When speaking to them, Uri used his Lebanese-Arabic, which alerted no one.

Finally, it was time for the Friday evening service, and Uri found the mosque to be packed with congregants. He saw many new faces, of course, as he found a spot at the back of the crowded prayer area. This service was longer than the others; and, as was standard at the Friday evening service, an offering box was clearly available near the exit. Uri was prepared for this and proudly placed a ten-dollar bill on top of the stack. The attendant's eyebrows raised slightly as he saw this generous gift; no doubt the imam would be apprised of the newcomer's kindness.

Uri made a point of being among the last to leave as the service ended. The imam caught his eye as the congregants poured into the street. He had a middle-age, portly man standing beside him. "Farid, I would like to introduce you to Mr. Hazerian," the imam said in English, as the man extended his hand with a warm smile. "This is the newcomer I told you of, Farid Refai." The man was nearly bald, but with a curly, mostly grey, well-cropped beard.

Uri took the man's hand in greeting, noting it was warm and moist.

"Mr. Hazerian owns the 'Cyrus Café' just two blocks from here on Third Street and is need of some help at the moment. Have you familiarity with Iranian food?" The imam quickly turned to the large, imposing gentleman. "Farid is from Jordan but has experience in many food businesses."

Uri blushed gratuitously and quickly stated in English, "I have worked as a waiter in my village, where there are a few Persian restaurants."

"And you speak Farsi and Arabic, I understand? We have customers from all over."

"I do, yes," Uri replied in Farsi, accented as it was. He assumed the man would not be totally familiar with a Jordanian manner of speech.

"Our menu is simple, the usual: Olivieh salads, Kashk kabobs, Dolmeh, Maust, Torshi, Khiar. With some tasty Persian sweets, as well!" Hazerian patted his ample belly and smiled. He seemed ready to give this stranger a tryout.

"Yes, I am quite familiar with all these salads, chicken skewers, yoghurt dishes and vegetarian plates. I can start tomorrow, if you wish," Uri stated firmly, showing his acceptance of the unstated offer.

"We open at nine, and you will work through lunch until five," the well-dressed man said. "Of course, you will have ample time for meals, in our slack times. I'm afraid the wages are somewhat meager, but our delicious food is included and the tips are quite bountiful," the man boasted.

"Of course!" Uri replied at once, pleasing both Hazerian and the imam. A match had been made.

Chapter 32

Uri made his usual appearance for sunrise services the next morning, Saturday, much to the delight of Imam Ali, and received a hearty greeting. Returning home to shave and change into his work clothes, he showed up at quarter to nine dressed in a clean shirt and jeans. He presumed he would be given a full-length apron, as was customary in Persian restaurants. "Farid" wanted to be early; first to make a good impression, and second to study the menu and ask any questions before the customers arrived.

The owner, Hazerian, was already there, bustling around in the kitchen, arranging chairs and making sure all was in order before opening. He seemed very pleased to see his new hire, Farid, early and eager to start work. "Good morning, Farid, I am glad to see you." He spoke in English, as was the custom. They didn't want to scare away any American business. "Here, we have an apron for you," he said, handing Uri a clean, starched white linen to fold and wrap around his waist, pinned in the back. "Please look over the menu. Our wonderful cook is already hard at work. Please say hello to Hossein."

A burly man of middle age, with a huge, rather frightening mustache gazed at Uri disdainfully. *He has probably seen new waiters come and go*, Uri thought to himself. Keen to please, Uri thrust out his hand, and said in Farsi, "Hi, I am known as Farid. Pleased to meet you. I hope I can be of good service."

The cook condescendingly took Uri's hand, gave it a limp shake, mumbled something and went back to work, chopping onions and other vegetables.

One other waiter, a young man named Omar, seemed pleased that he had some help, and graciously showed Uri around the place. "We share the tips," he pointed out immediately, showing Uri the glass jar just behind the wall separating the dining area from the kitchen.

The day began smoothly, as regular morning customers appeared right after opening and ordered coffee and pastries. Uri smoothly operated the coffee urn, which was already full and hot, pouring out small cups full of the strong, bitter brew. The pastries were on open display in a glass case from which the customers could choose.

Although he greeted the people in English with a cheery "Good morning, how can I help you?" the clients often replied in Farsi, pointing at the sweets they desired. Hazerian watched surreptitiously from behind the cash register as his new hire quickly and efficiently met their demands. The restaurant was relatively small, just ten tables, easily handled by the two waiters. Uri left it up to Omar to choose which customers he served. No doubt he knew the good tippers. Uri doubted that the "tip jar" was rigorously maintained.

The customers were mainly men, but a few women with strollers did come, always escorted by men, undoubtedly their husbands. All wore colorful abayas and hijabs. The women looked either down, at their husbands, or at the tots in their strollers. Uri never even glanced at them, for fear of offending both the woman and her husband.

There was a pause in business mid-morning and Uri had a chance to grab a little breakfast and talk with his new co-worker. Omar arrived two years ago from Iran with his family, had an argument with his father, and moved to this area from San Diego to see if he could make enough money to start a family of his own. He told "Farid" about some approved Shia places to meet chaperoned young women on

Saturday nights. Uri nodded, promising to go with him sometime, but not tonight.

Lunchtime was busy with many regulars mixed in with tourists. He greeted all in English, which worked well with these customers. As he expected, the tipping was meager, but he assiduously placed all of his in the jar. Omar watched in approval.

The afternoon was slow, but picked up well before the time for evening services. As in the morning, the clientele were regulars. One couple was especially friendly to the new waiter. A middle-aged man and woman greeted "Farid", identifying themselves as Zurvan and Fakhra, respectively. They spoke to him first in English, but then were pleased when he responded in Farsi. As the restaurant was getting busy, Uri could not stop and chat, but they said they came in practically every day and hoped to see him again.

Uri finished up around five, did not bother to check the tip jar, and said goodnight to Omar, Hazerian, and Hossein. The first two said goodnight warmly; the cook merely grumbled. Uri had taken the opportunity to eat some delicious baked chicken, rice, and salad in the slower part of the afternoon, and so was not hungry as he left to change for the sunset service. He arrived at the mosque in plenty of time, finding a much smaller crowd than on Friday. Imam Ali greeted him, eagerly asking about his first day of work at the restaurant. "It went quite well," Uri said in English, as the imam had requested.

"That's wonderful, praise Allah!" The pleased imam headed off to lead the small gathering in their evening prayers.

The rest of the night proved uneventful, the handful of regulars merely nodding to the pious newcomer. Uri then made his nightly sojourn to the parking garage to check in with Yehudi. He took an even more circuitous route this time, as there were considerably more people, many tourists, on the streets. As always, he continuously glanced at himself in store windows, often doubling back on the other side of the street and even going around the block on occasion. He could not jeopardize his mission with a stupid mistake, especially when he had such a fruitful beginning.

The call to Yehudi was taken on his satellite phone, as usual, probably at his home, Uri surmised. After the usual greetings, Uri immediately asked about Lara. "No news, I'm afraid. She did check in with Mary; still going through the list of eager bachelors," the consul reported. "And you?"

"Quite well, actually," Uri responded. He told Gold of the day in the restaurant, and of the friendly couple he had met there.

"That's great!" Yehudi said. "Any contacts you can make are all for the good."

"Agreed. I have tomorrow off work. I'm going to look around town some more. Shalom."

As promised, after morning services Uri took to the streets, memorizing the names of shops and buildings. There were signs in English, Arabic and Farsi, advertising medical and dental services, bargain clothing, hardware, fresh vegetables and meats, insurance and loan agencies; all aimed at the overworked, underpaid, immigrant population.

As he strolled around, he was surprised to see the friendly couple from the restaurant, Zurvan and Fakhra. They spotted him immediately and approached him with friendly smiles. "Farid!" the man said. "How nice to see you out and about. I was afraid Hazerian was going to make you work on Sunday, too." They were regulars in the restaurant, as he suspected.

"It's nice to see some friendly faces," Uri said truthfully. "Are you doing the weekly shopping?"

"Oh no, we go bargain hunting on Sundays. Lots of places have special deals. How about you?"

"Oh, I'm just looking around, getting acquainted, you know." All this conversation was being carried on in English. Uri hoped as always that his Israeli accent wouldn't betray him. But they themselves had heavy Middle Eastern accents; they seemed either Iranian or Pakistani.

"So you are a newcomer to the neighborhood! From where, if I may be so bold?" Zurvan inquired. Fakhra, in her black headscarf, merely smiled modestly.

"I am here recently from Jordan," Uri replied in deliberately awkward English. The couple did not seem to pick up on anything strange about his speech.

"Are you really?" the man asked warmly, without suspicion. "We are ourselves here only a few years, from Zahedan in Iran. Do you know of it? I suspect not."

Uri did know of Zahedan in the southeastern part of Iran, close to Pakistan and Afghanistan. There was suspected nuclear enrichment going on near there, and a large medical school as well. "I bet you're a doctor, maybe both of you? Am I right?"

"The couple's mouths flew open. You do know of our humble origin, then!"

"Oh yes, my father was himself a medical doctor, before..." He paused for effect.

"The DAESH...?" Zurvan inquired respectfully.

Uri nodded, his head down at the mention of the Arab name for ISIS.

"You poor man," Fakhra sympathized. It was the first words Uri heard her speak. Zurvan glanced at her somewhat reproachfully, but Uri showed no immediate reaction.

"Yes, they are indeed the living Satans," he finally replied. He appeared bereaved, which wasn't hard for him, considering the slaughter ISIS was performing in the area. If these two had any inkling of radical Shia activity here, they may be inclined to share it, he speculated.

"Listen," Zurvan said somewhat impulsively, "you're here alone; why not come to dinner at our place, tonight?"

The couple seemed so genuine, Uri thought to himself. *Why involve them?* Then duty intervened. "That is so nice of you; yes, I'd be delighted. What can I bring?"

"Only yourself; this is America!" Zurvan hastened to set the time and give Uri directions to their house." Suddenly he inquired: "Do you go to evening *salaat*?"

"Yes, in fact I do, but that will give me enough time to get to your place."

Uri shook hands with the man, nodded to the woman, and went on his way.

Chapter 33

That evening, following services, Uri made his way to Zurvan's home. It was only a short walk in the pleasant, cool evening air. He felt somewhat embarrassed, showing up at this couple's house empty-handed, but he really had no idea what would be appropriate.

He arrived at their modest bungalow right on time, a small structure set between other similar buildings, only one block from a busy street. He rang the doorbell, which was answered immediately by a smiling Zurvan, dressed casually, as Uri had hoped. He welcomed Uri into the small living room, where he was greeted by Fakhra. She was also in casual dress, except for the obligatory head covering in keeping with being in the presence of a male non-relative. She smiled at Uri, but quickly dropped her gaze downwards, and did not hold out her hand.

It was only then that Uri saw there was another person in the room. There, on a straight-backed chair sat a young woman, dressed similarly to the hostess, Fakhra. "May I introduce you to my cousin, Ayra," Fakhra said. The woman in the chair blushed slightly, looking directly at Uri for only a brief second. "Ayra, being unmarried, lives with us." Zurvan shuffled his feet uncomfortably as they watched for Uri's reaction.

"Ayra, this is Farid, whom we told you of. He works in the restaurant..." There was another pregnant pause as Uri and Ayra attempted to assess the situation. "As I may have mentioned, Farid has only recently arrived here, from Jordan." All this conversation had taken place in English, albeit rather slow, apparently for the sake of Ayra.

It was quite clear to Uri, as it no doubt was to Ayra, that this was some sort of clumsy matchmaking. Uri took it in stride; he had no wish to embarrass either his hosts or the young woman. "It is my pleasure to meet you," Uri said with a timid smile, so as not to appear the eager wife-seeker.

Another awkward silence passed before Zurvan finally stated, "Well, let us all head in to dinner, shall we?" He held his hand out to Uri, guiding him to the small dining-room table, the women following discreetly afterwards. Uri found himself seated facing the clearly ill-at-ease Ayra, the hosts taking the opposing chairs. Another pause followed, broken only by Fakhra, excusing herself in Farsi, leaving briefly to bring in the food.

The meal was delicious; lamb steamed in some sort of thick, rich sauce, salad with yoghurt-based dressing, tabouli, and skewers of chicken. It was truly a feast. Only when the dinner was nearly finished did the conversation begin. Zurvan asked Uri, rather inelegantly, "You have a wife coming to join you soon?"

Uri had been prepared for this as soon as he had seen the young, unattached woman. She had her head down though all of the meal, but he had gotten some quick glimpses of her. She was rather plain, but with an apparently pleasant demeanor. "No," he responded sadly to Zurvan's inquiry. Seeing the sudden interest on the part of both women, he quickly added, "after losing my wife...in the, uh, you know, fighting in Jordan...I've sort of decided, in my middle age, to stay the pious bachelor." That ought to quell any further interest in matrimonial quest, he figured.

Seeing the quasi-proposal was not going to proceed, Fakhra quickly changed the subject. "Are you enjoying life here in the States?" she asked politely.

"Yes indeed," Uri quickly responded. "Although I am staying very busy." The bachelorette lowered her head even further, somewhat embarrassed at the subtle rejection.

The meal ended about 10:30, with Uri graciously thanking his hosts, politely nodding also at Ayra, who did not return his gaze.

It was the very next day at the restaurant when, during the noon rush, Zurvan showed up, smiling broadly at Uri. "That was a most enjoyable evening. We were so pleased to have you as our guest."

"Oh, Zurvan, the pleasure is all mine," Uri replied gracefully. "Please tell Fakhra how much I liked the dinner she prepared. It was most delicious. Oh, and please give my regards to Ayra, as well," he added awkwardly.

"I most certainly will." There was a pause as Zurvan looked as though there was something he wanted to say, but was uncertain. Then he said in a low tone so that the other diners would not hear. Motioning for Uri to bend closer, he said cautiously, "I know you go often to the mosque with Imam Ali Al-Naqi, where I first saw you."

Uri nodded, not knowing where this was headed.

"I needed to warn you...perhaps 'warn' is too strong a word...caution you of another mosque not far from there, just around the corner, actually..."

"Yes, please go on."

"Well, the imam there, Imam Zainal Abidin, is rather...how shall I put it? Radical? It may be dangerous...no, no, uncomfortable, for one so new to the States to visit there...perhaps I have said too much."

"No, no," replied Uri. "I appreciate any and all information you can give me about living in the States...and the neighborhood," He laughed lightly for the benefit of the other diners, to show that this was not any kind of serious discussion. "Thank you again. Now I must get back to my duties or I might lose my job." Zurvan seemed relieved to hear this light-hearted response from his new friend.

"You see, Farid, most of us, though serious about our Muslim faith, have little to do with these radicals. I must tell you, my friend," Zurvan said sincerely, placing his arm around Uri's shoulder, "these few, with their hostile words and actions, turn the non-Muslim Americans against us. There are only a despicable few who support the anti-Semitic actions that reflect so badly on all the rest of us."

Uri, sensing the honest feelings of his host, took these words to heart. So the warning given to Mary weeks ago about the neighboring radical mosque had some serious truth to it. He would report it. Today.

Chapter 34

"Farid" had several other invitations to dinner from men he met either in the restaurant or the mosque. Most dinners were similar to the first, although there was only one more clumsy attempt at matchmaking. As with the first encounter any possible romance was quickly snuffed out by the reluctant Farid.

Just once did the host family speak in Farsi. The Kabir family, Abdul and Ana, spoke in Farsi throughout the dinner with Farid. He had met the husband, Abdul, several times at the morning service. Finally, one day, at the conclusion of the service, Abdul approached Farid and inquired as to his familial status. When he found out Farid was alone he asked him to dinner, as had his other hosts. Contrary to the imam's exhortation for the members to speak in English, Abdul addressed Farid in his native tongue. Uri quickly responded in his ersatz Jordanian Farsi. Though he said nothing, Abdul looked at Uri quizzically for a moment. "Where did you say you were from?" he asked.

"Eastern Jordan," Uri quickly responded. "A very small village called Mahattat al Jufur."

"Yes, I know of it," Abdul replied, much to Uri's dismay. "It is away from everything; no wonder your accent is so strange to my ear...there is not much there in the way of industry," he probed.

"You are correct, I am surprised you even know of us."

"I know the DAESH went through there, slashing and burning."

"I lost everything: my wife and parents. Even our few sheep and goats," Farid said, dropping his head in grief.

Abdul put his arm around Farid's shoulders. "You must come to dinner with us; let us share bread and bring comfort to you."

Uri quickly accepted the invitation, but was somewhat alarmed at the man's sudden change in manner. Had he given something away?

At dinner the next evening Farid was introduced to Abdul's wife, Ana. There were no children. The couple was in their mid-fifties, Uri guessed. Both were nearly completely grey-haired. Contrary to the other few homes Uri had been in, the Kabir family had photos and art from their native Iran. They also exhibited a large amount of Muslim, especially Shia, religious objects.

Eventually, the dinner conversation, conducted completely in Farsi, with Farid's strange accent now seemingly accepted, led quickly to politics. "You must be very angry with the DAESH," Abdul said suddenly.

"Indeed!" Farid replied with dramatic intensity. "Not to mention the Zionists, who stole much of our land." He wanted to see just where this would lead.

Abdul glanced quickly at his wife. "So you are not fond of the peace accord your King made with the Israelis forty years ago?"

Farid shook his head, seemingly in remorse. "He gave up without a fight," he reminisced sadly.

For the first time, Abdul seemed genuinely pleased with his guest, but did not pursue the politics any further. Instead, he turned to more mundane matters, such as Farid's living arrangements and grocery shopping. At the end of the evening, they said good night, with the promise of seeing each other soon, either in the mosque or the restaurant where Farid was employed.

Walking home, Uri was secretly pleased, though not sure what the future might hold. He would certainly report the evening's proceedings to Yehudi tomorrow in his nightly phone call.

Chapter 35

Time passed uneventfully, Uri falling into a routine in his undercover life as Farid, a devout Muslim newcomer to the neighborhood. One evening, two weeks after the encounter with Abdul and his wife, there was a visitor at the mosque. He was introduced to the assembly simply as "Imam Javad," though something about either the man or the name rang a bell in Uri's memory.

"Imam Javad, I'd like you to meet one of our new members, Farid Refai," the resident imam Ali Al-Naqi, said after the close of service. "Farid joined us about a month ago; he is new to America and to California. He comes to us from Jordan." He said all this in English; as part of the indoctrination of the Shia community to American culture. They were, after all, expected to live and work among English-speaking Americans. "Farid, this is the blessed Imam Javad Abdouleh."

The two men smiled at each other, shaking hands. Javad explored Uri's face carefully, as if recognizing him from somewhere. "*Mar khaba, ahla w'sahla,*" he suddenly said, not in Farsi, but in Lebanese-accented Arabic. It was a standard greeting, roughly translated to "Hello, welcome."

This man Javad was, physically, the opposite of the unassuming Imam Ali Al-Naqi. He was tall, strong in appearance, with those predator-like eyes that can strike fear in a man. They were set above a sharp, beak-like nose, increasing the resemblance.

Uri quickly responded in Arabic, "*Tcharrafna,*" meaning "Pleased to meet you."

Actually, Uri was delighted to speak to this man in Arabic; he was afraid his English would betray his Israeli accent. But his Arabic was as Lebanese in nature as was Javad's.

"Kifak?" (How are you?) Javad responded, still apparently searching his memory for this man.

"Mni kha-khamdella." (Fine-thank God), Uri correctly answered.

"Chou esmak?" (What's your name?) probed the esteemed visitor, even though he had already been introduced to "Farid Refai."

"Esmi Farid Refai," Uri replied immediately.

"Men wayn inta?" (Where are you from?) Javad inquired.

"Ana men Jordan," Uri stated, in keeping with his introduction.

Javad gazed at Uri intently with his hawk-like eyes, as if studying potential prey. "No, I don't think so," he suddenly stated in his Arabic-accented English.

"What do you mean?" Imam Ali interjected, also in English.

"His Arabic is like mine, learned in Lebanon. In fact, I think I know this man!"

Uri was startled, but remained calm. He may finally be able to assume the Mohammed Azizi identity he needed to break into the terror group. But at the same time he feared, when he replied in English, his Israeli accent would betray him. It was now or never, he thought. He had to reply in English or they would suspect him even more. He got a brief reprieve as the imam interrupted: "What are you saying, Javad, are you certain!?"

"Wait just a moment, and I will show you something." Javad left for a few deadly minutes, the other two staring at each other in a sort of limbo, the resident imam clearly unsettled by this accusation of his new member. It was only then that Uri noticed his new friend, Abdul, his dinner host. Abdul was standing well within earshot, but not entering the conversation.

Javad returned, carrying an old, beat-up leather briefcase. He set it on a chair in front of them and dug through some newspaper clippings. "Yes...here we are, look at this!" He triumphantly held up a page taken from a copy of *Al Jazeera*, sold at many newsstands in the Los Angeles area. On it, Uri recognized immediately, was the story taken from *Ha'aretz*, of the escape of the notorious assassin, Mohammed Azizi, from an Israeli prison, just over a month ago. Uri's picture, taken at Mossad headquarters, scruffy beard and all, stared back at them.

"I thought so!" Abdul suddenly said, eyeing the article, attracting everyone's attention. Javad nodded in agreement.

"What can I say?" Uri said, attempting a sheepish demeanor. He held out his hands, palms up, as if to say "*You got me.*" Then he straightened up, assuming a commanding presence. "I am here to continue the work you have started," he said boldly. The time had come. His dinner with Abdul must have led to this introduction.

The two imams, along with Abdul, glanced at each other, studying the picture and the man in front of them. It all fit, they now realized: the stranger with the Lebanese accent, masquerading as a Jordanian to evade capture, was here to aid their cause. What could be better! Surely a gift from Allah himself, blessed be he.

The two Shia imams bowed to Uri in unison, taking his hand in turn, and kissing it. "*Ahla w sahla!*" (Welcome!). They were as pleased as Uri, who breathed a sigh of relief.

Javad then told Farid, now unmasked as Mohammed Azizi, of the action group housed in the nearby Ah Bayt mosque. It was, Uri realized, the mosque run by Zainal Abidin. "We have already conducted some operations," he said, not being specific. Uri, however, was reasonably certain that these men were at least part of the gang that had created the mayhem in Los Angeles: the slaughter of the children, the assassination of the rabbi, the Purim attacks, and the most recent attack on the Sunni mosque. "We meet almost every night after services at my mosque, just around the corner. If you agree to join us, which I dearly hope you will, I will see you tomorrow night." Uri nodded eagerly. His mission had really begun.

Chapter 36

Uri had been attending the daily briefings run by Javad for nearly two weeks, learning the fundamentals of Javad's plan to cause havoc within the Jewish community, casting blame on the Jews. He bragged about how well it had worked so far. His select group consisted of ten of the veterans of earlier assaults; on the synagogues and on the Sunni mosque.

Uri steeled himself against his natural urge to kill Javad as he spoke of the school massacre that had been carried out, not by him but by the "blessed" Imam Ali Muhammad in Los Angeles. He told them also, but not in detail, about other scourges that had been carried out by his and Ali's men. It was all he could do to keep from throttling the man there and then. That, of course, was impossible as well as counter-productive. He reluctantly forced these thoughts from his mind; but the urge for retribution lay dormant in his brain. He needed to know what was coming next.

This particular night, Javad finally exposed the next chapter in their revenge against the enemy, or enemies if one included the Sunnis. There was in place already a very successful campaign against the Zionist entity, here and abroad, called the "Boycott, Divestment, and Sanctions," known as simply "BDS." This campaign, Javad told his eager acolytes, had as its purpose the disruption of Israeli commerce, which was, he divulged, booming at the cost of innocent Palestinian lives. It had been ongoing for several years now, very successfully.

The BDS campaign consisted of a determined effort to boycott all Israeli goods, especially those coming from the "occupied" lands in the West Bank. This effort had been the most successful, especially in Europe, where all goods imported from Israel, if they were even allowed in the marketplace, were glaringly marked in bold red lettering, as though they were poisonous.

Divestment meant getting all financial holding companies and pension funds, especially those at liberal universities, to sell off all their Israel-based holdings, no matter how profitable they had been to the organizations. Many large financial institutions and retirement funds had caved in to this gambit in fear of large-scale demonstrations, mainly from anti-Zionist students.

"Sanctions against Israel have reached across international boundaries," Javad told his listeners. Many countries instituted punitive measures against Israel as a means of forcing them to give up the land they "stole" from the Palestinians. He didn't mention, of course, that these lands were almost totally part of the U.N. charter that established Israel in 1947, or that it was the Arab countries themselves who urged the Palestinians to flee. And also, Uri noted to himself, it was the Arabs who instigated the wars that culminated in their loss of the area. This somehow never made it into the discussions, even the public ones.

Uri could see the loathing this speech was conveying to his captive audience, who were, in the first place, itching to cause death and fear among the Jewish community, Zionist or not. Javad was an excellent motivational speaker, bringing his audience almost to a fever pitch, ready to carry out whatever he asked of them.

Javad now got down to explicit instructions. There was to be a huge "Israel Independence Day" celebration at a public park in Beverly Hills on May 15. This annual event was the largest such celebration in the U.S., expected to bring more than 15,000 people; mostly Jews, of course.

This date, May 15, corresponded to "Nakba Day," the day of sorrow for the Muslims, as they mourned the loss of Palestine. To take advantage of the expected press coverage of the "Independence Day" celebration, there was to be an unparalleled BDS counter-demonstration. The latter had already been quietly organized by the "Americans for Islam" committee with over one hundred volunteers. They were ready to march around the park with printed signs stating "Free Palestine Now", "Eliminate Israel" and similar slogans.

"What a fortunate opportunity," Javad told his eager listeners. "What we will do is dress like angry American Jews, aimed at disruption of the perfectly legitimate right of our people to demonstrate in support of BDS. Administrators at large institutions, such as the University of California and others, have shown they are easily swayed in any direction that would avoid further turmoil on their campuses. For example, they have allowed our forces to shout down 'pro-Israel' speakers, explaining that the students' right to free speech was every bit as permitted as the speaker's!" He smiled at the obvious absurdity.

The small audience burst into applause at the way Javad described how the Americans fell easily to this argument. They truly would always take the course of least resistance.

"Our 'Jews' will instigate a physical confrontation with the BDS demonstrators," Javad continued, "who will easily overcome the small band of 'Jews'; without, of course, causing them any real harm. At any rate, the police will be forced to quickly enter into the fray and remove the instigators from the scene. The blame for the interruption of the festivities will fall onto the band of 'Jewish zealots'. The news media will be delighted!" The audience smiled.

"What a glorious opportunity for the gullible press to observe: American Jews carrying out violent, aggressive actions aimed solely against perfectly innocent protestors."

Laughter and applause poured out of the enchanted group as they imagined the disruption they were to cause, and the wonderful anti-Israel press coverage they were to bring; even better than the attack on the Sunni mosque!

Javad dismissed the group, but motioned for "Azizi" to remain. Uri did so, wondering what the terrorist had in mind for him.

"You approve of this plan, Mohammed?" Javad inquired.

"Indeed, it seems most ingenious, Master," Uri replied.

"I'm sure you would like to take part, but I fear that you might just be recognized. We cannot take that chance with so valuable an asset."

Uri looked suitably humbled by this compliment, but said nothing, waiting for more information. Surely the man had some plan for him.

"We both, you and I, will be in the background, dressed as celebrants. Many of the religious Jews have facial hair similar to ours. And we will wear similar clothing; including the Jewish *kippas*. We will merely observe and report back. If all goes well, and I feel sure it will, the liberal American press will eat this up! Not to mention Al Jazeera." He smiled, bade "Azizi" goodnight and left him there to gather his thoughts.

Now knowing the plan, Uri could convey the details to the FBI and LAPD. Ordinarily the police presence would focus on keeping the BDS demonstrators separated from the Jewish celebrants. Never before had an outside gang of angry Jews assaulted a peaceful group of Palestinian demonstrators. This time, though, it would be different. If the police understood the situation, as he was sure they would, it would be the "Jewish" attackers who would be detained. Most importantly, he would stress to Yehudi Gold, he was certain that the angry mob would comprise members of the same assault teams that terrorized the synagogues and mosques. With any luck they might even get a DNA match with the blood found on the broken glass of the mosque!

After hearing Javad's plan for the anti-BDS demonstration, Uri (aka Mohammed Azizi) had an idea that he felt would defuse the demonstration, and perhaps even identify some of the members of Javad's gang of terror. But he would need the approval and help from the authorities to pull it off. In addition, he would need to convince Javad himself of the idea.

* * *

That night, as usual, Uri made the excursion to his car in the parking garage. He was especially slow in his pace along one of the indirect paths through the neighborhood, stopping a number of times at the newsstands, and once at an all-night market to buy a banana. He stopped at this particular store often when he chose this route, and was comfortable talking to the owner, a Persian he often saw at the restaurant.

Uri was in no hurry, pausing outside the shop, perusing the local newspaper as he slowly enjoyed the ripe fruit. This was his custom when he chose this particular path; it was one that brought him to his apartment, but also passed the garage that housed his car. At this time of night, there were few, if any, cars or pedestrians. But Uri had more than the usual reasons for his apparent dawdling. He held the newspaper in front of him, his mind racing with the details of the plan he was about to propose; not to Mary Robley, but to Yehudi Gold. Finally, after about fifteen minutes of this charade, he threw the banana skin into the trash bin, folded the newspaper under his arm, and headed leisurely on his way. The plan had taken shape—at least enough to propose it to Gold.

He made his way casually past the garage, halting twice to look again at the paper, but really to see if there were any onlookers. Satisfied, he entered the garage through a back pedestrian walkway and made his way to his Ford, covered as usual with yellow dust. Using the paper as a broom, he cleaned off the car enough to make it look as if it had been driven in the past week. This corner of the garage, on an upper level and far from the exit ramp, was only lightly occupied, and he noticed several other vehicles that appeared to be used only rarely, based on their layers of dirt.

Checking once again for onlookers, Uri withdrew his satellite phone from its hiding place, and started the car engine to charge the battery in the phone. The noise also covered his conversation, if anyone were hiding in the vicinity. Yehudi answered immediately; if Uri was to call it was always about this time of night. After the usual pleasantries, the customary check on Lara, and the negative reply, Uri got down to business. He detailed the plan Javad had described earlier that evening, adding his own ideas for disarming the situation.

"You're quite sure this counter-demonstration is set to happen?" Gold asked, clearly alarmed.

"Yes, it's all set. We just have to make sure the LAPD has some legal pretense to apprehend and collect these 'fake Jews' before any violence occurs. I feel sure that some of the individuals have taken part in other attacks in L.A."

"You think maybe even this last attack at the Sunni mosque?"

"Right," he responded, pleased that Gold had the same idea.

"And you think we might even get a DNA match with the blood we found there?"

"I think it's likely, if you can come up with an excuse to take mouth swabs from them, for example."

"Good idea!" he agreed. "I'll check with Mary and Mike Scanlon to see if we can come up with something...we have to!"

* * *

The next night, after Javad's meeting with his men, revealing more of the details for the May 15 attack, now less than a week away, Uri respectfully asked if he could meet privately with the leader. Javad, knowing of "Azizi's" experience with bold attacks against the Jews, was more than willing to hear what he had to say. "Come into my private chamber," the ringleader offered graciously. With that he led Uri into a small room in the back of the mosque. There was a desk, somewhat cluttered with papers, and three chairs. He was clearly not expecting visitors. Javad offered a chair to Uri and sat beside him.

"Please," Javad said pleasantly, "what troubles you, my friend?"

"It is not trouble that brings me to you, Imam Javad, but an idea that might bring even more and better attention to our cause."

Javad, realizing full well Azizi's history of successes, was eager to hear what he had to say. He leaned forward, motioning for the escaped terrorist to continue.

"Your plan is a good one, Master, there is no doubt of that. But I was thinking, after our last session, that instead of arousing physical confrontation between our 'Jews' and the BDS demonstrators, not to mention the authorities...might it not be better to avoid the violence?"

Javad was clearly intrigued. "Do go on," he urged his co-conspirator.

"Well, what if you instruct your BDS demonstrators to deliberately *avoid* any physical action at all, even in self defense, against this band of aggressive 'Jews'?" Uri paused to see Javad's reaction. He saw only interest and expectation.

"The police would then be required to forcibly remove the band of intruders and see to any injured BDS demonstrators. The impact on the press would be even greater than if there had been resistance. We only have to think back to the days of Gandhi and Martin Luther King..."

Javad could do nothing but smile at this wonderful contribution to his plan. This man Azizi certainly knew his business. The newly revised strategy would be explained to the troops the following night.

Chapter 37

May 15th, a Sunday, began peacefully enough. The morning was overcast, with the typical spring marine layer blowing wisps of cool fog in from the ocean. Hazerian had graciously granted Farid, his eager new worker, the day off. Uri drove north on the 405 freeway into Los Angeles, exiting at Wilshire, heading into Beverly Hills. Although the Independence Day celebration was scheduled to begin at noon, the large public park was already crowded with tables, banners, signs and people by 11 a.m. Uri parked several blocks away, being careful to avoid the "residents only" curbside spots. He could ill afford a parking violation. As instructed by Javad, he wore a plain black Jewish kippa fitted tightly on his head. A Jew, masquerading as a Muslim, posing as a Jew, he mused.

As he strolled back to the park he noted the difference in the neighborhood from where he had been residing the past month. He had already forgotten the affluence of Beverly Hills; its luxurious houses and swank shops. The trees and flowers were in full bloom, a riot of color on all sides. Lawns were green and large, despite the water shortage. All was relatively peaceful and quiet in the wealthy neighborhood.

When he reached the park, the noise level rose, as the Independence Day celebrants set up their booths and tables. There was a large sheltered platform near the center of the park for the speakers scheduled for the afternoon. All around, parents with their children had placed blankets and lawn chairs in order to hear the talks as well as enjoy the sunshine. There were, of course, many booths serving food and distributing literature. AIPAC, the American Israel Political

Action Committee had a prominent set-up near the bandstand, where they were accepting donations and handing out pamphlets. Other such organizations, including the Zionists of America, the Friends of the Israel Defense Forces, and the American Friends of Magen David Adom were also in evidence. The AFMDA was the organization that protected the public in Israel from terrorist attacks, and helped with the aftermath of such attacks. It was a grisly, but necessary job: collecting body parts for proper burial under Jewish law.

He looked around for traces of Javad or the "fake Jew" mob who were supposed to interrupt the BDS demonstration, but as yet they were not in appearance. That, of course, was to be expected. They were not scheduled to show up until the celebratory speeches had already begun.

The sound and excitement grew as the time approached 1 p.m., the park filling with upwards of 15,000 people, as predicted. It was then that a second well-disciplined group appeared: the BDS protesters with their "Boycott Israel", "Remember Nakba Day" and "Palestine for Arabs" placards. They quietly set up their signs at the fringe of the main crowd of Independence Day celebrants, avoiding any physical contact. A squad of LAPD crowd-control officers placed themselves in position to intercede any disturbance that might arise. The LAPD had, of course, been well prepared, having been briefed in advance by Uri, through Mary Robley and Yehudi Gold.

This was the scene drawing most of the local and national media, hovering just beyond the ranks of BDS demonstrators and police. The main stage with the Independence Day speakers and listeners was pretty much neglected. If there was going to be a story, it would be here. But as the festivities began, the BDS people remained remarkably in control, paying little attention to the angry stares from the crowd of celebrants. Neither side seemed ready to deliberately antagonize the other, and the festivities went on without incident.

After half an hour there was a dramatic change. A small group of men, ten in number, aggressively approached the BDS demonstrators, carrying their own banners. They were distinctly dressed in costumes, grey with gold Jewish Stars, made to resemble those of the Jewish prisoners of Dachau, Auschwitz, and other Nazi concentration camps. They wore ghastly stage makeup that turned them into macabre victims of the Holocaust.

Attention quickly shifted to the burgeoning confrontation between these angry, wraithlike reminders of the recent past and the disciplined group of BDS demonstrators. The newcomers carried signs that read "Never Again", "Arabs are the New Nazis", "Keep Israel Pure", and "Jerusalem for the Jews."

It seemed that a violent interaction between the BDS demonstrators and this small group of specters was unavoidable. But it was then the police went into immediate action. Their clear objective was to calmly remove this latest group of costumed intruders; without them the event had been peaceful. And so they rounded up the ten costumed "survivors", placed them in paddy wagons and removed them from the scene.

There was a mixed reaction from the crowd, but one of glee from the press. This was the sort of thing that sold newspapers. Radical Jews attempting to attack a peaceful BDS rally! The Independence Day speakers and celebrants were forgotten in the rush to capture images of ghostly Jews apparently provoking peaceful BDS demonstrators. The attention of the entire crowd was focused on the arrests. No one made particular note of the quiet disappearance of the BDS people and their signs. The Independence Day celebration reconvened, but with muted cheer.

Javad, who had been watching from a discreet distance couldn't have been more pleased. Certain that his group of ten intruders could not be held by the police for any length of time, he nearly danced back to his car. His new associate, Mohammed Azizi, was to be congratulated; his contribution to the plan had been brilliant. He would wait, however, to make sure that his ten warriors did indeed get released from custody.

Sure enough, within thirty minutes, he got a call on his disposable cell phone, from Mahmoud, one of his most trusted young men. He and his nine compatriots had been released by the police after only a brief interrogation. As instructed, they allowed themselves to be searched, but because they had nothing that could cause injury or damage, not even identification cards, they had no cause to be held. All were released, but with a warning that this kind of behavior could "create public animosity to your cause."

Javad was delighted at this news. The networks would certainly take this story and show a peaceful rally had been disrupted by Jewish extremists. Luckily, the police had been there to avoid any bloodshed.

Before cutting the connection, Mahmoud added that, as a precaution, all of them had their mouths swiped with cotton swabs. Javad's blood curdled at this news. "What reason did they give for this!?" he shouted into the phone.

"They said it was standard practice now to test non-residents for the presence of the 'Zika' virus. No problem."

"You gave them your false Jewish names and addresses?" Javad was trembling.

"Yes, but we haven't been bitten by any mosquitoes."

Javad hung up, but he was ashen-faced. What was going on, he wondered?

Chapter 38

Lara, for what seemed like the hundredth time, went over the events that had led her to her present captivity: a tiny cell in an unknown location.

She had gone through, again and again, her newly arrived-at roll of prospective marriage proposals. She had narrowed the list down from the hundred or so responses she had received from her replies to the advertisements on the Muslim websites. Now that she knew the perpetrators were Shia jihadis and not Sunni, she had refined her search. She then tapered it to about twenty who were clearly Shia imams, based on their names and the names of their mosques. By reading through the literature for each mosque, it was quite clear which was which. The prayer schedules were the main identifier, as they were quite different for the two sects. This made her choices much slimmer, as only about ten percent were Shia.

Each of the prospective "bridegrooms" insisted on a face-to-face meeting, under thoroughly regulated conditions. They all included pictures of themselves, in addition to the grainy photographs on the website. They also showed their families and their mosques. The pictures were obviously doctored, so they were of little consequence. However, the man she had finally chosen was based at a mosque that had a long history in the area, even though this particular imam, Ali Musa, was not listed. Lara had often made decisions based on her instincts, and this was one of those times. Then things had made a disturbing turn.

Lara remembered waiting nervously at the bus terminal, dressed in the traditional black abaya and hijab, complete with veil, as ordered by her "intended." On her feet were running shoes, hidden by the long robe. She was equipped with the tiny electronic device supplied by Mary Robley. The Los Angeles office, she'd been assured, was tracking her every move and ready to pounce were she to run into a "situation." There was a pressure-sensitive switch that allowed her to just squeeze it, and the agents would be there in a flash—they promised. Well, Hadley had permitted nothing less. He was not about to take more risk than he could possibly explain—if necessary. They could not take the chance of allowing her to carry a weapon; if that were found, she was finished, of course.

The device was small, simple and foolproof, she was told. Rather than having it in her clothing, which might have been searched, it fit in her hair close to her scalp. It was tiny: only one mm in diameter, and similar in appearance to her hair itself.

She fidgeted with the scanty belongings she had hidden in her robes as she checked the street in both directions. They consisted of the bare necessities, should she run into trouble: some money in bills, a nail file, and a packet of tissues. It was near twilight and a gentle breeze wafted cool, moist air in from the ocean. Traffic was starting to dwindle from the earlier rush-hour madness here in the Wilshire district. A few men passing by gave her the once-over, but she dismissed them quickly with her no-nonsense manner. There were, after all, quite a few Muslim women dressed as she was on the streets of Los Angeles these days.

Finally, some fifteen minutes after the agreed-upon time of 7 p.m., a large, black limousine glided soundlessly to a stop directly in front of her, in a distinctly-marked "red zone." The rear passenger-side door opened and a dark-complexioned man beckoned her to approach, as he slid away to give her room to join him. In the shadowy twilight it was impossible for her to compare his appearance to the grainy photograph sent along with his email proposal. She noticed, to her relief, that there was also a woman in the vehicle, wearing a traditional Muslim burka, similar to the one worn by Lara for the occasion. *It was now or never. Be there for me, you guys,* she prayed as she stepped into the limo.

It was a relatively short ride to their destination, near the downtown area. The other woman slid out of the limo and guided Lara gently over to a nondescript concrete building, which they entered from the small parking lot at the side. At this time of night, the area was relatively quiet, and she saw no other people, as she gave one nervous glance at the surroundings. Well, her FBI "escorts" would hardly make themselves noticeable. She just had to depend on them being there as promised.

The small entourage entered the building through a metal side door into a lushly-furnished room, replete with Persian rugs, curtains and ornaments. There were six people already there, three men and three women. The women were all dressed in robes similar to Lara's; however, unlike Lara, all their faces were uncovered. The men rose, smiling as she entered and even bowed slightly to welcome her. The last to rise, she recognized from his picture, was Imam Ali Musa. He was large for an Iranian, over six feet tall, and heavy-set. Lara's stomach did a light flip-flop as she thought the unthinkable. "Lisa," he said in English with a heavy accent as he gestured for her to be seated, "please, make yourself at home. I, as you must have guessed, am Imam Ali Musa." Lara nodded in return, not exactly sure where this was going.

"First," he said quickly, "let us make sure we recognize each other. You, of course know me from my photograph. Now, as is appropriate with the female members of my family present, you may lift your facial veil. Lara had read enough about Shia custom to accept this as proper, and so delicately lifted her veil. There was an immediate flash of reaction as the members of the group saw her fair complexion, blue eyes, and blond eyebrows. "Yes," Ali said, "you are every bit as beautiful as your picture. He smiled cordially and asked, "Tell me again about your conversion to Islam. Your email was so brief."

Lara was ready for this question, and was actually put at ease by it. It seemed a natural request. "Well, as I said, I was living in Minneapolis and met these very nice young Somali men who introduced me to it. I was curious about the religion after reading so much about it in the press..."

"The *American* press...?" the imam said questioningly.

"Yes, I know how biased our media are, and I question almost everything I read. I am always eager to hear the other side of things. And, well, there had been so many Muslim immigrants to Minneapolis, and they have added a nice diversity to the city..."

"So your curiosity got the better of your fear of the unknown and..."

"Exactly," she added eagerly. "I was taking some night classes at the local community college and these two young men asked, very nicely, I might add, if I might want to visit a service at their masjid. They explained how Shia Islam made up just a small minority of the Muslims in Somalia, but that it was gaining popularity...and, well, they seemed so earnest and welcoming, I figured I have nothing to lose, so what the heck." She blushed charmingly at this last exclamation, hoping she had not offended the imam.

"Just so," he quickly interjected, clearly taken by her modesty. "And so you joined this masjid..."

"No, not immediately. I mainly was interested in their history and culture. Then I took some classes in Arabic, so that I could understand the prayers." This last she said in rather good Arabic.

"And you say this conversion took place over a period of five years?" the imam interjected. "I'm sorry, what did you say the name of this masjid was?"

"Yes, it was a long process. And the masjid was called Al Gama'at. Maybe you know of it." There was no hesitancy in her reply; she had been ready for the question. She even had the names of the imams there, had he pursued this line of questioning.

"Well, there are so many Shia masjid here in the U.S. now..." clearly impressed with her answers and her presence. Lara was gaining confidence.

"And tell me," the large man continued, quickly changing the subject, "did you have a romantic relationship with any of ..."

"Oh, absolutely not! They made it clear that an American girl like me should marry only someone noteworthy in the faith." Blushing again, she added, "...and when I moved here to Los Angeles and saw your notice on the web, well, I was certainly interested in learning more..."

"Your story is most charming, Lisa...may I call you that?"

"Certainly, I would like that."

"There is only one more formality before we can proceed with our...relationship." He rose and motioned to two of the women, gesturing towards Lara. "We must make certain your application is entirely honest. My cousins, Ghazal and Ana, shall be permitted to look upon your face and hair completely; in private, of course."

Lara knew this meant she must prove her blondness. At least she had the privacy of submitting only to the scrutiny of two women, out of sight of the men. The men in the room, she had noticed, had been most eagerly listening to this dialogue, no doubt hoping for such luck for themselves. That, and more, she had no question.

The two women gently took her by the hand and shoulder, leading her through a rear door, where there was a flight of concrete stairs leading down, presumably to a basement. This came as a shock to Lara; *would the tiny transmitter in her hair be at all effective through several feet of concrete?* She had been counting on the security provided by the agents who, she was sure, were close by, waiting for any distress signal from her. She merely had to squeeze the device sharply. But now... Her mind raced as she followed the two women, as slowly as possible, down the impossibly long stairwell.

They finally arrived at the lower level which held several rooms. At the end of the hall, there appeared to be an emergency exit, probably required by law. The trio proceeded to another steel door, which entered into a storage area of some sort. There were foodstuffs, tools, empty wooden boxes, pieces of furniture; even, she was alarmed to see, a small cot. Another door, left ajar, opened into a crude bathroom, containing a toilet and sink. The two Persian women closed the door behind them and said, trying no doubt to allay her fears, "Do not be afraid, we merely want to see your hair. The blessed imam wants to make certain you have been totally truthful about its...'blondness'."

Lara was anything but appeased by this disclaimer, but allowed them to gently remove her head scarf. "Oh," both Ana and Ghazal exclaimed, as they saw her beautiful, straw-colored hair in the harsh glare of the room's single bulb. This better be the end of the physical exam, Lara thought grimly, as the two Persians looked at her from all angles, but did not touch her. "Yes, you are most definitely a natural blonde, as is in keeping with the Master's wishes!" This exclamation was made in Farsi, which Lara understood immediately. She relaxed just a bit with the hope they would now return upstairs with their positive verdict. She took back her veil, and, as calmly as possible, headed for the door.

Suddenly, the door burst open, and there stood the imam himself, looking even more menacing in the harsh light. One of the women must have signaled him somehow after the "exam." "Well," he said calmly, taking the veil from her, "you certainly do pass the test." The two Persian women quietly fled from the room, closing the door. "Now, I must make sure that you are everything as advertised...Miss Edmond! Did you think we were really so stupid as to not see through your crude charade!?" This last was thrown into her face in perfect English, and it set her trembling. Quickly she grasped for her hair-transmitter, but before she could reach it, the bulky imam moved with surprising quickness, grabbing her hand and examining her scalp.

"Well, what do we have here, one of your crude FBI devices?" He laughed as he pulled it from her hair and tossed it aside. "You are buried, you might say, in twelve feet of solid concrete. I don't think your saviors will hear your plea for help."

Lara was desperately thinking of her options, trying to recall any and all of her training for these types of situations. Her heart was pounding audibly, it seemed, as she gathered herself. It had happened so fast...

"I must say, you certainly are as blond as advertised. Let's see just how lovely you are..." With this, he threw her roughly onto the cot, fell on top of her and proceeded to tear at her clothing.

Lara heaved a deliberate sigh of defeat as the huge imam pinned her to the iron bed, relaxing all her muscles as her defiance seemed to drain from her. Sensing victory and the fruits of his battle, the imam kept her pinned with his legs, as he took his hands from hers and started to remove his tunic. Waiting until she sensed the relaxation in her captor, Lara tried to banish the odor of his stale breath as she readied for her final surge. Rising with her upper body, using first her right hand, she gouged the imam's left eye sharply with her index finger. The imam gasped as the eye burst, viscous fluid spurting forth. In less than a second, she dropped her right shoulder back to the bed and bounced back up, using her left hand in the same manner, impaling his right eye. This was a technique she had learned years ago in her training, a Krav Maga move that used multiple strikes rather than the single strike taught in most martial arts.

The effect on the startled imam was exactly as she had expected. He screamed in pain as he brought his hands to his ruined eyes. Simultaneous with this, Lara brought her right knee, which he had released in his pain, sharply up into his groin. He howled again in agony, completely unconcerned now with his former prisoner. Lara took this opportunity to slide out from underneath him, gather up all her strength, and strike him sharply in the back of the neck with her elbow, aiming as best she could, at his sixth cervical vertebra. There was a clear cracking sound as at least one vertebra broke, and her assailant lay limp on the bed, fluid seeping from his eyes.

Panting from her effort, but realizing she was only part way to freedom, Lara rang a red bell she had noticed on the wall, hoping to generate some activity and confusion. She grabbed a crowbar that lay in the corner and waited at the side of the door, trusting that only one assistant at a time would respond. In less than ten seconds, the door opened, a man entered, and she crushed his face with the crowbar before he could say a word. He dropped to the floor and lay writhing in pain, blood coursing from his mouth, emitting unintelligible grunts.

Lara grabbed her meager belongings: her robe and headscarf. She turned, saw the open bathroom door and took a few seconds to wipe the detritus off her hands with a towel. She headed out into the hallway, when she noticed that the guard, who lay unconscious on the floor, had dropped a key-ring with two keys on it. She picked it up and clenched it tightly in her fist; but before she could get out the door, another guard rushed into the room, saw the ugly spectacle on the floor and cot, hesitated in confusion and mumbled some sort of epithet. Lara didn't wait for him to gain his senses. This man, a slightly-built youngster, received the curved end of the crowbar under his chin. He dropped, like his associate, onto the floor, blood mixed with bits of broken teeth flowing from his ruined face.

Fleeing into the hallway, she saw the emergency exit at the end of the hall. By this time there was the sound of multiple feet rushing down the stairs toward her. She guessed a general alarm had been sounded by now. Rushing to the exit, she found, to her dismay, that the door was locked. She realized she was still clutching the set of keys; she only had time to try one of them before the noisy group of men would reach her. She got lucky; the door opened and she burst onto a flight of stairs leading up to the street level. Lara urgently slammed the door closed behind her, just as the gang of angry Shia men reached it. Even as she hurried up the metal stairs, she could hear the Farsi curses from the hallway. They were unable to open the door.

The stairs ended at the street level, but there was no exit. Instead, the concrete floor took her several feet to her right, through what appeared to be a passageway into the next building. An opening had been cut through the firewall between structures, and the floor became wooden, rather than concrete. A few feet along this wooden floor led her to an apparent door to the street. This exit had a panic bar on it; the occupants had clearly disguised this way out to lead only from the building directly adjacent to the one serving as the "mosque."

There was no place to use a key, so she prayed the door would respond to a blow to the bar. No other option, she realized as she smashed her arms, with all her weight, into the bar. The door swung open and she was greeted with the foggy stench of a typical downtown alley. Never had the rancid odor of alcohol, urine and rat feces smelled so good. Lara had no idea where she was, so she picked the direction toward the more well-lit street. By now, an urgent alarm siren blared from the open door behind her. She was glad she had worn the running shoes as she dashed to the end of the alley. So far, there was no one chasing her.

As she exited the alley and turned into the street, she quickly recognized it as a part of the downtown skid row. A "resident" of the street sat there leaning against the brick wall of a building, next to a large cardboard box, sipping from a bottle hidden in a paper bag. They looked at each other in wonder. He, in an alcohol-laden stupor, she in a strange mix of Muslim clothing, running shoes, covered in a blend of blood and other bodily fluids. It wasn't until then that she realized she must look like some sort of ghoul from the next world, as the alarm continued to blare insistently from the alley behind her.

It was at that point she noticed an overcoat lying next to the rather inert man. As he gazed at her in wonder, she reached into the pocket of her robe and pulled out a few bills. "Fifty dollars for your coat!" she yelled at him. He seemed unaware of the alarm or anything other than the strange creature in front of him.

"No deal," he responded, "it's my best coat."

"Fifty bucks!" she repeated, waving the bills in front of him. "Think how many jugs of Muscatel you could buy with that."

"Muscatel!" he spat out derisively, "I wouldn't drink that if you..." Before he could think of an appropriate rejoinder, Lara threw him the bills with one hand and swept up the overcoat with the other. "What the hell..." he muttered, even as he counted the money. It was, in fact, sixty dollars, he recognized, more than he had seen in some time.

Lara covered herself with the overly large coat; she had no identification, little cash, and no means of communication. Her one connection to the outside world was the little in-hair device that now lay somewhere in the basement room she had just escaped. She reached the corner, recognizing the cross street as one that had a Metro stop. She hesitated, seeing that the long block leading toward the Metro station was very dark. Los Angeles, she remembered, had lowered its street-lighting standards some time ago as a cost-cutting measure. There was quite a commotion among the populace, worried about increased crime.

As far as she could see, though, the sidewalk was deserted; there were no cars, no people...

Chapter 39

Mary Robley was incredulous. "What do you mean, you lost contact!?" she cried out to the agents in charge of the observation.

"Everything seemed to be going normally," Brad, one of the young men stammered, "she was stationary, didn't give any distress calls, there was some movement, like I told you, then stationary again, still no distress call, so we…"

"Decided to do nothing!" Mary was beside herself. Lara had been equipped with the most modern, powerful microtransmitter in the service, one that could penetrate steel, concrete, miles of traffic…and they had lost her. "No one left the building?" she asked, unbelieving.

"No, we had the doors covered, there was no activity for about an hour, and still no change in signal strength or movement, just as we said. And no distress call, so we had been instructed not to interfere with the operation…"

"And then?" Mary asked, still stunned.

"There was still no emergency call, but she left the building by an alley way, and was driven west, towards the I-110 north on-ramp. We have two agents following. The sedan has out-of-state plates, Nevada, we're checking with them now. But meanwhile we have a tail on the car. It does not seem to be evading pursuit. Should we apprehend?"

"Didn't you have the alley door covered!?" Mary implored.

"There wasn't an alley door leading from the mosque building," Brad answered weakly. "We had a man on the roof earlier. The back wall of the building was solid concrete…"

"Then how the hell…!" Mary thought for a moment, considering her options. If Lara were in the car, but had not given a distress call, she might have matters under control. But if she weren't… "Make visual contact, see if she is in that car!"

"We've already tried that, no luck."

"What do you mean?"

"The windows are totally shaded. There are four adults in the car, but we can't tell if one of them is our agent. The transmitter is still broadcasting."

"Crap!" yelled Mary, in total frustration. "Alright, then in ten minutes, apprehend the vehicle, get all the occupants out, search the trunk if necessary. Give them some excuse, like 'missing child', if they resist. Be prepared to take them into custody. And let's hope Lara is alright."

Mary paced nervously, waiting to hear back. Her other senior agents were out checking leads at the scene of the Purim attacks, but were ready to act as soon as she gave the word. They had depended on the team stationed downtown, perhaps unadvisedly… Just then she got the call from Brad, in the chase vehicle. "We have the suspect vehicle. Two adult Caucasian couples, headed to Van Nuys. Trunk is clean, except for some beach gear. License plate checks with driver's DL. Wait a minute, Chuck here just found the transmitter taped to the outside rear panel…"

"*Oh my God,*" whispered Mary, as she dropped into a chair. "Get that building locked down and searched now!"

Chapter 40

On his daily trip to his car and satellite phone, Uri found a message waiting for him from Yehudi Gold in Los Angeles. He quickly returned the call.

"Are you sitting down, Uri?" he asked. Uri, already seated in his car, waited, expecting the worst. Hearing no reply, Gold continued: "First off, Lara is missing. The FBI and LAPD are searching for her." Uri let out a sigh of desperation; this is what he had feared.

"What happened to her, do you know?" he demanded. She had been talking of seeing an imam downtown sometime soon as part of her idea of marriage proposals...

"Yes," Gold muttered after a pregnant pause, "Mary Robley asked if I had heard from Lara. She hadn't checked in after some sort of 'engagement' last night, in the downtown area." He paused before saying anything else, waiting for the inevitable.

"Shit!" Uri shouted, quite uncharacteristically. "What the hell!!? They were supposed to have her covered..."

"Yes, she told me. Apparently something got fouled up. A blind exit to the building, something like that."

"My God," he cried, "*they lost her*!?"

"Only temporarily, Mary assured me."

"Oh, that's great," Uri mumbled. "Anything else?"

"Yes. A Muslim man was treated at one of those small, downtown "Urgent Care" facilities last night," Yehudi continued. "He gave his name as Ali something, but had no

ID on him. They have to treat everyone, of course, and his condition looked emergent, that is, in need of immediate help." Uri nodded; he knew what that meant. "He had received blunt trauma to both eyes, and they were both ruptured. That was the worst of it, but two of his cervical vertebrae were cracked. There was no nerve damage, so they put him in a collar and told him to see a specialist as soon as possible. Oh yes, and his testicles were both severely bruised. He claimed it was an attack by a street gang, but he didn't want to report it to the police. He said it happened downtown."

"What about the eyes?" Uri asked, trying to piece things together.

"Fortunately for him, the eyes are apparently pretty tough organs; they can take blunt trauma, as long as the nerves don't detach. He was lucky; they'll recover in time, but maybe not to full use. He can already make out light and dark. He was taken away by the two men, apparently Persian, who brought him in. They promised to get him to an ophthalmologist as well as a neurosurgeon. The medical facility said they couldn't keep him against his will. Oh, yes, one of the people in the waiting room reported he heard one of the men call the victim 'imam'. Luckily, these incidents have to be reported immediately to the police, so we got all the details. Mary asked me to get in touch with her as soon as you..."

"As soon as I what!" Uri retorted angrily. "I'm stuck down here in Orange County posing as a Shia assassin. "I bet that 'street gang' who got that 'imam' was none other than one pretty mad FBI agent. And the FBI lost her! She was supposed to be under complete surveillance and protection!"

"Call in to the FBI right away," the consul instructed, as comforting as possible.

Uri immediately called Mary at FBI headquarters. "What in the world!?" he shouted.

"You've spoken with Yehudi, I suppose," she replied as tactfully as possible under the circumstances. "Believe me, we have all our resources out looking for her."

"Yes, I would hope so! What about that tracking device?"

"Somehow they must have found it before she could sound the alarm...but believe me we have a rescue plan in motion....How is it going on your end?"

"A hell of a lot better than on yours!" He said angrily, breaking the connection. *I hope the damn transmitter pin works better for me....*

Chapter 41

Yousef, one of the injured imam's most faithful lieutenants, held him in his arms as he listened to his curses and calls to action. The women had been dismissed, and the men had carried the imam to their limousine for transfer to their own Islamic medical facility just a few miles away. The surgeon had been called. "That FBI Jew slut!" the imam muttered. "We must get word to Imam Javad!"

"Your eyes, master, your eyes..." the acolyte pleaded.

"They are of no matter now, we must get word out to our brethren!"

"Master," Yousef asked, after a moment's thought, "you said the woman had some sort of signal device in her hair?"

"Yes, so...?" the critically injured imam asked, touching his ruined eyes. He barely had any feeling in his hands and no movement at all in his legs. He trembled with rage as he thought of the female FBI agent, and how she had tricked him, left him so utterly disabled and humiliated. He must get revenge...

"Master, if we can find that little transmitter we can set the FBI on a fruitless chase, while we complete our evacuation of this building. Surely they must have known she was here..."

The imam thought for a few seconds, realizing the desperate position they were in. They had rented this unused warehouse building specifically for terror operations, under assumed names, of course, and now must leave it immediately. Imam Ali would be able to help, but first, Yousef was undoubtedly correct. They must throw the authorities off the track....Even through the pain and sightlessness, the imam remembered the little yellow pin in the slut's hair. He had discovered it and... "In the basement room, where we were...I picked the pin from her hair and threw it..."

Yousef phoned Farshid, who along with two others, was still at the makeshift mosque, urging them to search the area for the transmitter. Meanwhile, the whole building was being vacated. All other personnel left by the rear alley door and were headed to a safe location downtown.

"We found it!" came the call to Yousef a few minutes later over his disposable cell phone.

"Take it and attach it to some moving car," came the immediate demand.

Farshid understood at once what was to be done, and ran out into the alley with adhesive tape on the transmitter-pin. Racing to the street corner, he slapped it onto a moving sedan, yelling "out of my way," then returned to the alley. "It's taken care of, Yousef," he said proudly. "The pin is on its way north, out of the city!"

"Alright, good work. Now all of you get out of there. Head to location A-4, understand?"

"Yes, Yousef, how is the master?"

"Not good; he cannot move his legs, but somehow, Allah be praised, he seems to have some vision in his eyes, even though the fluid..."

"The doctor is a good one, he will bring the blessed imam back to us..."

"Praise Allah."

"Wait," Yousef commanded suddenly. "The Jew whore could not have gotten far. She escaped out the door to the alley. Take Hamid with you in the black sedan and see if you can find her!"

Farshid saw Hamid carrying some documents to the incinerator. The large Syrian had already changed into street clothes for his escape from what was now certain discovery of their location. "Drop those papers and put on your overcoat. We must find the woman," Farshid commanded. He headed out the door to the street, where the sedan was parked, Hamid rushing to catch up. The two, now both in black overcoats, jumped into the car and headed through the back alley. As they reached the cross-street, they saw the vagrant shouting in agitation at someone in running shoes, wearing a filthy tan overcoat, many sizes too large. The person, even in the dim light was clearly a woman, stumbling to run in the oversized coat. Even as the two men watched, she appeared to hesitate as she reached the next cross-street to the south, leading to a major thoroughfare. Just as she headed in that direction, the black sedan purposefully followed.

Lara made her way as quickly as she could along the long, dark street, hampered by the large coat. She was about halfway to her goal of the busy street ahead, as a sleek black sedan glided to a halt next to her. She hadn't even heard it approaching. Its headlights blinked at her, the occupants waving to her from the dark interior. *Could it be*, she asked herself anxiously, *a government vehicle?* The interior was too dark for her to see more than two men in dark overcoats. The window on the curb side opened and the occupant clearly said her name: "Miss Edmond...it's alright, we've come to rescue you!" Farshid, a long-time U.S. resident with some time in community college, had perfected his American accent for just such occasions.

Lara, considering her alternatives, realized if these were not friends, she couldn't outrun them under these conditions. *They must have gotten a signal from the pin-transmitter, after all,* she hoped! The two men exited the sedan slowly and approached her in a friendly manner, it seemed. It was still too dark to see them clearly…and then it was too late. Lara, totally fatigued from her grueling evening, did not even sense the rag going over her nose and mouth, as she fell into total blackness…

Chapter 42

Lara awakened to find herself in what appeared to be a prison cell. She was lying on a thin mattress attached to a steel cot along a wall. The robe she had been wearing had been replaced with a prison-type blue jumpsuit, but she was still wearing her running shoes. Her head was throbbing, her throat dry. She looked around her surroundings, seeing bars on two sides, concrete walls on the other two. A typical jail-cell door was set into the bars of one wall. A crude toilet and sink were attached to another wall, with only a flimsy curtain providing a modicum of privacy. A dirty towel hung by the sink, she noticed with a jolt of disgust.

Rising from the bed, she found she could walk, but with some pain in her right leg. She managed to get to the sink, and making a cup with her hands, drank as much water from the tap as she could. She realized she needed to use the toilet, doing so after draping the curtain around herself as well as she could. Slightly nauseated, she made her way back to the cot and lay down. She replayed as much as she could remember from the scene in the mosque. She remembered the fight in the basement and the flight into the street. Also the sedan pulling up next to her and the men… and that was it. *How long ago was that?* She had no way of knowing. Right now she just wanted to rest, maybe to sleep…

An unknown time later she was awakened by a woman in Muslim clothing, including complete head and face covering. Only her eyes were visible, two small black lasers piercing into Lara's brain. Lara was terrified; she had no immediate recollection of where she was or what had transpired. As she came to her senses, she realized the woman was holding a tray of food, gesturing for her to take it. Lara took the tray from the woman, realizing this may be the only food she was going to get. She felt a sudden pang of hunger as she smelled the meal, an assortment of lamb, rice and flat bread. There was also a plastic cup filled with cool water, which she eagerly drank, even before touching the food.

She ate quickly, perhaps too quickly, feeling somewhat nauseated afterwards. It was only then, in her discomfort, did she fully recollect the events that had led her to her present dilemma. She immediately became depressed. *What was going to happen to me here?* She thought ruefully. They, whoever "they" were, knew who she was, no doubt about that. And would the FBI or LAPD have any idea where she was? Or Uri, she thought, out in Orange County, posing as a terrorist. Suddenly crying, something she had not done in years, she put the tray of half-eaten food on the floor, curled up on the cot and went back to sleep. Never had she felt more helpless and alone.

Lara was awakened from a fitful sleep a few hours later by, apparently, the same veiled woman. "Do you need to use the facilities?" the woman asked, in English, gesturing at the tiny toilet. Lara shook her head. "Come upstairs with me," she added, again in highly-accented English. "We have better...there. Also he would like to talk to you."

Lara had no idea who "he" was, but she was pleased to hear there was a real washroom, apparently upstairs. She followed the woman, noticing the food tray had disappeared from the floor. A large, imposing man accompanied them. The cell door was left open, she noticed, as she followed the wraith-like woman and her escort up the concrete steps to the next level. Here the floor was carpeted and the walls covered with pictures of mosques, apparently from the Middle East or possibly Iran or Pakistan. There were also bookshelves against the wall, containing titles in Arabic and Farsi. She didn't have the chance to look closely.

"Here," her attendant said suddenly, pointing at a blank wooden door. "Knock when you are finished." She then opened the door for Lara, and closing it behind her, latched it from the outside.

Lara gratefully made use of the relatively modern bathroom, taking time to wash her face and hands. Looking in the mirror, she was shocked to see a haggard stranger peering back. "*Oh, my God,*" she thought to herself. And this was only one day, or at least she thought so. After the initial fright wore off, she took the opportunity to examine the room for anything she might use. There were no windows or other doors. There was just a single bar of soap, a clean white towel, and tissue paper. There was no stall, only the bare toilet. Nothing useful presented itself.

Lara knocked on the door as instructed, and the same woman unlocked the door, letting her out into the hallway, the male guard standing silently by. "You will now talk to him," the woman said, leading her to another door, this one also of wood, but much more elegant, with multiple panels of rich, dark walnut. Lara's attendant knocked lightly, and a deep male voice ordered, "Enter!" in Iranian-accented Farsi. The woman opened the door for Lara but did not enter herself. Lara got the hint and walked into a gloriously-furnished office. A large Persian carpet graced the floor, with Persian prints filling the walls. At the far end of the room sat a dark-complexioned man at a large wooden desk. He was heavily bearded and wore a white turban and robe.

"Welcome, Miss Edmond," he stated, this time in English, but with a heavy accent. "Let me introduce myself. I am Imam Zainal Abidin." He rose gracefully to his full, imposing height and stared at her with intensely black, intimidating eyes, set well back in his face. His massive, heavily-bearded jaw added to his fearsome presence. He was indeed like something from her worst nightmare.

"I hope you are reasonably comfortable. You have eaten and, ah, made use of our…facilities?" he added, standing and smiling. He motioned for her to sit in a padded chair that faced his desk. She sat, not saying anything, and waited for her captor to go on.

Not getting a reply to his opening remarks, he sat, cleared his throat gruffly and continued, albeit in a less friendly tone. "You see we know who you are. You will be treated fairly while you are here, much more fairly than those who are imprisoned by your government and their allies." He paused again.

"When can I get out of here?" she asked bluntly.

"Ah, you do not like your accommodations, I see," he said, chuckling lightly. Lara did not respond. She had gone through similar situations, but only in training, and knew what she must do, and also what not to do, or say. After another brief pause the bearded man said, "I am the Imam here, and what I say goes, as you Americans put it." Another pause, then, "We want from you only some information. If you answer truthfully, and only when we have 'checked it out' as you say, you will be released. You will not know where you are, nor where you have been. Oh, and by the way, you may be interested to know that the little device you had in your hair was of no use to your employers." He sat back in his chair, pleased with himself.

Lara said nothing, not wanting to give anything away, knowing he would continue with his demands. She knew now that her transmitter device had proven useless.

Another moment passed, then the imam stated, more forcefully this time, "You will tell us who, exactly, you are working for, and what they know of us."

"I have no idea who you are," she said almost truthfully. "I only know that I am being held against my will, and I will be found eventually. I feel sure I am still in the United States, at least."

"You are lying, Miss Edmond; don't insult my intelligence. We know you were sent to answer an advertisement as a 'wife' for a Shia imam, by the FBI. We know, as you do now, that you failed in your endeavor, and are now at our mercy. Tell us exactly whom you work for, what they know of us, and what they suspect, and we may release you."

Lara noticed that the imam's English improved as the session wore on. But before she could even answer, the now angry man added, "Oh, and one more thing. We want to know where your Israeli partner and lover, one Uri Levin, is hiding!"

This set Lara back a bit. *So they knew of Uri, too.* That was not good. What was good was that she now knew that they had no idea where he was, nor what he was up to. This last gave her a glimmer of hope.

"Do not gain any comfort from that information, Miss Edmond," the imam added. He must have detected something in her attitude. She would have to be more careful.

"First, let me tell you I have no idea where Uri is." Realizing they already knew he was in the U.S. and on the case, she might as well appear candid. "I don't even know if he is in the Los Angeles area."

"You are lying; you certainly know where your compatriot is! You think we are stupid?" the imam shouted angrily. "Let me also inform you that your contact in Los Angeles, the Persian Jew dentist, Emelkies, has been found murdered."

Lara was jolted by this news; but, of course, knew of no reason to believe him. She merely avoided the news, going back to the previous discussion, of Uri. "It's true Uri was in Los Angeles. But we have been out of touch for some time. I have no idea where he is nor what he is doing," she said matter-of-factly.

The imam looked at her with irritation, which slowly changed to resignation. "All right, we'll see what a few weeks in your cell will do for your memory," he said smiling. Imprisonment, he had found, works wonders on the pliability of captives, especially women. He hit a buzzer on his desk, and the attending woman accompanied by her escort appeared almost at once. "Take her back," Abidin said simply. The woman approached Lara, who stood up, resigned to her fate.

Chapter 43

Lara was still in her cell two days later with no change to her situation. She had been allowed, once a day, to come upstairs and use the washroom on the main floor of the building, which she assumed was some sort of mosque. The same woman escorted her each time, accompanied by her dangerous-looking companion. Although she had no way of calculating the time, her meals seemed to be served three times between visits upstairs. Also, the single light bulb dimmed for a few hours after what seemed to be the evening meal. It brightened again just as the dawn call to prayer sounded. Further, she was aware of what seemed a call to prayer, in Arabic, two other times each "day."

Lara was growing increasingly apprehensive about the chances for her rescue. If the homing device had not performed correctly, she had no optimistic view of how she could be found. The imam had not called for another "audience" with her; she assumed he was waiting for her to volunteer information in exchange for release. No chance of that, she told herself. They must be out there, somewhere, searching for me, she assured herself.

It was three actual days after her capture that a stranger showed up at evening prayers at the Orange County mosque where Lara was being held by Imam Zainal Abidin. He was clearly Iranian, and identified himself as one Ahmad Mohammad, a common enough name. But this Ahmad Mohammad, dressed in standard American clothing: blue jeans and running shoes, asked particularly for the imam. He said he had "some important news for 'His Reverence'."

He was brought to the imam's study, where he introduced himself. "Ahmad Mohammad," he stated simply, seating himself on a large cushion in front of the imam. "I have heard many good things about you, Master Imam Zainal Abidin," he said smiling.

"Yet I know nothing of you," the puzzled imam cautiously replied.

"But I am certain you know of my father, The Grand Ayatollah Seyyed Mohammad Hussein Fadlallah, hero of the Hezbollah, blessed be his memory." Ahmad showed the imam a large gold ring, on the face of which was a seal with the likeness of the Ayatollah Khomeini, father of the Iranian revolution. On the back-side of the ring were the words, engraved in Farsi: "To my loving wife Najat and my son Ahmad. May the revolution continue." It was signed: "Seyyed." The imam was suitably impressed; the young man did indeed have the likeness of the Grand Ayatollah, and spoke in the manner of the South Lebanese Shia elite.

Along with the ring, Ahmad produced a faded newspaper clipping from the Beirut daily "An-Nahar," dated March 23, 2009. There was a photograph showing the Ayatollah Fadlallah with his arm around his son, Ahmad Mohammad. There was no doubt his visitor was indeed the son of the late Grand Ayatollah. Abidin was awed beyond words.

Ahmad, seeing the impact the objects had on the imam, pressed forward. "I have something else to show you, blessed one, something you will be pleased to see." At this point he reached into his backpack. The imam's assistants, who were standing beside him, quickly reached down and grabbed the stranger's arms.

"It is alright, Turan," the imam said, gesturing at the large, bearded Indonesian man who had hold of Ahmad's right arm. "But just bring out whatever you have for us, slowly, so as not to distress my associates." Ahmad looked back at Turan and the other man, who was smaller, but dark and fierce, with glowing black eyes. "Turan and Hamid are very protective of me, and are easily provoked. We do not often have esteemed visitors such as yourself."

Ahmad slowly produced from his backpack a single man's running shoe, handing it to the imam, who refused to touch it. Instead, he gestured for Hamid to take it from Ahmad. The little Yemeni took it gingerly and looked it over; it seemed harmless and ordinary in every way. He showed it to the imam with a puzzled look on his face.

"And what am I to make of this, ah, piece of footwear, my friend?" The imam was puzzled.

"If you will look at it carefully, Master," Ahmad replied, smiling graciously, "you will see it bears the brand and size of the missing Dr. Emelkies, as noted in the newspapers."

The imam, his curiosity ignited, spoke quickly to the Indonesian, "Turan, the file," he said, gesturing toward a file cabinet at the rear of the room. "And if it is as you say," he said sharply to Ahmad, "what is it supposed to tell us?"

"The deed is done, Master, we have eliminated the Israeli spy who has created much trouble for us in Los Angeles, giving aid to the Mossad for many years."

For the second time, Abidin was shaken speechless. He presumed the dentist-spy had been killed, based on the newspaper reports and information he had received from sources in Iran, but this…

"And just who is this 'we' you speak of?" the imam inquired forcefully.

"His daughter, Sarah, and I. With the help of one of my associates, we killed him and dumped the body into the rain canal. Sarah will be here soon, to corroborate my story."

"Even if I were to believe this outrageous tale, why would the daughter participate? Was she not a Jew, like her father?"

"She was, but she saw the light and converted to the true faith three years ago, unbeknownst to her spy of a father. She has been aiding our cause, anonymously, ever since."

At this point, Turan reappeared with a file of newspaper clippings. Ahmad caught a glimpse of the headlines and crime-scene photos. He noticed that the imam was especially interested in a picture of the dentist's daughter, who, the headline stated, had become named as a suspect. "And this is the woman you say will appear here?" he inquired of the stranger. Ahmad nodded, apparently convinced of her imminent arrival.

The imam continued scanning the material, looking for anything to do with the clothing found with the body discovered in the drainage canal. There was a sharp intake of breath as he examined one particular paragraph, and he reached for the shoe. "Yes, the article says that only one shoe was found. And how did you get this one?"

"It fortunately slipped off his foot as we dragged him from the car. Afterwards, we were about to discard it, when we felt it might come in handy at some point. And here it is."

At that moment, Hamid entered the room, breathless. "Excuse me, Holy One, but there is a young woman at the door—she says she is Sarah Emelkies!"

"Bring her in at once!" the imam commanded.

Hamid left briefly, then returned with a young woman, dressed in similar fashion to Ahmad, jeans and running shoes, with a small rucksack. The imam gestured for her to give him her pack, searched through it quickly; then, finding nothing of interest, handed it back to her. He noticed her appearance; it agreed, at least superficially, with the missing dentist's daughter. She was attractive, Persian in nature, with jet black hair and dazzling blue eyes.

"And who might you be?" he asked gently.

"I am Sarah Emelkies, Holy One," she replied at once in unaccented Farsi, bowing slightly.

Abidin was briefly taken aback by the ease with which she spoke the language; seemingly as a native Iranian. "You know this man, who calls himself Ahmad?" he finally posited.

Sarah glanced at her young companion. "Yes, of course. We have conspired to rid the world of my accursed father, servant of the Jews."

There was a long pause as Abidin considered the treasures that had just fallen into his lap. Sheikh Nasrallah had often spoken highly of the blessed Ayatollah Fadlallah. Now the Ayatollah's son, Ahmad, had appeared with evidence of the death of an Israeli spy and the complicity of his daughter! To the imam, this evidence was overwhelming. "What you have shown me and told me is of the highest importance. How can I repay you?" he said gently.

"Sarah is now a suspect in her father's death," Ahmad replied. "We could definitely use a place to stay, at least until the intensity of the search abates."

Abidin was delighted to be able to compensate these young conspirators in any way he could. Hezbollah would be eager to hear this news, and grateful to both Abidin and the dentist's assassins.

The imam rose slowly and declared, "Of course, you may stay here as long as you wish! You have done our cause a great service!" Then, on the spur of the moment he had an idea. He would impress these youthful warriors with the status of their benefactor. "Come with me, please. I would like you to see someone," he said, swollen with pride. He motioned for his servants to accompany him and his new guests. The strange party proceeded through curtains at the back of the imam's office, into a hallway and down two flights of concrete stairs, arriving at a jail-like set of rooms, only one of which was occupied. In it sat a disheveled young woman, with blond hair. She looked up, puzzled and in obvious distress. "Is this woman known to you?" Abidin asked arrogantly.

Sarah knew at once this was the missing FBI agent, Lara Edmond, but feigned ignorance. "I don't think so, Reverence, but let me get a good look at her." She moved around the side of the cell, examining the prisoner.

Suddenly, Ahmad began sneezing and loudly blowing his nose into a handkerchief. "Oh, excuse me," he said, drawing all attention to himself, and away from Sarah. "It must be this dry climate." Ahmad had cleverly moved into position to obscure the imam's view. Simultaneously, Sarah retrieved a note from her pocket, rolled into a very small ball. As she passed out of the imam's view she tossed the tiny missile at Lara's feet. Lara quickly stepped on it.

"No, I've never seen her before," Sarah declared innocently after a few moments' hesitation. "Who is she?"

The imam glanced back at the clearly distraught FBI agent, who sat on her cot with her head in her hands. "This is none other than the FBI 'agent' who attacked one of our clergymen! She has been a nuisance to us for some time now." After a moment of triumph, the imam, pleased by his performance, led the party back upstairs.

As soon as the group had gone up the stairs, Lara reached down and opened the note. It read, in English:

Then Mordechai commanded to answer Esther: Think not with thyself that thou shalt escape in the king's house, more than all the Jews.

This quote from the Book of Esther could only mean one thing: they had come to rescue her. It would mean nothing to the guards or even the imam, if found, she figured. Anyway, she wasn't about to find out. She swallowed it. It was better than the food, she told herself. She sat back on her cot, her spirits soaring. She had no idea what was coming, but the FBI had certainly sent this pair to find and release her; it was now only a matter of time.

* * *

Sarah and Ahmad returned with the imam to his elegant study.

"Well," Zainal Abidin said, rubbing his hands together, as he gazed gratefully at his two guests. "You two have certainly been of enormous help in our cause. How else can I be of service while we wait for further instructions?" He was extremely pleased with the status of the situation. The "dentist" Mossad spy had been eliminated, and the FBI whore had been captured. Javad would be pleased. Now, what to do with them? He surely would hear from Javad soon; the man had not been in touch since the raid at the Beverly Hills Park on May 15, "Nakba Day." That had gained international attention. Not all good, to be sure, but their Shia allies were certainly pleased.

Ahmad and Sarah glanced at each other. *How to proceed?* was in both their minds.

Seeing their indecision, the imam offered, "Since I assume you have no place to stay, as I said, you may stay here until I hear from our…higher ups. I presume you are not married…to each other, that is."

With only a second's pause Ahmad said, "That would be must gracious of you, certainly!" Sarah nodded her approval.

The imam pressed his buzzer and Turan, the big Indonesian man appeared. "Show our two friends here to the guest rooms on the second floor," he commanded.

Sarah and Ahmad thanked the imam in fluent Farsi, bowed, and followed Turan out of the study, into the hallway. He led them up a carpeted stairway to a hallway on which there appeared to be four rooms. "May we get our bags?" the two guests asked, almost simultaneously.

"Wait here and I will see." The big man hustled back down the stairs to get instructions from the imam. Sarah and Ahmad took the opportunity to check out their accommodations. The rooms were modest, a small bed in each, a table, and private bathroom. They returned to the hallway, Sarah putting her finger to her lips as Turan approached. "The master agreed. You may go to your vehicle and retrieve your things. I will go with you."

The two agents followed the man back downstairs and out to their car. There Turan watched carefully as they each removed a travel case and returned to the building. He examined both, finding nothing but clothing and toiletries. Seemingly satisfied with their conduct, he escorted them back to their rooms. "Breakfast will follow the morning prayers," he informed them curtly. "Also, the master says you may enjoy to walk through our gardens during the day." As always, he said this in broken English, apparently to show his skill, as he had already heard the two strangers speak in Farsi.

After a restless sleep, the two arose at the call to morning prayer, joining the imam, the two male attendants and one woman, who didn't speak to them. The large, sparsely furnished prayer room was curtained from floor to ceiling, no doubt to act as a sound absorber. Following the short service, Sarah and Ahmad proceeded to a modest dining area, where they were joined by the imam, but not the others. The woman, covered fully save for her eyes, served them a meager meal of unknown cereal grain and yoghurt. There was only water to drink. As they finished, the imam said, "I hope Turan told you about our garden. I do not want you to feel like prisoners, like our friend down there," he said, gesturing toward the stairs leading to the cells in the basement. "You will find it sculpted in keeping with our homeland."

This would be their chance to make a plan, they both thought to themselves. "Yes, thank you, that is most kind, we would like that." Ahmad replied happily. The two agents returned to their separate rooms without saying a word and changed into clothes suitable for walking outside. They noticed Turan watching as they left through a side glass door into the garden, which lay within the walls of the mosque. Apparently satisfied they were not about to try to flee, he disappeared from view, and, more importantly, from earshot.

As the pair courteously examined the Persian flowers and tinkling waterfall, they were able to finally exchange some conversation. The noise of the bubbling water would cover their talk, Sarah hoped. They leaned close, and she offered, "At night, I think there is only one guard sitting in that chair by the stairs. The other, I believe, is stationed outside. Tonight we should try it!"

Ahmad nodded, apparently intrigued by the flowers next to the cascade. "Let's wait until midnight, then you can approach the inside guard, asking for some stomach remedy. I will take him out, and we can go from there. I assume he has the key to her cell," referring of course, to Lara.

They nodded in return, as though, agreeing on the beauty of the garden, and after a leisurely stroll around the small enclosure, returned to the mosque building. There, just inside the glass door, stood a dour Turan, looking for anything that ought to be reported to the master.

After the noon prayer, heralded by the Arabic intonation, apparently from a recording, there was a simple lunch. This was attended only by the pair of agents and the other male guard, Hamid, a little Yemeni man who spoke little to no English. The pair, however, did not dare speak, other than to comment on the beauty of the grounds and the generous, delicious food. They spoke in Farsi, but elicited no comment from their Yemeni companion.

It was Ahmad who decided to ask Hamid if they might peruse the library; he was sure there was one. Hamid, after a pause to consider the appropriateness of their request, showed them along the hallway to a large, windowless room opposite the imam's study. "Here, you may go," he said, "I will tell Master."

"Thank you," Ahmad replied in perfect Farsi. The two took the opportunity to look over the selection, mostly religious books, written in both Arabic and Farsi. There was even one section, they found, of religious literature, Muslim of course, written in English. Ahmad and Sarah muttered only briefly as they took various volumes to the comfortable, cushioned armchairs to read in the fluorescent-lit room. There were no other visitors.

* * *

It was while the two agents were in the library that Imam Zainal sent Hamid down to fetch Lara once again to his study. She was brought in, haggard, hungry and apparently downcast. The imam ordered her to sit, then abruptly stated, "You may be interested to know that the two strangers whom you just saw, are in fact, the murderers of your friend the Persian dentist. They even brought me evidence of his remains." He then showed her the shoe and the newspaper account.

Lara was visibly stunned by this news. The picture of the dentist's daughter certainly looked like the visitor she had just seen. All the evidence certainly seemed to implicate her in the dentist's death. Yet, the note dropped at her feet.... The imam was pleased at the effect this news had on his captive. "Perhaps now you will decide to help us. As you can see, you have little choice!" He abruptly sent her back downstairs to her prison cell.

* * *

A large grandfather clock toned out the excruciatingly long minutes until dinner. The pair had no inkling of the fact that Lara had been within a few feet of them. At one point Sarah asked Hamid, who was stationed just outside, if she could use the restroom. Hamid, after the briefest of pauses agreed, pointing to a bare wooden door near the staircase, guarded by the Muslim-clad woman. The woman wordlessly let her into the room, locking the door behind her. Sarah took a few minutes, during which time she looked around for anything that might be useful to them in their escape. She knocked lightly on the door. She had found nothing. The woman attendant wordlessly showed her back to the library.

The imam appeared after another hour or so to inquire as to how they liked the library and garden. Sarah and Ahmad eagerly voiced their approval. "You may wish to have a rest and change for evening prayers and dinner," he said in the true manner of a host.

"Yes, indeed," Ahmad said, as he and Sarah headed upstairs to their rooms, every movement observed by the large Indonesian. Turan had apparently replaced Hamid at guard duty. They each entered their rooms without a word, sharing only a glance. The hour of action was fast approaching, yet felt an eternity away.

* * *

Meanwhile, downstairs in her cell, Lara fidgeted constantly. *They must be here to release me*, she told herself for the hundredth time. The news the imam had just given her, concerning the apparent death of the dentist, had dampened her enthusiasm, to be sure. But she clung to the hope of her rescue.

She had asked to use the upstairs restroom once in the afternoon, but the woman attendant, for the first time, raised a finger, cautioning her to wait until, apparently, she received permission from someone. After only a few minutes, she returned with the bodyguard and led Lara upstairs into the bathroom. Lara looked around and noticed something was different: the towel, instead of being on the rung where it had been, was now laid on the edge of the sink. Her hopes rose again: *was this a signal?*

Lara ate the simple dinner given to her by the silent woman with even less appetite than usual. Her adrenaline was flowing with expectation. The woman picked up her tray, noted the remaining food and gave her a look of disdain. *How dare she leave this generous offering of food on her plate?* was the impression seen by Lara. She sat anxiously on her cot, waiting for any sounds that might indicate imminent rescue. After several hours, the light dimmed, signifying night-time.

* * *

Upstairs, Sarah and Ahmad went through the motions of evening prayers and dinner with the imam and his guards. Little was spoken; the pair of liberators was eager to get on with the rescue; the imam was anxiously awaiting word from Javad. Hamid and Turan rose from their places at the table just after the imam. When the imam went silently to his rooms, Turan, the large man, took his place at the foot of the stairs. Sarah and Ahmad said nothing to him, merely nodding to him as they headed to their accommodations. They each had a wristwatch in their suitcase, which somehow had been left there by the persons who had no doubt searched their possessions. They had no weapons with them; they realized guns would have immediately been confiscated and compromised their status as fugitives. They had, however, secreted handguns in the undercarriage of their car. Had they been asked, they would have said they felt individual protection was necessary in the Los Angeles area.

At the agreed upon hour, Sarah left her room, went downstairs and asked Turan if she might get a cup of yoghurt; she was feeling a little nauseated and yoghurt was helpful to her. The big man rose, grunting, and led her to the small kitchen down the hall from the stairwell. As he opened the refrigerator, he was unaware of the barefoot presence of Ahmad behind him. Sarah kept him distracted, bent over searching for an open container. "There," she said loudly, pointing at a large white carton. At that instant, the base of a desk lamp crashed down upon his head, sending him wordlessly to the floor. Being already bent over, he had not far to fall. "Thank you so much, Turan" she said loudly, just in case anyone might be within earshot. The pair was sure that Hamid had drawn outside guard duty, but they had no idea of the location of the silent, dark-clad woman. She was not at her chair by the first-floor washroom.

Sarah and Ahmad smiled conspiratorially at each other as they set about tying the Indonesian to the sink with silk cord they had found in the prayer room. They taped his mouth shut with packing tape found in the kitchen. Sarah used a tiny syringe hidden in the lining of her travel case to inject him with a mixture of Xanax and Ambien, dissolved in alcohol, enough to keep him asleep but hopefully not kill him. They had agreed with the FBI and LAPD to carry out this mission with a minimum of fatalities. The press would exaggerate any violence that resulted, even for the release of a kidnap victim.

Next, they had to take care of Hamid, whom they assumed was outside the front door or in the parking lot, standing guard. There had been no sound of opening doors or footsteps. The imam's rooms were similarly silent. Sarah gingerly exited the main door to the mosque. Looking to the left toward the parking area, she saw Hamid casually sitting on a folding chair, reading under a streetlamp. She went briskly toward him, gesturing urgently.

"What is it," the small, dark Yemeni asked earnestly, rising from his chair.

"I think something is wrong with Turan," she said, her voice filled with concern.

Hamid quickly followed her into the building, only to be stopped by the same lamp as his companion, wielded by the same assailant, Ahmad. The pair of agents tied up and disabled him as they had with Turan, placing his limp body in a hall closet. Due to his small size, they gave him a commensurably smaller dose of the sleeping potion.

While Ahmad was outside, Sarah had gone through Turan's pockets, retrieving a set of keys. Now they did the same with Hamid, finding another set. Surely these would allow them access to the basement and the prison cells. They hoped.

Chapter 44

Downstairs, Lara was dimly aware of strange sounds emanating from the floor above. Ordinarily at this time of night things were very quiet. Suddenly she saw her specter-like female attendant hurriedly trying to open her cell and arouse her. Lara was afraid the woman had seen the escape attempt in progress and was trying to remove her to another location. At the same time, the two avengers appeared at the top of the stairs, alarming the black-clad attendant. As the door to the stairs slammed shut, the woman desperately tried to impede their progress, flinging her set of keys into a trash can. A slight cry emitted from her lips. It was the first sound Lara had heard from her captor in some time.

With the help of Sarah, Ahmad tied a loose ring of silk fiber around the woman, trying to sooth her nerves with some calming words in Farsi. But she suddenly fell limp in his arms. During this time, Sarah was frantically trying to find the keys to the cell door. Lara, meanwhile, was so excited by the arrival of her saviors, she could do or say nothing, just watched as the drama unfolded.

When the two agents finally managed to open the cell door, Lara leaped at them, hugging them even before they identified themselves or placed the now-unconscious female guard on the cot in the cell. The three of them, under the direction of Sarah, silently climbed the stairs, hoping to find no angry men waiting for them. Opening the door, the hallway was clear and quiet. Motioning silently for Lara to remain still, Ahmad raced noiselessly up the stairs to the second floor and retrieved their luggage. It was only when they had gotten into the car and left the parking lot that they were able to talk about their adventure. Lara, of course, was ecstatic, urging them to stop at a fast food restaurant, even before calling in to Mary Robley in Los Angeles. There she gorged herself on hamburgers, fries and a quart-sized soft drink, followed by a trip to the ladies' room.

They got hold of Mary at home on the satellite phone. She was groggy but enormously elated at the news of Lara's rescue. She insisted on all the details once she was convinced of Lara's well being. She further ordered them to return immediately to Los Angeles, where she would meet them at headquarters. A physician was called to do a thorough work up of Lara's physical and mental condition after her wretched experience.

Ahmad drove while the two women sat in the rear seat where Lara went over her ordeal. About halfway through her narrative, as she tried to recall every detail, she suddenly asked about Sarah's father, the dentist-sayan. Sarah laughed, relieving Lara's tension. Sarah then described for Lara the pretense of her father's murder and the placing of a body at the exit to the canal. It had actually been that of an unidentified derelict, donated by the coroner, which otherwise would have gone to a medical school. Her father, Sarah told her, was well on his way to Israel. It all seemed to fit together. Relieved of that heaviness, Lara looked forward to contacting Uri. That is, as soon as her physical exam and debriefing with Mary Robley had been concluded. She promptly fell asleep, leaning on the rear door of the car.

Lara slept through the two hour trip to the FBI building on Wilshire. There, in the absence of her two new companions, Sarah and Ahmad, she described to Mary, every aspect of her ordeal, starting with her ride to the Los Angeles mosque and her battle with the amorous imam. Mary broke in at this point and showed her a picture of the injured man, his eyes evidence of a brutal beating. "He'll live," Mary told her, "but he won't soon forget his 'engagement party'."

Lara nodded in recognition. Then she continued with a description of her imprisonment until being interrupted by the female physician, who insisted on an immediate examination. An hour later, after being deemed amazingly healthy after her cruel confinement, she returned to Mary, who had now been joined by Mike Scanlon. He had apparently been brought up to date by Mary while Lara was getting her physical with the doctor.

Lara continued where she had left off, describing even the questioning by the imam of Uri's whereabouts. At this, Lara noticed a meaningful, if not disturbing, glance between the two law officers. Lara immediately interjected, "What is it? What's happened to Uri?"

"That's right," Mary said as controlled as possible. "You've been out of touch for a while." She then went into the Israel Independence Day events, including, of course the BDS demonstration and its aftermath. The counter-demonstrators had been apprehended and tested for DNA, she continued, although the results had not been made public. "...but there was a match with the blood samples found at the scene of the Sunni mosque massacre..." There Mary paused, to let Lara process this news.

"And Uri...?" Lara pleaded apprehensively.

"We held the counter-demonstrators downtown on suspicion of complicity of murder, but..."

"But...?" Lara pleaded anxiously.

"The leader of the group, one Imam Javad Abdouleh, and some of his lieutenants, were not apprehended and we haven't caught up with them yet..."

"And Uri...?"

"It was Uri who tipped us off about the upcoming confrontation at the Celebration. He had been in daily contact until that day..."

"And since…?" Lara was about to faint, only partly from lack of sleep and nutrition.

"Nothing. But…his locator is still functioning, hopefully better than yours. We have every hope that he is where it says he is…in Orange County."

"Can't you send a Hostage Rescue Team down there to get him?" Lara begged.

Mary looked meaningfully at Mike before saying, "Recent anti-discrimination actions against the FBI and LAPD have made it difficult, if not impossible, to 'invade' a predominantly minority - in this case - Muslim neighborhood without a very tight court order. I'm afraid we don't have the time to…"

"My God," Lara cried. "You mean you're we're helpless? He could be in serious trouble, or worse!"

"I've spoken with Yehudi Gold, the Israeli consul, and he's contacted Mossad, in Israel.…You know, Sarah's father has been secretly moved there…and they all agree that we need to extricate Uri with as much caution as possible. None of us wants another 'Dubai' embarrassment. Which means that we're limited in what resources we can use…"

"Meaning me, I guess that means," Lara interjected.

"Get some rest. Then the *three* of you," referring to Lara, Sarah and Ahmad, "will be our best 'resources' in getting Uri and this guy Javad back here."

Chapter 45

Sheikh Nasrallah was frightened. Having the Iranian prime minister summon him again was most disturbing. Fortunately, the fighting in Iraq had left the DAESH forces severely depleted, so this journey was less worrisome and far less time-consuming. Still, he was shaking as he waited for his benefactor in the sumptuous lounge. A servant, a young, handsome boy, brought him some coffee and sweets, distracting the sheikh for just a moment.

Finally, after what seemed like hours, but was actually only about fifteen minutes, the Iranian walked slowly into the room and planted himself in his opulent chair opposite the Hezbollah leader. The same servant brought him refreshments and silently left the room. The two men sipped their coffees in silence, the sheikh trembling visibly now.

"First, I have some wonderful news to share with you," Abbasi, the Iranian prime minister, said heartily. At this, Sheikh Nasrallah calmed considerably. He had, apparently, worried for no reason. *Things were fine.*

"We have concluded our arrangements with our allies, the Russians. An intermediate range ballistic missile will shortly be launched from our western shores, deep down the Persian Gulf!"

The sheikh, totally at ease now, grabbed a particularly large sweet and took a huge bite. His fears had been for naught. The plans were proceeding beautifully. The Americans and their stooges, the Israelis, would be sent into total panic with the news that the Iranians had the means to destroy the Zionists with a single nuclear strike. "That is magnificent news, indeed, my brother!" he said leaning back in his chair, enjoying his treat. He waited for even more wonderful information. "But, my friend," Nasrallah added, "how will you prepare the missiles that will rain down death upon the Zionists? Don't tell me the Russians will supply you with the weapons to do that!?"

Abbasi grew pensive, as though trying to determine whether to share some other secret with his guest. Finally, he clapped his hands twice and a servant appeared instantly. They exchanged a few words and the man left, only to reappear moments later with a television monitor and remote control. It was the same setup he had used in his earlier meeting with the sheikh. "I have something else to show you," he said, flipping on the monitor with the remote. A DVD began playing a scene from something that looked like a science fiction movie.

"Remember how I told you the Russians were helping us modify our nuclear reactors?" The Hezbollah leader nodded; he was certainly no expert in these matters, but was eager to see what the Iranian had to show him. "Well, this is what we have done with our Bushehr nuclear station and other reactors the Americans have had us remove, under the so-called 'agreement'."

Nasrallah watched in awe as some strange machinery came into view. "This is what is called a 'BN-600 fast-breeder reactor' developed by the Russians. Basically, it converts inert, depleted uranium into weapons-grade plutonium."

"Depleted uranium?" the sheikh asked, totally out of his depth.

"Yes, that is uranium from which nearly all the weapons-grade material, the U-235, has been removed, leaving only the inert part, the U-238. That stuff is generally considered useless for weapons. The Americans are not concerned that we have tons of the stuff; it can be used for a variety of other purposes, like building materials."

The sheikh just nodded, not knowing where this discussion was headed.

"The Bushehr reactor has been converted into one of these BN-600 'breeder' reactors. You see," Abbasi said patiently, "this normally inert U-238 turns into powerful plutonium fuel when bombarded with what are called 'fast neutrons'." The sheikh still looked bewildered. "These reactors produce fast neutrons from a small amount of low-grade U-235, the type used in standard power reactors. They have been allowed us by the agreement with the Americans." The sheikh remained still, waiting for the punch line.

"Rather than the water used in normal power reactors, the BN-600 reactors use liquid sodium as a coolant. What happens then is that, instead of just producing electric power, the surrounding inert U-238, is converted into Pu-239: weapons grade plutonium!"

The sheikh was clearly stunned, impressed by this news.

"We then, of course, have to split the plutonium from the rest of the material, but that procedure is relatively simple. It's a standard chemical separation that looks to the outsider like any other chemical process, like making fertilizer, for example."

Nasrallah was finally catching on. Without knowledge of the BN-600 reactors, the international inspection team would see only a standard chemical plant.

"Then," Abbasi continued, "we have another facility, hidden in the mountains, that takes this plutonium and casts it into lethal warheads. We will soon have enough weapons to annihilate the Zionist state several times over!"

The sheikh mulled this over for quite a while before offering: "But surely the U.S. would retaliate on Israel's behalf immediately after any strike such as this...no?"

The Iranian smirked at his guest's naivety. "Certainly we have considered this. That is why we also have a 'demonic' plan to counteract such a strike," he said with a conspiratorial grin. "I cannot give you the details, but the Americans will be aware that any such action will result in widespread nuclear war! They wouldn't dare risk such a thing on behalf of such an insignificant country. It would be a *'fait accompli'*. The world would just have to accept the destruction of the 'State of Israel' as a means of keeping world order."

The Hezbollah leader seemed unconvinced. "Look," the Iranian continued, "the 'Israelis' would not want to take the chance on living in their little, vulnerable country any more. There are, after all, many places they could go instead—the United States, for example, as well as several of the European countries. They belong there anyway," he finished dismissively. "This is our world; always has been. The Jews have no business here."

Nasrallah certainly had no argument with that; he would be delighted to be rid of the Zionists. Their freedom and high standard of living had made a mockery of the rest of the region, stirring unrest and instability. He settled back, resigned for the moment to accept the Iranian's proposition.

"Well, my friend," Abbasi finally said with a smile, "and how is *your* plan proceeding?"

The sheikh, reassured somewhat by the Iranian's news, replied, "Quite well, I understand. Our men made quite a significant splash at the 'Independence Day Celebration' in Los Angeles, as I'm sure you have read."

"Quite well, you say?" The Iranian replied.

"Why, yes. The 'Celebration' was completely disrupted. The local paper reported that the BDS demonstrators were aggressively confronted by a group of Jewish extremists— our men! The Americans are outraged."

"You fool!" the Iranian roared with virulence. "There is a spy in your midst! The police know your men for who they really are. They took DNA samples from them and compared them with their actual names and immigration forms. They will all be picked up and interrogated. It is only a matter of time!"

"But how...?"

The Iranian spelled out the facts for the astonished sheikh. He also told him what must be done. And soon...

Chapter 46

Javad was still basking in the glow of the success of the mission to demolish the "Israel Independence Day" celebration as he spoke with his colleagues at his Orange County headquarters. The newspapers had made the most of the apparent disruption of the peaceful BDS demonstration by orthodox Jewish zealots. Even the escape of the FBI whore, Lara Edmond, could not totally dampen his spirits.

There had, however, been some unnerving developments in the past few days since the event. One by one, members of the "Jewish zealots," the core of his gang at the mosque, had disappeared. He knew they had been "swabbed" for their DNA the day of the demonstration. But what possible connection could link them to any other activity, he wondered? And how could they have been located so quickly? There was no crime in what they had done at the celebration; otherwise, they would have been charged then and not released.

What he didn't know was that at the time of their detention each had been surreptitiously "tagged" with a new, tiny electronic marker invisible to the naked eye. The LAPD had then been able, under the guise of immigration control, to pick them up, one by one, and bring them to police headquarters. There they were being held, incommunicado, for questioning related to the BDS event.

Suddenly, an innocuous phone call came in to the mosque announcing they had a visitor, recently arrived from Lebanon "on business." A man calling himself "Ammar" had arrived at the clothing store used as a front for urgent matters relating to the Shia cause. The owner of the store had phoned, saying this visitor had arrived, needing to speak with "James." This was Javad's pseudonym known only to Nasrallah and his closest associates.

Javad told the man to come and meet him at "Location M," which would be known to him only if he were authentic; it was used by Javad for only the most critical meetings. After only thirty minutes a middle-aged man, clearly Middle Eastern, arrived, giving the restaurant owner the appropriate greeting. He was shown immediately to a small room in the back. Javad was already there waiting nervously for him. Any message requiring this degree of confidentiality must be truly important, and, most likely, bad news.

He was not mistaken. The man, Ammar, quickly got down to business. He recognized Javad from a multitude of photographs he had seen in Beirut. "There has been a serious development," he told Javad, after the perfunctory greeting. The man was still agitated from his long journey. "We have an informer inside Rimonim prison in Israel," he told Javad without any prelude.

Javad merely nodded, not knowing what to expect, motioning with his hands for the visitor to get on with his story.

Ammar took a deep breath and blurted, "He tells us that the man, Mohammed Azizi, *is still there*, in prison! The story in the newspapers about his notorious escape is a fraud..."

There was silence as Javad tried to assimilate this news. "You're quite sure of this?" he said, looking deeply into Ammar's face for any hint of deceit.

"Quite sure. Sheikh Nasrallah says it is urgent you take all necessary steps. He said you would know what that meant."

Javad did, indeed, know what that meant. The man who had been posing as Azizi could only be the man they had been seeking: Uri Levin. What a fool he had been, Javad berated himself. Right there under his very nose! Suddenly he realized that the absence from religious services of a number of his men was no accident. They had been arrested somehow. The DNA swabs, of course! The police must have some evidence…he searched his memory for any link with their other activities…

Well, there was nothing to be done about that at the present. What must be done immediately is to apprehend the Azizi imposter. He called over to the mosque, reaching Turan. "Apprehend our friend Azizi as soon as you can, and hold him in the basement; use the storage area for now!"

"But master…" the Indonesian replied, amazed by the order. Azizi was their trusted associate.

"Just do it! I will be there in a moment," he replied curtly.

Chapter 47

Uri was barely aware of the motion behind him, as the padded weight struck him with nearly full force in the back of his head. He crumpled to the ground, scarcely conscious. Only his subconscious reaction to the movement saved his life, he realized later.

He didn't know how long it'd been until he gained consciousness. It seemed like hours, but was probably only minutes. There was a dull throbbing in the back of his head that felt like a jackhammer. Colored wheels spun in his eyes. Sounds around him came as though muffled through many layers of cotton. Several pairs of rough hands picked him up off the floor. It was then that he realized his hands had been duct-taped in front of him, and his mouth taped shut. They lifted him up bodily and set him into a wooden chair. Then they taped his ankles and torso so that he was like a sitting mummy. Then, apparently satisfied that he was immobilized, his captors left through a door that was right in front of him.

It took him only a few minutes to re-create the action that had preceded his current predicament. He had entered the mosque, dressed as Farid-Azizi, as usual. There was no one there for the evening prayers, which struck him as very odd. He went back behind the prayer room…then the blow to his head…

The Shia leader and his men must have realized he was not who he claimed to be, though he wasn't sure if they knew his precise identity. He hoped not; if they knew he was, in fact, a Mossad assassin, he was in big trouble. In any case, it was clear he had to get out of here; they most probably would be back with designs on finding out all they could about his identity. Fortunately, he was not blindfolded; that indicated they were not overly concerned about his ability to escape. He was able to turn his head enough to see that he was in an empty room with a lone light bulb, no windows, and just the single door. The walls were concrete, the door, steel, with no bolt. He could see the knob had a simple lock mechanism. If he could free himself, he might just be able to open it...

His first move was to try to free his hands and arms from their constraint. It was well-known among professionals that duct tape was very strong in tension, but weak in shear strength. With the proper sharp, outward, diagonal motion, one could start the tape tearing at an edge, and quickly continue the tear to completion. But it had to be done with strength and speed. He took a deep breath and brought both elbows sharply away from his body. Luckily, he had perfected this move years ago back in Mossad training. To his great relief, the tapes tore away with a sharp cracking sound. He then performed the same maneuver with his hands; both were released in an instant. With his hands and arms free, it was a simple matter to pull away the remainder of his bonds.

Now to get out of here. He figured he didn't have much time before his captors returned with an interrogation team. Reaching into his pants pockets, he found the thin length of wire hidden in the lining. As he expected, everything else had been removed. He rose, careful not to knock over the chair or make any other noise. He was relieved to find they had left him with his running shoes. His only other clothing consisted of a t-shirt, underwear and slacks.

He made his way quietly to the door, a distance of only about ten feet. Then he studied the door lock. It was a simple key-activated mechanism from either side, not a dead bolt. He recognized it immediately; it was a Weiser 5-cylinder design, available everywhere. Uri had practiced on this lock in school many years ago, and was certain he could open it.

He first tried the knob to see if, indeed, it was locked. As expected, it was. Then, using the concrete floor, he bent the end of his wire so that there was about a five-mm hook. He inserted the hook into the lock and felt for the most inward cylinder. When he could go no further, he twisted the tool in both directions. Happily, the cylinder opened with an audible click. He moved the wire out to the next stop, and repeated the maneuver. Another click. Three more and he would have it. The last cylinder was balky, but with sweaty persistence, it yielded.

Uri tested the knob; it moved as anticipated, and the door opened slightly. The hall outside was lit. He considered his next move; *get as much advantage as possible,* he told himself. He decided to knock out the overhead light bulb. That would keep them guessing; they would at least have to find some other light before entering the room. Using the chair, he was able to swing one of the legs into the bulb, which exploded in a shower of glass. Now the only illumination was from the crack in the door.

Uri ran noiselessly back to the door and opened it cautiously. The hallway outside, concrete, like the room, was empty. He carefully closed the door, stepped out and looked in both directions. *Pick one and go,* he told himself. He went to the right and hoped for the best. He had no idea where he was, but immediately came to a short staircase that led up about one flight, ending at another door, this one wooden, as was the floor. Opening it, he found himself in a paneled, carpeted room, filled with books and religious icons, clearly Islamic. The room was only dimly lit. Hopefully, he was now on the first floor of whatever building this was. Probably Al-Naqi's mosque, he hoped.

Before he could make his next move, the door at the other end of the room suddenly opened and two men, chattering noisily, entered, spotting Uri instantly. There was nowhere for Uri to hide, so he waited for their approach, instinctively moving into his defensive stance. Unafraid, the two men, one considerably larger than the other, charged directly at him. Checking their hands, he saw they carried no weapons. The larger man headed for Uri's right side, the smaller to his left. Uri waited until they were within one stride of him, then attacked the larger of the two. Bending quickly at the waist, he stepped hard on the man's right instep, simultaneously snapping his right elbow under the surprised man's chin. His yowl of pain stopped short as his glottis burst. He dropped like a stone.

The other man, taken aback by his companion's sudden removal from the fray, considered his options and headed back the way he had come. Uri was not in favor of this; he stopped him by grabbing his long, greasy hair and throwing him to the ground. He recognized this man as one of those who worked at the mosque. Was he still there? "Where are we?" he ordered the terrified man, who was Pakistani in appearance. The man's eyes were wild with fear; he seemed unable to speak. Uri slapped him, hard, across the face. "Are we still in the mosque?" he commanded. The man just trembled. Uri could see a stain spreading across the man's trousers. The man was frantic now, seemingly in shock.

Uri was considering his alternatives when two doors at opposite ends of the room suddenly opened and he was confronted with Javad and four others, two of them very large. All were carrying weapons. Before he could even consider his options, he was grabbed from behind and a rag stuffed over his nose and mouth. All of his limbs were immobilized by the overwhelming number of assailants.

Chapter 48

Lara with her new teammates, Sarah and Ahmad, were given a minimum time in which to sleep and get prepared for their trip back to Orange County. The doctors' reports on all three were good; even Lara had not suffered unduly during her ordeal.

The situation was desperate; Uri was undoubtedly captive. Somehow Javad had found out his true identity, Mary, Mike and Yehudi concluded. There was no other reason why he would not have contacted Mary by now. Her best guess was that the detaining of the fake "Jews" at the Independence Day rally had alerted Javad that there was a spy within his fold. "Azizi" would be a prime suspect, having so recently arrived. Perhaps he had even received word somehow from his bosses in Lebanon that an imposter was in his midst. At any rate, they had no recourse but to attempt to locate and release him, at once.

Mary was adamant; using a force of police to invade a predominantly Muslim neighbourhood was out of the question, being "politically incorrect." But armed with a variety of weapons, communication devices, and tools of the trade, the three of them stood a reasonable chance of catching the criminals by surprise. At any rate, they hadn't the time to organize any sort of intricate effort; Uri might not survive long enough.

The trio had the distinct advantage of knowing where Uri was being held. His locating transmitter continued to operate, hopefully better than Lara's. It was a different model, made for emitting a shorter, higher-frequency signal at longer intervals, but over a much greater period of time. Mary hoped he had secreted it in the waist band of his underwear, as instructed. They were confident of its condition by the fact that it correctly indicated when he was at his car in the long-term parking garage. It had tracked him there every day, as he called in on his satellite phone. The twenty minute period between signals had been sufficient to adequately track his movements—so far.

But now, for the past thirty-six hours, he had been stationary, within just a few feet. He was almost certainly under some sort of restraint. The three rescuers were ordered only to locate him with certainty—they could not afford another embarrassment like the affair with Lara, her transmitter taped to a car.

They did have with them weapons for immobilization; even if not deadly, they should be sufficient to leave their victims helpless until the police arrived. They were far superior to the Tasers used by law enforcement. Unlike Tasers, these were actual handguns, but loaded with non-lethal projectiles. Lara, who was a trained FBI agent, however, was also armed with a lethal Sig Sauer, to be used only as a last resort. The worst thing that could happen was a scandal involving officers killing innocent Muslims.

Each of them was equipped with several types of restraints, similar, but stronger, than the typical plastic ties used by police. They also had a variety of gas grenades, to be used only if confronted with a group of assailants. Each of the three had a small backpack that looked like a typical tourist accoutrement, loaded with their contrivances.

On the way down to Orange County, Lara went over with her colleagues every situation they might encounter. From the apparent location, as close as she could tell, Uri was being held in the same prison as she, just days ago. They had all altered their appearances so as not to be immediately recognized. The two women wore typical Muslim dress, complete with headscarves of different colors. Ahmad wore clothes similar to that seen on the streets there: drab shirt and jeans, with old tennis shoes. He wore on his head a white kufi. The appearance they were to project was that of a Muslim man accompanying his wife and sister, perhaps, as they walked casually around the street, shopping and sight-seeing. All three were fluent in Farsi, of course, and reasonably conversant in Arabic. If spoken to in English, they would resort to Farsi in reply.

As instructed, the trio headed straight for the garage that housed Uri's Ford. Mary Robley had given Lara a spare set of keys, hoping of course, that the assailants had not gotten hold of Uri's. Even if they had, of course, they would not know the location of the car. There, indeed, they found the car, backed into a space on the fourth floor, covered with a thick film of yellow sand and dust. Knowing exactly where Uri had hidden his gun and satellite phone, they gathered them up and immediately called Mary, informing her of their location. She sounded relieved that they had gotten this far without difficulty. The three rescuers were instructed to head for the suspect mosque; Uri's signal continued to pulse its reassuring tone. They drove rapidly to the location of Uri's beacon. It was the mosque where Lara had been held captive; the mosque of the despicable Imam Zainal Abidin.

Chapter 49

"**W**here the hell are we?" was all that Uri could to think to ask, as he slowly regained consciousness. He was aware of Lara standing there, holding a wet towel to his bleeding forehead.

"We're in the basement of the mosque—you remember them taking you here?"

"I remember a fight, and being knocked out, then moved, by car, I think...but it seems like days ago." Reality was slowly forcing its way through the fog. He remembered a scuffle, some sort of noxious gas, incredible amounts of noise, and then someone covering his face with a rag. Then nothing but blackness, a void, passage of an infinite amount of time, then suddenly a light, and an incredible amount of dizziness, a floating, then pain, all through his body, but especially in his head. He remembered retching, gagging, fighting for air. After that, he remembered a relaxation, then slowly a return to consciousness.

"The mosque... you mean the radical Shia mosque...Sarah, the dentist's daughter...?"

"You're back among the living! How much do you remember?" Lara asked.

"I was bound and gagged. They were asking me all kinds of questions. Then suddenly there was all this noise and confusion...that's it."

"We found you from that little transmitter you were carrying. It's lucky they never spotted it. Anyway, we saw a few of them as we busted in the door, but I'm afraid they're just the little guys. They ran off through the back, but we were too concerned about you to chase them."

At that moment, the front door burst open; Lara and her cohorts had failed to lock it in their haste to get to Uri. In came Javad and three of his assassins. All were carrying machine pistols. The rescue team had left all their weaponry in their car, and so was powerless to stop them.

"Well, what do we have here?" Javad said gleefully. "All of our American and Israeli friends." Javad held his captives at gunpoint while the others made a cursory search of them for weapons. He motioned for his men to bring the two men and two women ahead of them, at gunpoint.

The four prisoners were hustled out of the mosque by the rear door, heading toward two vans parked behind the building. It was only then that Uri realized that this was a different mosque than the one where he had attended religious services these past few weeks; rather it was the one where he met with Javad and his team of marauders. The mosque belonging to Zainal Abidin.

Just as Javad opened one of the vans and was pushing his prisoners into it, a man turned the corner of the alley and shouted, "Farid!" Uri recognized him immediately as his host for the friendly, if somewhat awkward, dinner some time ago, the man named Zurvan.

Startled, Javad hesitated for a moment as the stranger came up to Uri and shook his hand vigorously. He motioned for his three assassins to put away their weapons. Reluctantly, they did so. This was a matter that could be handled without the need for gunplay.

"Where have you been? I have not seen you in some time, my friend!" Zurvan said with surprise as he took in the entire scene. "And who are these men?" Seeming to recognize something was amiss, Zurvan challenged Javad and his men, "What exactly do you think you are doing?!"

Uri nodded at Lara, who took his lead and smashed her knee into her captor's groin, simultaneously driving her elbow into his nose, breaking it with an audible snap. Blood came gushing forth, drawing the other assailants' attention, just for a moment. At the same time, Uri drove his heel sideways into Javad's knee, snapping it, sending the leader to the ground; he had no chance to draw his weapon. Sarah took advantage of her young captor's apparent reluctance to strike a woman and let out a shriek that was certain to be heard in the street. Not being trained for such a situation, the young man hesitated for a second, then sprinted out of the alley. He was no doubt recalling that his comrades detained after the "Nakba Day" demonstration had not been heard from again.

Ahmad followed suit, bringing his hands up and clawing at his captor's eyes. It was fortunate that none of the assailants had taken the initiative and unholstered their weapons. Javad, however, was not about to let the sudden appearance of this stranger foil his plan. He brought forth the Glock concealed under his jacket and, from the ground, fired in Uri's direction. Fortunately for Uri, but sadly for his friend Zurvan, who had come to his aid, the 9 mm slug struck him squarely in the face, killing him instantly. Uri kicked the gun loose from Javad's hand and searched for an escape.

The burly Persian guarding Ahmad grabbed him and headed for one of the vans. Uri, seeing only one possible flight route, lunged for the back door to the mosque and opened it, shouting to his rescuers. Lara and Sarah immediately followed his lead and dashed into the mosque. Seeing their leader in distress on the ground, the other assailants rushed to his aid, deciding their captives would be easily recaptured in the mosque. Javad, screaming in pain and frustration, yelled at his men to forget him and go after the transgressors. The men paused for a crucial second. It was just enough time for Sarah and Lara to bolt the door behind them. They hoped Ahmad could manage on his own.

Ahmad, in fact, was able to disable his captor during the disturbance caused by the injury to his leader, Javad. As the Persian turned to see what was going on, Ahmad thrust his left hand sharply into his captor's back, knife-like directly into his right kidney. The blow was strong enough to penetrate between the man's ribs and burst a large blood vessel. The large Persian staggered with the impact and the sharp ensuing pain, reaching back impulsively to see what had struck him. This was barely enough time for Ahmad to flee, after first finishing his captor with a blow to the back of his neck, followed by the pressure of his thumb into the hollow below his ear, penetrating the man's brain.

Unfortunately, the rear door of the mosque was already locked, eliminating that escape route. Instead, Ahmad ran in the darkness to the corner of the alley and sprinted into the street.

Ahmad's assailants were torn between chasing Ahmad and aiding Javad. There were just four of them now, including the injured Javad, who insisted on continuing the pursuit, limping badly on his damaged leg. One of the others helped him to his feet and they tried, without success, to enter the rear door to the mosque. "Go through the front door, quickly," Javad screamed at his men. "Then get back here and open this door!"

"But Master," one of them pleaded, "They may find the phones, they will call for help!"

"We will hold them hostage, threatening to kill them one by one. They will not sacrifice two women and the Israeli. Just follow my orders!"

Two of the men raced around to the front door of the mosque, one of them remembering to gather up the keys from Javad. The other, young, thin man called Kaveh, stayed with his leader, standing guard with his pistol in hand. As yet, no other strangers had entered the alley.

The two assailants ran around the corner and, not seeing Ahmad, proceeded to unlock the front door to the mosque and rush inside. In their haste, they neglected to re-latch the door. Inside all was dark and quiet. The elder of the two attackers, a man called Dalir, took command and headed, from memory, toward the back door, not knowing immediately where to turn on the lights. His compatriot, Shahin, followed blindly in the dark. After just a few minutes Dalir found the door, which was lit with a red "Exit" sign, and opened it. Shahin ran to join him, not knowing what, nor who was waiting in the dark surroundings. Javad, limping badly now, with the aid of the young, untrained Kaveh, entered the rear door and immediately resumed command. "Get the lights," he ordered Dalir, the most senior of the three of his remaining aides. "The switches are in the metal box just inside the front door."

The others remained on guard, pistols at the ready, not knowing what was in store. Three minutes later, the main prayer room and hallway blossomed into light and Dalir returned to the group, smiling at his successful venture. All of them looked to Javad for instructions. He told Dalir and Shahin to search the whole building for the three surviving enemies: Lara, Uri and the Persian Jewess, Sarah. He had no way of knowing that Ahmad had survived the fighting in the alley and was now on the premises.

Javad was helped by Kaveh toward his small office, hidden behind the imam's elegant study by a blank wall. Here he would make a quick internet call to Sheikh Nasrallah in Beirut. It would be early morning there, and he hoped the sheikh would understand their operation was in jeopardy and take appropriate measures. He realized this was not the most secure means of communication, but the U.S. authorities were certain to have been completely alerted by now. All he could do was minimize the damage—and eliminate the Israeli and his American whore. Sarah, the dentist's daughter, was of secondary concern.

Javad was determined to save himself and his men. He had set in place emergency measures for such a situation as this. He had a small launch in Los Angeles harbor, filled with necessities, arms and communication equipment. They could easily make their way into Mexican waters, where they would be safe until picked up by Hezbollah operatives. But first things first—the villains must still be hiding here in the mosque building. They couldn't last long.

As Kaveh helped Javad as best he could, Dalir and Shahin continued the search for their three adversaries; they were unarmed and somewhere within reach. Each of Javad's assassins was equipped with a Glock-19 pistol, a 9mm weapon with capability for fully automatic fire, complete with fifty-round magazines.

The building was not large. The main floor comprised first the prayer room, which lay right inside the front door. As a precaution, too late as it turned out, they dead-bolted this door, something they had neglected to do upon entering. Along the wall leading to the left of the prayer room were the restrooms. They checked each of these, carefully, as they had been taught in training. As Dalir waited outside against the wall, Shahin dove in through the door of the men's room first, his pistol at the ready, set for automatic fire. The light switch, he knew was on the wall, to the right of the door. Flipping the toggle, bathing the room in light, he saw no one. There were no stalls, just a urinal and toilet; no place to hide.

His heart beating wildly, Shahin whispered an all-clear to his waiting partner, and repeated the procedure in the ladies' room. Here there were two stalls, which he broke into with his foot, his pistol again at the ready. Once again there was no one. They retreated back into the hallway and quietly discussed their next move.

Adjacent to them were the library and garden, opposite the imam's study. They saw the light from under the library door and entered it quickly, but noiselessly. There was no concealment available, and a glass door that led only to the garden was locked and chained from the inside. Still, they peered into the small garden through the glass door, seeing nothing amiss. There was also a door leading to the garden directly from the hallway, but this too, was locked and bolted.

To the right, along the hallway, were the kitchen, dining room, and laundry. The lights were on in all three areas, so all was clearly visible. The two assassins checked out the kitchen and small dining room first; again there were no hiding places. They quietly entered the laundry room, where there was an industrial-size washer and large dryer. There were also open areas of linens, cleaning supplies, and hanging garments. The washer was open and empty. Next the dryer was checked out; it was large enough to harbor a fugitive or two. But it, also, was vacant. They were about to examine the two large bins full of linens when they heard Javad calling for them.

They fled back into the hallway toward the sound of their master's voice. They found him, holding his broken leg, mumbling in pain, supported by the tiny Kaveh.

"What is it, Master!?" Shahin and Dalir cried out in unison.

Seeing his two men standing there dumbly, he yelled, "Have you not found those Jews yet!?" They just shook their heads. "Check the kitchen and upstairs bedrooms; they must be somewhere! Quickly! We haven't much time. Remember, take them alive if you can!"

The two admonished men headed for the stairs.

Chapter 50

As Dalir and Shahin ran noisily down the hall, fearing their master's wrath, Uri and Lara took the opportunity to emerge from their hiding places in the bins of dirty linens. Sarah emerged from her alcove behind the large dryer. They stared at each other, aware at how close they had come to capture.

Unseen to Javad and his men was Ahmad, who had hidden in the street and seen the front door being opened. Hoping they had not locked it from the inside, Ahmad had crept silently in, hiding in the rear of the prayer room until the lights came on. He held his breath as Shahin had opened the rear door and let in the wounded Javad and the young Kaveh. He also heard the instructions given by Javad to his men and waited for them to start their rounds. As expected, the inexperienced Dalir and Shahin were less than noiseless as they made their predictable investigation of the first floor. He saw Kaveh and Javad headed, limping, toward the imam's chambers, but was afraid, unarmed as he was, to follow them further. Instead, he watched the two other men, Dalir and Shahin, checking out the restrooms. He stayed hidden as they examined the kitchen and laundry, then heard the call from Javad and saw them head toward the imam's study behind the prayer room.

It was only then that Ahmad joined his comrades; Uri, Lara and Sarah as they emerged from their hiding places in the well-lit laundry to his right. They hugged each other briefly and whispered their strategy. None was armed, but they had the advantage of knowing the location of their enemies. They also had the benefit of being in close proximity to some ersatz weaponry: large carving knives and cleaning chemicals in the kitchen. Uri quickly mixed up a deadly potion of drain cleaner and bleach, pouring it into a bucket. He handed this to Ahmad. He, meanwhile, picked out a vicious-looking pair of long, sharp, meat-carving knives for himself.

Presuming they had a few minutes grace, they peered out into the now-lit hallway. Uri's plan was to catch the inexperienced Dalir and Shahin and ambush them on their way back down the stairs. Finding nothing in the upstairs rooms or corridor, and having cleared the main floor, they would be ill-prepared as they descended back down.

His instructions were simple: when the pair came down the stairs, hopefully together, Uri would take out the one on the right with the two knives. Ahmad would simultaneously throw the contents of the pail in the other's face. Lara and Sarah would wait on either side to help finish them off. For this they had armed themselves with a couple of small, steel fire extinguishers.

Uri's team was well in position as the two rookie assassins noisily made their way downstairs, muttering softly to themselves about what to do next. They were, however, not alongside each other, but in tandem. Dalir, the older of the two came down first, a few steps ahead of the slender Shahin.

As soon as Dalir showed his head at the bottom of the stairs, to Uri's right, he was met with Uri, thrusting both carving knives upwards into the man's midsection, slicing his aorta and piercing his heart. Dalir went down without a sound; merely a gush of blood. The astonished Shahin, carrying his machine pistol, stopped in his tracks. Ahmad had no time to waste; he turned the corner of the stairwell and threw the deadly mixture right into the man's face, no more than five feet away. Blinded and gasping for breath, the young killer instinctively pulled the trigger of his Glock 19, sending a spray of 9 mm slugs directly into Ahmad. The young agent was cut nearly in two. Not waiting for the others, Uri stepped up and finished Shahin off with a slashing of his neck, severing his carotid and jugular.

The three surviving members of the rescue team looked in horror at their dead compatriot, Ahmad. Uri and Lara, with their battle experience, took no time to ponder the situation; they gathered up the two Glocks now at their disposal. They then set out to hide the three bodies as best they could. Sarah, while shaken to the core, followed their lead, helping drag the three victims into one of the restrooms.

With his team clustering together in the men's room, Uri assessed the situation: the gunshots would no doubt have been heard by Javad and his young assistant, Kaveh. They would shortly be out in the hall to investigate, fully realizing they might meet armed resistance. To preempt discovery, Uri, with one of the recovered Glocks, proceeded directly to the imam's study to locate Javad.

Lara, armed with the other pistol, crept to the left side of the prayer room, which also had access to the study. Between them, they should have Javad trapped. Where his remaining assistant, the young Kaveh was, remained a dangerous unknown. Sarah was to post herself as lookout at the street-side entrance to the prayer room, where she could signal the police, who must be on their way by now. Having no better tools for self defense, Sarah picked up the most useful objects at her disposal: the fire extinguisher and one of the long knives. She then hid among the curtains in the prayer room.

Chapter 51

Javad heard the sound of machine-gun fire. It was from one gun only, he realized. Either his men would be shortly coming in to the communications room, or...the other alternative was the one he feared. Hearing no sound of his men coming to greet him with good news, it took him only a few seconds to decide on a course of action. "Kaveh, my friend," he said to the trembling young man. "You must take your weapon and help your mates capture the usurpers." He looked the frightened young man square in the face. "It is your duty! When you are finished, return here and we will make our escape. Allah, in his grace, will protect you. Your time for martyrdom has not yet come!" Javad knew, at this point, of course, that there was little likelihood of his young acolyte ever returning.

"*Allahu Akhbar!*" shouted the neophyte, as he ran out the door.

Meanwhile, down to business, thought Javad, most probably now on his own. He continued rapidly assembling the papers and computer discs he had been drawing together in preparation for the retreat by sea from Los Angeles harbor. The rooms he had been using as his office were, in fact, the chambers of the Imam Zainal Abidin.

Abidin had realized he was under pursuit from Federal agencies ever since the "Nakba Day" disaster; he had removed his papers and other belongings, making his escape by sea.

Now it was Javad who must finish clearing out the ultra-secret plans for the destruction of the Zionist State. It was essential, at any cost, that the enemy not gain access to the intricate schemes that had been assembled.

* * *

A highly-charged Kaveh left the study and aimed for the hallway. He immediately saw the dark trails of blood leading to the men's room. He listened carefully and, hearing nothing, opened the door and viewed the ghastly spectacle. Not knowing exactly what to do, the now frightened youngster entered, as quietly as possible, into the prayer room. Kaveh immediately spotted Lara, stealthily headed toward the entrance to the study. Seeing that she held one of the captured machine-pistols, he shouted: "Drop it at once or be shot!" He knew that Javad would be pleased to capture this FBI woman and hold her hostage to aid their escape. He waited for her to turn and see that he was armed, and then comply. Glancing quickly, Lara, did, in fact, see the eager assassin, armed and grinning at his victory. But she also saw Sarah, silently creeping along the curtained wall, armed with the deadly knife and fire extinguisher.

Lara dropped her pistol and raised her hands. She turned slowly to meet her clearly-panicky attacker, drawing Kaveh's attention away from Sarah, approaching him from the rear. Lara had a look of resigned defeat on her face as she awaited capture. Kaveh, excited by his sense of victory over an FBI opponent, albeit merely a woman, said to her as she slowly approached, her hands in the air: "You stupid Jew bitch! You think you can outwit us?" He laughed loudly as he motioned for her to get down on the floor. He would take pleasure in searching her for any other weapons.

That was his last thought as Sarah thrust her knife mightily into his back. He turned, startled and mortally wounded, dropping his gun. There was no sound other than that of a ripe melon being crushed, as the thoroughly furious Sarah rendered his head into a bloody pulp. Lara instinctively jumped aside as Kaveh's lifeless body slumped to the floor. Silently, she motioned for Sarah to drop the fire extinguisher and instead pick up the Glock, which lay unfired on the floor by the victim's feet.

* * *

Javad, hearing the shouting and other noise from the prayer room, waited hopefully for an appearance by his young apprentice. When Kaveh didn't emerge, he feared the worst and hurriedly finished throwing his papers and discs into a large attaché case. It was then that Uri materialized at the door from the study leading into the small communications room. Both men assessed the situation wordlessly, Javad seeing the Glock in Uri's hand. With a look of futility, Javad dropped the case he was holding and thrust his hands quickly into the air.

Uri was, unfortunately, unaware of the hidden infrared beam that this motion of Javad's had on the Persian rug at his feet. A spring-activated lever silently jerked the rug just a few inches forward, pitching Uri to the floor. It was a last-ditch measure of protection the always-cautious Javad had installed in case of such a situation. Uri's head banged against the desk as his Glock fell uselessly to the floor. He was instantly rendered unconscious. A triumphant Javad hovered over his nemesis as he assessed his next move. Without waiting to see what had happened to the rest of his team, he would take Uri as his captive and head to the waiting car. He would have help as soon as he arrived at the harbor; having already signaled the resources there. They were ready for the journey into friendly Mexican waters.

Laying down his Glock, Javad hastened to bind the unconscious Mossad agent with plastic ties, and drag him outside. He would immediately return for the papers and discs. It was only then, his hands occupied with Uri's immobilization, that Sarah and Lara materialized at the door.

"Don't even think about it," Lara stated firmly, as Javad reached for his pistol.

"You FBI slut!" Javad shouted as he instinctively brought the pistol up from the floor.

And those were his last words, as both Lara and Sarah blasted the terrorist with their automatic weapons. The pistol fell from his lifeless hands, his eyes still open in rage.

Chapter 52

Mary Robley sat at the head of table in the conference room on the top floor of the FBI building on Wilshire. The Homeland Security representative in Los Angeles, Bret Williams, sat on her right, Mark Higgins and Mike Scanlon from the LAPD on her left. A few other high-level officials from both the FBI and LAPD made up the rest of the select group.

There was another government representative as well: Oscar van der Waals, from the local Central Intelligence Agency Office. It was not often that such a high-level CIA official showed up at multi-organization meetings such as this. These desk agents seldom saw the light of day.

All the people at the meeting had received the necessary security clearance to share the sensitive information under discussion. Under emergency conditions such as these, clearances could be rushed through the bureaucracy.

"I'll tell you what I know so far," Mary said firmly. "The State Department confirms that a medium-range ballistic missile was fired from the city of Bandar in Ganaveh County, on the west coast of Iran. That's on the Persian Gulf. The missile flew nearly a thousand miles, striking the ocean just east of Oman."

There was silence around the table as they waited for more.

"And that's contrary to the agreement set out by our government. Iran is not allowed to have missiles other than defensive ones, limited in range to 100 kilometers," Williams quickly broke in. He also had been extensively briefed about the missile firing by Homeland Security and the Defense Secretary.

"That's not the worst of it," Mary continued. "On impact, there was an explosion in the range of ten kilotons." She waited for the force of her words to be completely absorbed. "As you all know, as does the whole civilized world, these actions are in complete conflict with the terms of the contract signed by our two countries, permitting the nation of Iran to recover the one hundred fifty billion dollars we have held frozen since 1979..."

"There's more," Williams interrupted. "This is information limited to your ears only; not to leave this room." He looked up at the stern, white faces. "We sent up a reconnaissance flight off one of the carriers in the sixth fleet. They gathered samples from the plume."

The assembly, including Mary who had not yet heard this report, sat in stunned silence, waiting for the bad news.

"The isotope distribution in the blast is indisputable. The weapon was definitely nuclear in nature." Everyone in the room shifted in their chair: *an atomic weapon!*

"Worse...the isotopes collected firmly indicate the fuel was plutonium, not uranium!"

Everyone was astonished at this news. "What the hell?" Scanlon cried out. "Where would they get a plutonium weapon? The Russians? They sure as hell didn't make that themselves."

Williams waited until the group had quieted a bit. "They could only have gotten it from the Russians, unless..." Everyone held their collective breath. "...Unless the Iranians had somehow cheated on their agreement and managed to build a plutonium-producing reactor; a heavy-water type, for example."

"But wasn't the International Atomic Energy Agency supposed to be monitoring them?" Mary asked, somewhat skeptical.

"That's what we've been led to believe," Williams stated. "Now we've got a whole new ballgame. They're essentially rubbing our noses in it, saying 'What are you going to do about it now'?"

There was a frightened buzz around the table as these words sank in. "Naturally, State, the Agency, and of course, the president and Joint Chiefs are meeting as we speak. No one wants this to be the start of a nuclear World War," Williams continued. "But both the range of the missile and the nuclear payload indicate complicity of another government. As far as we knew, Iran hadn't the capability for either of these 'achievements'." The implication of these words was clear to all at the table. Either the Russians had participated in such an overt act of aggression, or the Iranians were able to go at it on their own. Either possibility was frightening as hell.

"But what could the Iranians possibly gain by an overt act like this?" Mike Scanlon queried.

"That's a good question, and one we don't have an answer to," Williams replied. "All we do know is that there has been a great deal of electronic and personnel traffic between Iran and Russia over the past few months. That, combined with the increased military activity of the Russians against ISIS, or as they call it, 'DAESH', suggests a combined strategy to wipe out the Sunni Caliphate, at the very least."

"Why do you say 'at the very least'?" Mark Higgins asked.

Williams was ready for this one. He quickly responded, "Our satellites and drones have picked up increased electronic traffic between Iran and Lebanon recently. Iran has been aiding the Hezbollah there, as well as Hamas in Gaza, as all of you well know. We have a feeling that this is connected to Iran's stated threat to eliminate the State of Israel!"

"Wait a minute," Higgins protested. "That's a pretty big stretch, isn't it?"

"Not if you consider that the anti-Zionist activities here and elsewhere have severely escalated in the past three months," Mary chimed in.

"What exactly do you mean?" Higgins asked.

"The attacks on the schools, synagogues and the Sunni mosque have all been tied to Shia extremists—though that fact has not been made public, for obvious reasons," Mary explained. "The Iranians could be threatening us with nuclear blackmail..."

"Wait just a minute!" Higgins protested. "If I follow what you're implying, the Iranians are trying to make us believe they would take on the U.S. and our allies with nuclear warfare if we don't allow them to wipe out Israel! That's not even possible, let alone likely!"

"I have to agree, Mark," Williams interjected. "The Iranians and Russians all know we have immediate retaliation capability following any action against one of our allies, NATO member or not. It's almost like the scenario in 'Dr. Strangelove'!" Everyone at the table was intimately familiar with the hypothetical "Doomsday Machine" in the 1964 classic movie, where an attack against the Soviet Union would trigger an automatic, world-wide nuclear holocaust.

"This is different," Mary pointed out. "The Iranians may be threatening a devastating blow against only the U.S.—if we make a retaliatory strike at Iran..."

"There *is* a problem: hypothetical, of course," the CIA official suddenly interposed. Oscar van der Waals was a small, unassuming man in his late fifties, but with a resume impressive to all those familiar with it. According to Agency scuttlebutt, van der Waals, as a young man, had penetrated the East German Stazi organization prior to the 1989 toppling of the Berlin Wall and the subsequent breakup of the Soviet Union. His small, well-trimmed grey mustache added a note of authenticity to his European appearance and manner. He was clad in a plain white shirt, bow tie and vest.

He, single-handed as the story goes, disrupted the chain of command to the guards at the Berlin Wall, countermanding the order to repel potential transgressors. Without his actions, the East German guards would have received the order to fire on any dissidents who tried to leave East Berlin on that fateful day. The rest, of course, was history. Once the dam broke, so to speak, there was little the Soviets, let alone the East Germans, could do to stem the tide. The Soviet Union was history.

Van der Waals now had everyone's attention; he described the "fail-safe" mechanism in place, ordering a massive retaliatory strike against Iran, should they be so bold as to attempt an attack against the Jewish State. It was only this reassurance, well-known to the Israeli heads of state, as well as their enemies, that precluded any preemptive strike by the Israelis. Only a direct order from the U.S. president could overrule the retaliation.

After a long pause, during which all the others carefully considered this news, it was Mike Scanlon who finally inquired, "So how does this impact the situation we have on our hands now, in Orange County?"

"This missile-firing in the Persian Gulf is an overt demonstration by the Iranians, and Russians, to see how we react. Do nothing, and the next step would be a more dramatic...maneuver. The Iranian leader, Abbasi, is like a crafty child. Seeing how far he can push us." As van der

Walls concluded, the mood at the table became very somber, indeed.

Chapter 53

Prime Minister Abbasi of Iran received an irate call from his Russian compatriot just as soon as the Iranian missile test-firing was revealed. He used the new Qatari-built satellite phone, guaranteed to be secure, but limited to the most urgent matters. This apparently was one of those times.

"Are you out of your mind!?" Kazakov roared in an out-of-character tirade. "I thought we had agreed that the missile test firing was to be an innocuous demonstration of your medium-range rocketry, not a threat of nuclear war!!"

The Iranian was speechless for a moment. He had presumed his Russian counterpart would be impressed by the success of the missile and payload.

"Don't you realize the Americans have an electronic-activated nuclear strike system in place that could obliterate your country if they fear you are committing an aggressive nuclear assault!?" Kazakov continued.

The Iranian was taken aback by the vehemence of the Russian's objection. But he responded after only a moment. He hesitated only in fear of the security of the communication..."I know well of their so-called 'secure' retaliation scheme. You should know that we have a counter-measure ready for them. I cannot go into detail even on this phone, but be assured that we, and you, will be safe from any attack from the Americans or their so-called allies!"

There was a long pause as the Russian considered what he had just heard from the Iranian. He realized that any American counter-measure would hit the Iranians first, and with deadly force. He would give Abbasi enough time to set up a meeting where they could safely discuss exactly what the Iranian had in place. "All right," he said, more calmly. "The Americans would never attack without further provocation. But you have certainly now put them on high alert. I want no more demonstrations of this kind, is that quite clear!?"

"Certainly, my friend. You will see and I am certain you will agree!"

Chapter 54

Yehudi hurriedly stepped out of Mary's office; he had been brought over as soon as her top-secret meeting with the CIA and LAPD had concluded. After being brought up to date on the urgent situation, he used a private office space to confer with his New York office over their secure line. David Peretz was ready, expecting his call. "So you heard all the bad news, Yehudi?" David said.

"You bet I have! So it's true; the Iranians have shot off a plutonium-powered nuke? Right down our throats!?"

"It's true, Yehudi. But that's not the end of it. Jerusalem has been in constant contact with Washington ever since the news broke. The U.S. has been watching the area, by satellite, where the missile launch occurred. They've spotted at least two silos with other birds ready to fly! Presumably filled with deadly payloads, well within range of our homeland!"

"What's our plan, David? We can't just sit back and let them destroy us!"

"What I've been told, and I have to agree, is that this is a bold effort on Iran's part to threaten us, that is, Israel, with extinction, anticipating the U.S. will do nothing about it. The Americans have no stomach for another Mideast war, the thinking goes..."

Yehudi's stomach turned at the thought of war, especially nuclear war. "So what is going to happen...?"

"A little good news, my friend," he reassured his colleague. "A sort of agreement has been reached. Israel is going to be allowed to knock out the missile silos in Iran with an air blitz..." Yehudi sat down hard into his chair, his hands shaking. "...while the U.S. has agreed to demolish the Iranians' missile defense ring, their SAMs, around the missile base, just before our boys fly in there!"

Yehudi could only marvel at the speed at which these decisions must have been made.

"The Americans had a quick emergency meeting once they found out the Iranians cheated on their commitment not to enrich fuel in their reactors. There is simply no other way they could have gotten enough plutonium. Especially in the few short years since the agreement was put into place."

Chapter 55

Uri awoke on the floor by the imam's desk to another blinding headache. His eyes failed to focus well, but he was delighted to see a smiling Lara looking down at him, holding his head in her hands.

He then noticed four police officers standing behind her, looking concerned, but just a little bewildered. He noticed they wore insignias from Orange County.

"Are you conscious enough to take a look at some of Javad's papers and other material we found?" Lara asked.

"Yeah, I think so, what have you got?" Uri managed to reply, his lips dry and swollen.

"Take a look at these," Lara said. But Uri's head was still spinning too much to make much sense of what she was showing him. Because the police were not cleared to hear the rest of this conversation, she politely asked them to leave the room. They did so, albeit reluctantly.

"Lucky they kept pretty good records of the meetings they were having down here. The leader, Javad Abdouleh, was the coordinator between the Mufti, Sheikh Nasrallah, and if you can believe this—the Iranian prime minister! From what I can make out, and I've just started going through their notes, it appears they were getting ready to launch widespread attacks in the U.S. The imams from several Shia mosques were carrying out campaigns aimed at getting their congregants to condemn ISIS, and, in fact all Sunni Muslims. They were using the new rapprochement between the U.S. and Iran to show that we were all on the same side."

Uri could only shake his head in amazement.

"From what we can tell, Iran has used their apparent 'peaceful intent' to construct a whole network of some kind of reactors to produce plutonium. They've buried these under schools, hospitals, and other public venues, and have already produced enough for several kiloton-size weapons!"

Uri considered, as well as he could in his half-conscious state, what Lara had just told him. It was terrifying, to say the least; but she had not yet finished. There was a pause as she continued to pore through the raft of documents.

Lara peered closely at one particular set of computer printouts she had discovered. "These look like the descriptors for computer malware," she said with some excitement.

"Mal, as in malicious?" Uri replied, still in a haze.

"Exactly."

"Why do you suppose they're written in English?" Uri asked.

"English is sort of the standard language of computer geeks," she mumbled, continuing to examine the diagrams and descriptions. The more she read, the more excited she got. "Do you remember the STUXNET virus that disabled the Iranian enrichment program about ten years ago?"

Uri thought for a moment. "Was that the joint U.S.-Israeli virus that caused their uranium centrifuges to spin out of control and destroy themselves?"

"That's right!" she replied, encouraged by his alertness. "Actually, it's what the tech folks call a 'worm'. Once it gets into a computer operating system it replicates itself and brings everything down. When it got into the computer that runs the centrifuges, it ordered them to spin out of control until they eventually disintegrated."

"Did the Iranians ever figure out how their computer got infected in the first place?"

"Not really. But it seems like almost everyone in the world uses the same basic operating systems, so that it's pretty easy for someone skilled in the art to insert a worm or virus into a system through an innocuous-looking message."

"Sounds incredibly dangerous," Uri said.

"Yes, it's spawned a whole new business in 'malware' detection. Government computers especially need to be scanned constantly for sabotage. Malware has the potential to shut down entire industries, or even nations!"

"But getting back to what you found here, what makes you think it's some kind of threat?"

Lara helped Uri to carefully rise and sit in a chair. He needed the assistance. She was obviously getting ready to explain something important. "Did you know that the United States has a 'fail-safe' nuclear retaliation program?" Uri shook his head; he had no idea what she was talking about. Lara went on: "Only the president, vice president, or chairman of the Joint Chiefs can order a nuclear strike in retaliation for a pre-emptive attack on us. But just in case such an order gets through by accident, or purposeful intervention by a third-party, the president, and only the president can give the command to nullify this order."

Uri nodded. "That makes sense. We don't want to have an accidental 'retaliation' when, in fact, no first strike has taken place."

"Right," Lara confirmed. "But if an enemy, say Iran, was certain no retaliation would take place, they would feel free to make a preemptive strike against us or one of our allies, like Israel."

"That makes sense, too" Uri replied. "But how could they be sure, the Iranians, I mean, weren't going to suffer a devastating counter-attack?"

270

"That's the point of all this malware here!" she exclaimed. "They have a STUXNET-type worm, a 'zero-day' type ready to *rescind* any retaliation order. And it will look as though it came from the president!"

"Wait a minute," Uri interrupted. "What the hell is a 'zero-day' worm?"

"It's one that acts without warning," she explained. "When Iran gets the signal that the worm is in place, it knows it can attack Israel, for example, with impunity. Any order to retaliate will be rescinded, apparently by order of the president!"

"All right, say all this is true," Uri replied. "Iran should know that Israel would retaliate immediately, and with full strength. Plus it has the protection of its 'Iron Dome' system."

"Iran can bombard Israel from several nuclear missile locations. The Iron Dome system, as good as it is against Hamas or Hezbollah rockets, would be no match for the type of advanced nuclear weapons Iran seems to have developed." She glanced at him with dismay, hoping he understood the gravity of the situation. "Iran would be willing to accept the loss of a million or two of its citizens if it meant the complete destruction of Israel."

"Are you telling me that the U.S. and the rest of the world would then just stand by and see Israel obliterated?" Uri implored.

"It would be a *fait accompli*," she explained. "No nation would be willing to start a world war over the destruction of tiny Israel. Certainly, refugees would be taken in, but the huge Muslim majority in the world would be grateful that Israel was no longer a thorn in their side."

The blood drained from Uri's face as he recognized the truth in what she was saying. One didn't have to look back very far in history to see a similar situation.

"And that's not the end of it," she continued. "Iran could now, with the assistance of Russia, of course, attack *our* nuclear reactors, naval vessels, including submarines, all with the same impunity garnered by this worm."

"Now wait a minute," Uri argued. "You're not trying to tell me that Iran, even with the help of Russia, could get off that kind of massive attack against us without facing immediate destruction?"

"The Iranians have unprecedented access to our military establishment. It's all come about since we signed the anti-proliferation agreement with them. They have all their frozen assets back, and now they purport to be our ally in the fight against the ISIS Caliphate! They've been providing false information on ISIS to our CIA, Homeland Security, and military intelligence, all under the guise of being our friends in the fight against ISIS. All the while it has been the Iranians who have been master-minding the murder of our children, and committing other atrocities."

"You can't prove any of that," Uri responded weakly.

"Maybe not all, but the facts sure point in that direction."

Uri sighed. "This is a pretty bleak scenario," he said woefully. "What sort of plan can we present to stop it?"

"The way I see it, the bad guys have not implanted the zero-day worm in our Defense Department's operating system—yet. If they had, it would've been all over by now. But they're obviously close."

Uri thought about that, then asked, "how do they go about, uh, 'implanting the worm'?"

"Simple. They've got to have an agent who can get a USB flash drive into one of the NSA computers that are connected directly to the main operating system."

"We need to get this to Mary, Mike and Yehudi right away, even before we leave here," she added.

"You've got my satellite phone?" Uri asked.

"Sure," she remembered, reaching for it. At that moment, something seemed to disconnect in Uri's brain. He got an intense headache, the room turned over, and he fell unconscious. Lara jerked open the door and implored the Orange County cops: "Please," she urged, "get him to an emergency room *now!*" Even while two of the cops hastened to the task, Lara turned back to her trove of documents. "Listen," she said to the remaining police, "No offense, but I have to ask you to leave. I need to make a secure call here."

The Orange County officers looked at each other, shrugged and left the room. They were getting a little tired of taking orders from a woman, Fed or not.

"Mary!" Lara shouted as the FBI chief picked up. "Are any of the others there?"

"We're all here waiting for you!" Mary replied. "Everyone OK?"

Lara paused and considered their dreadful losses. "Not quite; we lost Ahmad, but Uri, Sarah and I made it…. Listen, I have something that needs to get to Washington poste-haste. Yehudi there, too?"

"I'm here," the Israeli consul said, terrified of what might be in store.

"I'll only be able to give you the basics, but it appears from the paperwork and computer material I've been able to gather…"

"Just a minute, Lara" Mary interrupted. "What about the ringleaders—Javad and his jihadis?"

"Terminated. All that's left are the files and discs they were trying to get out of here. I've been able to skim through it, no details yet, but it appears they have sophisticated software—malware—ready to go in place to nullify our strike counter-measures..."

"Wait a minute, you're getting ahead of us," Mary said as she looked around the room at her colleagues. Lara, of course, was on the speaker phone. Mary knew, that as one of the FBI's top computer experts, Lara had been the originator of the government's network of listening programs that had hacked into the Hezbollah and other terrorist organization electronic communication systems. She would know what she was talking about, and it must be deadly serious for her to be this alarmed.

"It looks like they have found out about and are prepared to disrupt 'POTUSTOP'!"

It was only Mary and Bret Williams, from Homeland Security, of the Americans in the room, who knew what Lara was talking about. POTUSTOP was the ultra-secret program that permitted only "POTUS," the President of the United States, to *halt* a pre-set retaliatory nuclear strike against an enemy. Its main purpose was to dissuade any foreign power from making a preemptive attack on the U.S., NATO members, or other allied countries.

But it appeared that Yehudi Gold, also, was privy to this information. The Israeli prime ministers, past and present, had been reassured by the threat of this retaliation and had agreed to set aside any plans for a preemptive attack on, say, Iran, for example. This, despite Iran's constantly stated threat to "annihilate" the Jewish State. He sat up, clearly frightened by this news from Lara. He also was well aware of her computer skills and so took her warning very seriously.

Lara went on to describe the "worm" program she had discovered in Javad's papers, asking that Bret contact Washington and inform his chief of the severity of the threat.

When the call was finished, Yehudi, very concerned now, made a secure call to his prime minister's office in Jerusalem, where it was early morning. He spoke rapidly in Hebrew, gesturing and wiping his brow. When he concluded the call he turned to his colleagues on the conference call and stated, "Our prime minister has confirmed the request from your president, the authority, I should say---the *permission*, to disable any missiles the enemy already has on the launch pad. The Americans will also provide whatever military air support their country can supply!"

Chapter 56

Seth Moscowitz looked out over the desert landscape and checked his instruments for the twentieth time. Everything in order. He had just left Israeli airspace and headed south over the Red Sea. His wingman, Gershon Lieb, was right where he was supposed to be. They tipped wings to each other, but maintained radio silence, as ordered.

Seth, at twenty-two years of age, was a small, dark, wiry man, carrying a lot of the features of his Russian grandparents. His hair was thick and curly, his spirit ebullient. He looked forward to the chance to make a heroic effort in his country's behalf.

Gershon was, physically, the opposite of his squad leader Seth. He was tall, over six feet, with a fair complexion and light brown hair. He was a quiet man, just twenty-one years old, and quite popular with the ladies. His quick, gentle wit endeared him to almost everyone.

The entire mission should take a little over two hours, each way. But they would have to be refueled on the way home. Seth worried more about that than anything else. With nothing to do for the moment, he recalled the chain of events that had brought them here.

It began only one week ago, he recalled. He and Gershon were ordered to report to General Schoen's office ASAP. The general was the tactical head of the Israeli Air Force, whom neither young pilot had ever met before. As usual for the Israeli military, uniforms were rather casual, as was the etiquette. "Sit down, gentlemen," the general said briefly, after shaking each of their hands. "You may recognize Avi Nachman," he said, gesturing towards a man in civilian clothes, sport shirt and slacks, already seated at the general's right.

They did, in fact, recognize the newly-appointed defense minister, a solid hawk in every sense of the word. He was a "Sabra," as were the two young pilots, born and trained in Israel. Nachman was well-known for his escapades with Mossad in his younger years, a deadly assassin.

"Let's get right down to business," Schoen began. It was typical in the IDF, the Israel Defense Forces, to eliminate extraneous conversation. "I'm sure you are both aware of the situation with our neighbors," he said to the two pilots, clearly referring to the Iranian crisis. "You have been selected for a most important, though dangerous, mission from among all your colleagues training with the new F-35 Lightnings. What I have to tell you cannot be shared with anyone; you will soon see why."

The two pilots strained forward in their hard wooden chairs as the general continued. "You may know, or gathered from the gossip going around, that our Iranian friends have threatened us continually. For annihilation. Now it appears they have the actual means: the test of that medium-range missile you have no doubt heard about has nuclear capabilities."

The young men brought their gaze from the general to the defense minister and back again. He was serious; this was no drill.

"We are preparing for a unique strike, one that can not, *must* not, fail." The general continued. "It will be similar, but far more involved, than our strike against that Iraqi reactor nearly forty years ago." Everyone in Israel, if not the whole world, was familiar with the bold air attack on the Iraqi Osirak nuclear reactor in 1981. What few knew was that General Schoen, a young lieutenant at the time, had participated in that raid.

"The flight path will be more involved than the one we used back then," he continued, pointing at a large map on the wall. "To reach the missile complex at Bandar, on the Persian Gulf, you'll have to fly down the Red Sea to just south of Sharm el-Sheikh, then due east across Saudi Arabia to the Persian Gulf, south of Kuwait. From there it's a short hop up to the target. About 1100 nautical miles, overall." He paused, noting the anxious looks on the young pilots' faces.

"I know the F-35 has stealth capability, but you mean we're going to fly across five hundred miles of Saudi air space!?" Seth asked incredulously.

"A little more than that, actually. But don't worry; we have full cooperation from the Saudis. They don't like the idea of the Ayatollah having these weapons any more than we do..."

"But isn't that missile complex covered by SAMs?" Seth, as well as everyone in the air force knew where the Iranian rocket compound was located, and that it was guarded by surface-to-air missiles.

The general had expected that query and was ready for it. In fact, he would have been disappointed if the pilots hadn't asked. "The Americans, after a long series of talks, have agreed to take out the SAMs with Sparrow or Phoenix-type missiles from their Sixth Fleet in the Gulf. Should be nothing left for you but some smoldering ruins."

"What will we have with us?" Gershon, the younger of the pilots, asked.

"The main armament will be two-2000 pound JDAMs each." The pilots knew these were the "Joint Direct Attack Munitions" that had a range of fifteen miles. They would have to get in pretty close. "You'll also have two AIM 120 missiles for air-to-air protection, and even your GAU-22As with a thousand rounds of 25 mm cannon fire."

"But we won't be able to make it back after that long a flight..."

"Right," the general answered. "You'll have to refuel. We'll have a KC-135 ready for you over the Gulf with enough gas for the return trip!"

* * *

Seth was now, once again, going over the whole battle plan in his head; the re-fueling was the part that concerned him. He had only practiced this difficult maneuver once, and that was in the friendly skies over the Negev. He was brought back to the present by rapid chirping in his headphones, signaling approach to target. He had been on flight control using the pre-programmed flight design on his plane's computer.

Looking down now, he could see the coast of Iran on the Persian Gulf, a stark contrast of brown desert against the intense azure blue of the Gulf. He glanced over his starboard wing and saw Gershon's F-35 about 200 yards behind and below him. They were now less than 50 miles from their targets: the ballistic missile installations at Bandar.

Seth could now see plumes of black smoke rising into the clear air above the desert. These would have to be the SAM installations, taken out by the U.S. Navy, as promised. He was about to enter the prescribed flight path to the missile silos themselves when he got a different, more insistent warning, both in his headphones and on his visual display. There at ninety degrees east and 1000 yards, he saw four Grumman F-14 Tomcats headed his way. These were the fighter jets sold to Iran by the U.S. over thirty years ago. The distinctive double vertical stabilizers were visible, even at this distance.

His alarm system now warned him of air-to-air missiles headed his way. He knew these had to be the old "Sidewinders" dating back to the sale by the U.S. As practiced many times before, he and Gershon split off from each other and engaged their anti-missile defense systems. The Israeli F-35's automatically evaded the aged, slow Sidewinders, which drifted down into the Gulf below.

The four Iranian Tomcats closed in, two at each of the two Israeli Lightnings. Seth picked the port-side enemy headed his way and released one of his modern AIM 120 air-to-air missiles. He then pulled his craft into a steep dive, combined with a tight left turn. As the enemy Tomcat passed above him, he saw it burst into flame as his missile struck home. He could see that neither of the pilots had a chance to get out of the burning plane.

Figuring that Gershon could take care of the other two enemy planes, he focused on the remaining Tomcat, now on his tail. The Tomcat had only his old Gatling gun, with its 20 mm rounds, and no modern aiming system. Rather than fire his remaining AIM, Seth pulled his craft into a tight, right turn that he knew couldn't be matched by the old, slower F-14. He had to give the guys credit, though. The pilots attempted, vainly, to match his maneuver. This put him, as he had planned, below and behind the enemy plane. He could imagine their frustration as they realized their vulnerable position.

Before he could even fire his cannons, he saw the canopy of the F-14 release, and two parachutes appear, as the pilots safely ejected. Only when they were well out of range, Seth fired a few of his 25 mm slugs into the empty enemy plane, seeing it explode and disintegrate, as he swept by.

Keeping the mandatory radio silence, he now checked on his wingman, Gershon. There he was, 200 yards to starboard, waggling his wings to show all was well. Seth smiled to himself and returned the gesture. It was on to the target now. He still had armament to counter another threat, should it be necessary. The two pilots could compare war stories when they were safely back at base.

Seeing no other aircraft, and getting no warning from his detection systems, Seth headed directly for the target missile complexes. They were now inside the fifteen mile range of their JDAMs. Sure enough, directly ahead, were the two silos, capable of firing the Iranian medium-range nuclear missiles. At their briefing, Seth and Gershon had been assured that the missiles would not be "armed" until out of Iranian airspace. That is, there was no chance of a live warhead being triggered by destruction of the missiles and silos. The firing mechanisms were pre-set this way for safety.

Seth headed for the closer of the two silos, knowing Gershon would zero in on the other. At a range of five miles, well within the kill zone of the JDAMs, he locked his firing system in on the well-defined structure and hit the red button. Once the missile was released, he broke into a tight turn to port, hauling the nose of his plane upwards. This would get him well clear, both of his target as well as Gershon's.

The two attackers were within sight of each other as both silos ruptured and exploded in a shower of burning debris. Seconds later the sounds reached the pilots, along with a blast of air sufficient to push their craft noticeably askew. There was a "thumbs-up" from the teammates as they headed for the upcoming refueling over the Gulf. This was the part of the mission Seth had been dreading.

But before he could even prepare for the dangerous maneuver, they were alerted by their warning systems of another pair of oncoming enemy F-14s. It was clear that the enemy aircraft had split in their pursuit of the Israelis, one headed for each of them. Knowing his partner was capable of downing the other, Seth dove directly under the Iranian

Tomcat, not firing his remaining missile. Instead, he would rely solely on his cannons. But just as he dropped the nose of his F-35, he felt a slight shudder, and saw the tracks of 20 mm cannon fire rip past him.

Seth presumed he must have taken at least one of the slugs, hopefully in a non-critical part of the plane. In any event, he pulled up well above and behind the attacking Tomcat. The Iranian pilots were not, apparently, aware of his location. The old F-14 was notably deficient in visual sighting, especially to the rear. He didn't wait for the pair to eject this time. Seth poured a full second's worth of cannon fire into the doomed plane. It disappeared in a black cloud and flame as Seth roared past.

Glancing at his cockpit screen, Seth saw that his fuel level was dangerously low. There never had been any doubt that refueling would be necessary; they were well past the 1300 nautical mile ultimate range. Once again he saw Gershon off to starboard giving the "thumbs up," but pointing at the starboard side of the fuselage of Seth's plane. *"Must be where I got hit,"* Seth thought to himself. Anyway, there was nothing he could do about it now, and the control surfaces seemed to be reacting well to his commands. He shrugged at his partner, as if to say, *"Can't worry about it now,"* and headed off toward the rendezvous point with the KC-135.

The refueling plane was circling right where it was supposed to be, just off the Saudi coast, heading south. Seth, seeing his wingman closer to the huge KC-135, signaled with a flip of his wings for him to go first.

Gershon made a pass under the belly of the lumbering refueler, allowing the crew member aboard assigned to the task to prepare for the delicate operation. For this one maneuver, they had been allowed to break radio silence. It would be for only a few minutes, hopefully.

Seth watched from a position to port of the KC-135, and listened in on the conversation. "How are you today, sir?" the crew member asked.

"Fine, but going to need almost a full tank." Gershon replied.

So he's as starved as me, Seth thought to himself.

He watched as Gershon expertly dropped into position directly behind the tanker, then fell to about fifty feet beneath. He maintained his speed equal to the tanker, about 300 knots. He saw the tanker crewman begin to lower the flexible fuel hose into position. Connected to the hose was a "drogue," a funnel with small airfoils to stabilize it in the buffeting wind. It was now Gershon's job to eject the "probe" housed in the fuselage just to the right of the cockpit. He then had to insert the probe delicately into the drogue.

He was aided by two things: first, he had a display on the right side of his control panel that gave him a close-up view of the probe and the approaching drogue. Second, the tanker airman gave him a running estimate of how close the drogue was to the probe. "Twenty feet, ten feet, five feet..." Seth heard him call out. Then: "contact!" The probe was in place and the fueling began.

Gershon truly was a gifted pilot, Seth thought to himself. He was a true reflection of his grandfather, Gideon, who had been part of the IDF "Raid on Entebbe" back in 1976. Gershon, and everyone else, was rightfully proud of the way that the IDF had carried out that near-impossible rescue of the civilians trapped on a hostile airbase.

In just six minutes the tanker had filled the F-35 to capacity. "That's it, sir, you're full," the crewman said. "Good luck!"

Gershon had completed the entire refueling task in less than ten minutes, and fallen to starboard and accelerated away. It was now Seth's turn. He dropped into position aft of the tanker, keeping his speed to match. "How are you, sir?" the man asked.

"Just about dry."

"We'll fix that," he promised, lowering the fuel hose and drogue.

Seth watched on his display as the drogue came into view. He extended the probe, but was chagrined to see the drogue fly off to the right. "That's OK, sir, we'll give it another go." Seth cut his speed slightly and the drogue disappeared from his display, but appeared in his windshield.

"Alright, sir," the crewman said calmly, "you're about one hundred feet aft, but on target."

Seth lightly increased his speed as the crewman counted out the decreasing distance. "Fifty feet, thirty feet, twenty feet, ten feet..." Seth could feel the perspiration flowing over his body. "Alright sir, less than five feet now."

Seth tried once again to carefully insert the probe into the hanging, bouncing drogue. *"How had Gershon done this so easily?"* he mumbled.

"What was that, sir?" the crewman inquired.

"Nothing. Oh, I think I got it!" he replied as he saw the connection on his display. At the same time a red light turned green, showing the fueling had begun.

"Yes, sir, fueling has started. How much do you need?"

"A full tank, for sure, I'm dry."

"Right you are, sir." He counted out the fuel load as it went into the starving F-35. "By the way, sir, I don't know if you are aware that there appears to be a fuel leak out of your main starboard fuselage tank."

That's what had happened during that last air attack, Seth realized. He had taken a slug in the tank, causing the leak. "Thank you," he replied to the crewman. "Hope I can make it home."

"Yes, sir, you're full now. You can retract your probe."

Adding to his embarrassment, in pulling loose too quickly, he left the hose dangling in the wind, spraying fuel for a few moments. "Sorry about that."

"That's alright, sir, we got it covered. Good luck!"

"I'm going to need it," Seth thought, as he veered off to the west, over the Saudi mainland, headed home. It was a good hour's flight-time before he reached the Red Sea, he realized, trusting his fuel would hold out. It all depended on how bad the leak was. It seemed as though he could already see the level dropping on his instrument panel.

The flight west to the Red Sea was uneventful. Seth had dropped his speed and reset his altitude for maximum fuel economy, and was far behind Gershon by now. But by the time he reached the Gulf of Aqaba, he saw a red warning signal, informing him that his fuel was at the danger limit. He was virtually empty. He turned north, praying for a miracle, and broke radio silence again. "This is Aleph One, over," he declared.

"We've got you, Aleph One. You're a little late, but on track. Any problems?"

"Afraid so. I'm out of fuel, heading for Eilat, will probably have to ditch."

"Roger, Aleph One. We've alerted the sea rescue and the base at Eilat. Good luck."

This being said, Seth figured his best chance of saving himself, and any civilians on the ground, was to drop the craft into Israeli territory, and not where any enemy troops could reach him. The Sinai was crawling with Hamas, and other unfriendly forces were already aware of his dilemma. Breaking into Jordanian air space was not much better. Though Jordan was officially at peace with Israel, it would cause an "incident," at the very least.

Seth headed up the Gulf, hoping for the best. He was, in fact, within sight of the Israeli port of Eilat when his engine coughed, signaling lack of fuel. The control stick jerked in his hand, and then the only sound was the wind whistling past his doomed plane. *"Let's see if we can make it there from 40,000 feet,"* he said to himself, knowing these stealth jets were not designed for gliding.

He watched as the sea, the bustling port and the land on both sides, grew closer. He checked his ejection seat, making sure all was ready for a "punch out," which was now a certainty. He dare not drop below a thousand feet, or his parachute might not have time to deploy. The land, the sea and the port all were rushing at him at the same rate. He guided his craft slightly to port, to make sure he did not hit the populated area in and around Eilat, and prepared for his departure. As with most pilots, he had never practiced this maneuver, fearing it would not become necessary.

At one thousand feet, and the ground approaching fast, he saw that he was well west of the populated region, and that the ground was, in fact, closer than the water. He grabbed the handle that would eject him from his now-silent bird, thanking her for getting him at least this close to home.

The blast of air was worse than he had imagined. He was knocked briefly senseless. Looking up he was delighted to see the billowing blue and white parachute dragging him back and forth in the wind. Then he saw his plane, smoldering to his right, dug into the sand. *"Thank heaven for that,"* he thought. His next question to himself was whether he had made it into Israel, or was headed into the Sinai, and an uncertain fate. He didn't have to wait long, as the ground was quickly approaching. He had parachuted before, but not in a military chute. This one was made for the most rapid possible descent. The last thing he saw before impact was a cloud of sand headed directly for him.

Then he hit, rolled over, and clumsily attempted to knock the air out of the 'chute before it dragged him too far. His world spun as he lost consciousness, but not before he saw the jeep approaching him, the blue Star of David fluttering from its whip antenna.

Chapter 57

Uri awoke in a strange, sterile-looking room. He looked around, trying to get his bearings. His first reaction was to check his body parts. He seemed to be intact, as far as he could tell. Then he noticed all sorts of wires and tubes coming from his body, hooked to machines on both sides of his bed. His head was wrapped in bandages. It was only then that he became aware of a smiling nurse standing by his bedside, holding his right hand. The fact that she was smiling he found very reassuring.

He then felt a remarkably familiar hand holding his left hand. He had to turn his head to see who it was; his left was his blind side. Thrilled, he saw a smiling, though teary-eyed Lara, dressed in casual clothing: white blouse, blue skirt, with a blue kerchief around her neck. Her choice of colors struck him immediately; she might as well have been wearing a Star of David. She didn't say a word, but was forced eventually to bring a tissue up to her eyes. Uri hoped those were tears of joy and not the precursor to some bad news.

But before she could say a word, the door to the room burst open and an exultant Mary Robley and Bret Williams rushed to the foot of his bed. They were beside themselves in their eagerness to see him, it was clear. "The warrior awakens," Mary said first. Bret was calmly standing there, in obvious pleasure.

"What in the world...?" was all that Uri could muster. He noticed the nurse packing up some of the electronic gear that cluttered the room. He was delighted and reassured by the constant pressure of Lara's hand in his.

"You've been out for a while, my friend!" Mary began. "Those two 'clops' you took on your head did a number on you." Uri wondered where Mary had picked up the Yiddish word. "Anyway, you suffered a mild...ah, concussion." She chose her words carefully, so as not to cause the recently awakened Uri a relapse.

"Where are...?" Uri began.

"I'd better start from the beginning," Mary said with the tone of one about to begin a long story. "But it has a very happy ending!" Uri sank back in his bed, all ears. Except, of course for his left hand, which remained in the warm, comforting grip of Lara. "First off, we, or I should say Lara and Sarah, finished off our 'friend' Javad back in Orange County. I say 'back' because we're here now in the military hospital at the VA in Los Angeles. You were transported here right afterwards; we left agents to clean up the mess down there. They did recover the remains of Ahmad."

There was a slight pause as she added: "He is to be buried in Israel with full military honors, and our grateful thanks to his family...along with a handsome compensation and full residency."

Uri look bewildered by all this, so Lara took over. "You remember being trapped in that mosque in 'OC' with a bunch of bad guys—Javad's men?" Uri nodded lightly, trying to bring it all back. "There was a fight...guns, fire extinguishers, pails of lye, remember?"

It came back in a flash. Uri remembered going into Javad's office and then...lights out.

Seeing the recall on Uri's face, Mary continued the story. "Well, after Javad pulled the rug out from under you, literally, Lara and Sarah finished him off and recovered some mighty useful material." That jolted Uri back to the communications room in the mosque. "But then...the accumulation of the two blows you took to your 'kopf...'" The Yiddish again brought a weak smile to Uri's face. "...caused a swelling on your brain that put you out for a long time..." Uri looked up, startled. "Don't ask," she said dismissively. Uri felt as though he was listening to his mother. Suddenly, he had a terrible thought. "Zurvan..." he blurted out, searching Mary's face.

There was a dreadful pause as she considered what to say. Finally, she replied in a somber tone, "I'm afraid your friend didn't survive the gunshot." Mary saw the grief on Uri's face and quickly continued, "it was instantaneous; he never felt a thing...we, that is, the Bureau, have already sent a 'bereavement' team over to see his wife, Fakhra..."

"What could they possibly have told her...?"

"The usual, in cases like this. That he got accidentally caught up in a government 'sting' operation and we express our sincere regrets and a monetary compensation..."

"I'm sure she was totally understanding," Uri replied caustically.

"Actually, she was quite accepting of the situation, I'm told. A lot more than many would have been..."

Both Uri and Lara were clearly devastated by this; Lara, even though she already knew the awful truth. No one said anything for almost a full minute.

"Alright, back to the story," Mary finally continued. "With the help of all the intel Lara gathered up, we were able to piece together what the Iranians had in mind. Lara found a 'worm' they were about to insert into the DOD computer system, an order that would *countermand* any retaliatory strike against a nation that carried out a preemptive attack on us or one of our allies. It would appear to have come from the *president*."

"So the Iranians would feel free to *make* a strike against Israel, knowing they were immune from any retaliation!" Lara concluded. Mary nodded in agreement with this summary.

Hearing "worm" triggered instant recall in Uri's slowly wakening brain. That was the last thing he remembered Lara telling him before he passed out. *How long ago was that...?*

"The best part is still coming...if you're up to it?" Mary hesitated. Uri struggled to sit up for this; he certainly didn't want to miss the best part. Although it would be hard to beat having Lara this close beside him.

"We, that is Bret and I, along with Yehudi, contacted the State Department and told them what we discovered. Of course, we transmitted all the details Lara got from Javad's cache to their analysts at the same time. It didn't take long, twelve hours maybe, and the president and Joint Chiefs put the intel together with what they had from satellites and drones over Iran. The data on the plutonium...I omitted that part, I kind of forgot how long you've been out..." Uri grimaced at the thought, it must have been days.

"Wait a minute!" Uri said with a start. His face twisted as he struggled to remember something. "Amir and Izad!" he blurted out. "They are the culprits!"

"What are you talking about?" Mary asked, thinking Uri had some kind of relapse.

"Amir and Izad are the computer geeks Javad boasted to me about! The worm!" There was silence as the others watched Uri struggle to recall... "One night, meeting with his troops, Javad confided something to me. He had two jihadis working for a software firm in Hawthorne; they were doing contract work on some computer programs for DOD. Javad bragged that they had been able to burrow...excuse the pun...into the DOD's main operating system. That must be how Javad was able to set up this worm to disable the retaliation process!"

"Do you know the name of this company in Hawthorne?" Mary asked gently. She didn't want to cause Uri to suddenly lose this important information.

"I think it was 'Pacific Coast Software Solutions', something like that. Anyway, Javad was ecstatic. Apparently, these two guys, educated with the help of U.S. dollars, were able to dig deep into DOD operating systems while working on a minor accessing program, outsourced to this small company in Hawthorne. I think Javad even referred to a 'worm', though I didn't have any idea what he was talking about..."

Mary was clearly pleased with Uri's recollection. "Can you give our Homeland Security people all the details, whatever you can remember, about this company? They'll follow up and get hold of these guys...what did you say their names were?"

"All I know is Amir and Izad..."

"That's enough. We'll get on it! Meanwhile, to finish this Iran story," Mary continued, "they shot an intermediate range missile with a nuclear warhead down the Persian Gulf. Aircraft from our Sixth Fleet down there caught radioactive debris that positively showed the warhead was armed with *plutonium*!"

This brought Uri fully upright, totally alarmed. No one in Israel, to his knowledge, had ever imagined the Iranians had that level of sophisticated weaponry.

"The first thing the president did was to contact the Russkies." Bret Williams interjected. "They appeared to be as surprised as us. No way would they have given the Iranians any plutonium. They didn't go so far as to admit anything about the intermediate-range missile, however. But we figure that's where it came from. Anyway, they promised not to interfere in any reprisals we had in mind...within reason. Whatever that means."

"You mean to say the United States military carried out action against Iran!? All while I've been asleep in this bed?"

"Not quite," Williams continued. "It was your countrymen who did it," he proclaimed smiling. He knew Uri would love this part. "We took out their SAMs while the IDF blasted Iran's missile complex at Bandar, on their West Coast." He realized Uri would want more details of this raid so he went on. "Two F-35's hit them, flying over Saudi airspace, if you can believe that, then returning safely over the Red Sea. Beats even the 1981 attack on the Iraqi reactor!"

Uri's brain was spinning with all this news. Suddenly he thought of something. "What about the disarmament agreement—the one between the U.S. and Iran? If they've got plutonium, doesn't that mean they have some kind of illegal reactors going, like heavy water or something? I mean, other than just for power production?"

Bret looked at Mary, who shook her head. "We don't know about that end of things," she said. "That's above our level of classification. But I certainly assume so. Believe me, they're on it." After a short pause she added, "I can tell you that the guys at the NSA have been able to listen in on some pretty interesting conversations between Iran and Russia, and Iran and Hezbollah. They've taken to using these second-rate satellite phones the Qataris have come up with. But I can't tell you exactly what they've found—yet. My guess is that it has to do with the missiles as well as the plutonium."

"Don't forget one of the most important things, for our end, at least," Williams added. "We've picked up two of Javad's operatives; that is, two of the shooters at the Sunni mosque. They left some clean blood samples on the glass doors they broke on their way in. Their DNA then was matched with their mouth swabs from the BDS demonstration at the Israel Independence Day celebration. Good to about one in ten billion, the analysts say. Our Orange County crew say they have solid leads already on the rest of the attackers."

"So the 'Never Again' note at the Sunni mosque...?" Uri asked.

"Fake. Just like the costumes and Hebrew curses. All set up to blame the Jews."

Uri looked up at Lara, who smiled charmingly.

Chapter 58

The next day, after a long, peaceful sleep with Lara sprawled in a chair by his side, Uri awoke to a prim nurse who arrived briskly, "Well, believe it or not, you've been cleared to go! Your brain swelling has pretty much disappeared; and your EEG and other vitals are back to normal—for a man your age." Uri grimaced at that last dig. "After breakfast we'll let you walk around the halls a bit, and if you can handle that, the Israeli Embassy has a nice room for you in Westwood, across from the Federal Building."

He wolfed down the breakfast with a surprising appetite, outdoing Lara, did his walk around the halls with her at his side, and then packed up his meager belongings. With Lara always right next to him, a car was waiting to take them a few short blocks to a small, unassuming, but surprisingly luxurious hotel. The happy pair found he had already been assigned a room under his old pseudonym, Uri Cohen.

Entering the room, on the uppermost floor, they found the embassy had provided him with a full set of fresh clothes, shaving and toiletries, complete with bathrobes—for two. *Yehudi thinks of everything*, Uri mused. He noticed Lara blushing a bit. There were also, standard for these luxury hotels, two bathrooms, one on either end of the large bedroom.

Fresh from his hospital dressings, Uri took a long hot shower and shaved off the accursed beard he had lived with for more than a month. He then put on the bathrobe and awaited Lara. Impatiently.

She finally emerged from the other bathroom, skin aglow, with a disarming grin on her face.

Without a word, he stripped her of her robe and fell on top of her, feeling her warm trembling body beneath him. With a sense of urgency, he began kissing her mouth and breasts, while exploring her with his hands. His kisses became more ardent as she, with a cry of anticipation, grabbed him and brought him up to her. With a climactic burst, both trembled as they reached heights that staggered them.

Afterwards, they lay there, exhausted, kissing and fondling each other. "My God," she said, "that was incredible." He nodded in agreement, nuzzling her neck. "That makes up for that awful time in that cell…well, almost, anyway." They both laughed. After a while, she felt his arousal begin anew. She crawled on top of him, and very gently, began caressing him again, feeling his need intensify. When he was reaching a point where it was evident he could stand no more, she sat astride him, joining with him until he exploded violently.

After a long, luxurious rest, she snuggled up against him; he ran his fingers through her hair and delighted in her feel and scent. As they relaxed, cozy in each other's warmth, she was suddenly struck by a sense of déjà vu. They had been like this twice before in the past few years. Lightly stroking his arm, she looked him in the eyes and asked carefully, "So what's next for you?"

He didn't pause. "I've been meaning to ask you: do you think you could consider living in a foreign country, like Israel? Of course, it would mean putting up with an aging, cranky, one-eyed Jew."

She laughed and kissed him passionately on the mouth, not saying a word.

Epilogue

The events in Southern California had consequences far beyond the region. The Department of Homeland Security took immediate and drastic action against the possibility of hacking into their "fail-safe" nuclear retaliation program. The ultimate, computer-driven program that safeguards the government's ability to nullify any surprise attack was upgraded to a version that was "state-of-the-art." Further, its capabilities were made clear to friends and foes alike. Any action against the U.S. would not only be met with a crushing blow to the offending nation, but would be made public to the world. Offending regimes would suffer fatal political consequences.

Sheikh Nasrallah became the brunt of all the humiliation that befell Hezbollah, and even Lebanon itself, as his nefarious actions against both Israel and the rest of the free world became widely publicized. Military aid to Hezbollah from Iran was essentially terminated.

Prime Minister Abbasi of Iran suffered perhaps the most of all public officials. His complicity with Hezbollah, of course was a disgrace. But perhaps worst of all was his deception involving the highly-touted pact with the West; this brought shame upon the entire nation. Sanctions were re-established, bringing the wrath of the Iranian people to a fever pitch. The Ayatollah, fearing a counter-revolution, made a public show of the dismantling of all its "Breeder" reactors, and an end to its nuclear weapons programs.

The partnership between Iran and Russia regarding military affairs effectively concluded. Their collaboration in an attempt to destabilize the region was seen by most as both ineffectual and ludicrous.

Most of the perpetrators of the attacks on the Los Angeles area synagogues and Sunni mosque were brought into custody. Unfortunately, Zainal Abidin made his escape and was not heard from again. It is likely he surfaced in Iran to an unknown fate.

But the Los Angeles imam, Ali Muhammad, who was responsible for the despicable murders of the children and rabbi in Beverly Hills was brought to swift justice, with the help of an outraged Muslim community. After a speedy, but notorious trial, he was sentenced to fifty life terms without parole.

* * *

Lara Edmond did, in fact, move to Israel to become Mrs. Lara Levin in a small secular ceremony. She kept her last name as Edmond, and joined the military intelligence wing of the IDF: AMAN. Here she rapidly advanced Israel's ability to enter and disrupt the enemies' computer networks.

Uri maintained his desk job, monitoring the activity of the many adversaries of the State of Israel. The two spent much time together, of course. They were able to lunch often in bustling Tel Aviv during the work week. The newlyweds took frequent vacations, Uri showing her the amazing country called Israel, and its remarkable peoples.

Though the couple maintained an apartment near the beach close to Tel Aviv, their main residence was located in the mountains of the Galilee, near the Golan. Here they lived a near-anonymous existence in a tranquil setting, Lara quickly learning the language almost as well as her native tongue. Nights were spent learning more about each other.

They spoke of plans to visit her native Ohio, where her family was keen to meet her famous husband. He, too, was eager to meet them; to hear more about the Edmond family and its tradition of military service.

They spoke, too, of the possibility of their own family to come; another generation of patriots and warriors.

Author's Note

Devil in False Colors is a work of fiction, nothing more. The characters and events are all products of the author's imagination and should not be taken as anything else. There are, however, truths hidden beneath the fiction. Israel is a democracy, essentially the only one in that part of the world. Though many may not realize it, Israel was established as a "Jewish Homeland" by Britain, who, along with France, captured the entire region during World War I. After much haggling with the "League of Nations," the area set aside for the country which would become Israel, was far larger than the Israel we see today.

The boundaries established by the United Nations in 1947, in their historic vote, created a country with virtually indefensible borders. There were no natural barriers against the invasion by aggressive neighboring States that totally rejected the dictum of the U.N.

On May 15, 1948, the day that Britain left its "protectorate," armies of no less than four Arab countries poured across the borders with the avowed goal of destroying the infant democracy. Forces from Iraq, Jordan, Egypt and Syria falsely warned the Arabs living within Israel's borders to flee, lest they be massacred by the Jews, or even be killed by the invading Arab armies. The outcome of this invasion, as well as the other wars instigated by Israel's neighbors, is well-known history.

Despite these discouragements, more than 20% of Israel's citizens are indeed Arabs, most of whom are Muslim. They enjoy full rights of citizenship, total religious freedom, serve in the Parliament (Knesset), and one is even a member of the prime minister's cabinet! Contrast this with the status of Jews in the surrounding Arab countries. If you can find any.

Israeli Arabs have a much higher standard of living than their brethren in the surrounding Arab nations. Public polls consistently show that Israeli Arabs prefer, by a wide margin, to live in Israel compared with living in the neighboring Islamic countries. Yet Israel remains a thorn in the side of its most belligerent neighbors, perhaps because it shows how this arid land, devoid of most natural resources, can provide a prosperous, free life to its inhabitants. It is much the same situation that existed in Europe for most of the twentieth century and eventually led to the fall of the Soviet Union. It is no wonder why the leaders of Israel's bellicose neighbors indoctrinate their children from a young age with irrational hatred of the Jews.

The animosity of Islam toward Israel, and in fact most Western democracies, is well known, of course. What is less well-known is the animosity *between* the two main branches of Islam: the Sunni and the Shia. Based on two different interpretations as to who are the true followers of the Prophet Muhammad, blood has been spilled over the centuries. It is seen so dramatically now as the "Islamic State" Caliphate (Sunni) slaughters its neighboring Shia citizens.

ISIS (or ISIL) is the nickname Westerners give DAESH, the Sunni terror organization. It is currently the main threat against the free world. They have claimed responsibility for nearly all the horrendous acts of violence against innocent citizens around the world, most notably in Europe.

Perhaps not so well-known is the threat the "Islamic Republic of Iran" poses to the West. Iran was emboldened by the notorious takeover of the U.S. embassy in Tehran in 1979, so shamefully unopposed. Now the capital of Shia Islam, with its 46 million residents, ruled by militaristic religious leaders, Iran has audaciously vowed to "wipe Israel off the map."

Not limited by financial or military resources, the threat is quite real. Were they to be successful in this endeavor, their thirst for power would be unlimited. Iran and its allies are truly a force to be reckoned with.

*   *   *   *   *

Made in the USA
San Bernardino, CA
25 May 2017